STORIES OF MARKETING in INDIA

Anand Karandikar

Popular Prakashan
www.popularprakashan.com

Published by
Harsha Bhatkal for
Popular Prakashan Pvt. Ltd.
301, Mahalaxmi Chambers
22, Bhulabhai Desai Road
Mumbai 400026
info@popularprakashan.com

First Published 2022

(4539)
ISBN 978-81-950882-6-3

Cover design and layout: Anjali Sawant
Typesetting: Thinq Mediia

Printed In India
by Repro India Ltd.
Lower Parel
Mumbai - 400013

I dedicate this book to

Divakar Gorhe
Ashok Joshi
Arun Firodia
Ravi Kant

My research and consultancy work has been possible because of their encouragement and support.

Contents

Foreword

Case studies are now established as the best way of teaching management. A case study brings out the readiness of real life and can touch upon all the facets of reality that the manager faces in his work life.

There has been a paucity of good case studies for teaching management in the management schools as well as management development projects in India.

Dr. Anand Karandikar's book fills this void admirably. The case studies are from real life experiences. They all relate to the experiences of the author and therefore they have a ring of authenticity to them. They are Indian in all their aspects and are therefore very relevant to management education in the Indian milieu. Moreover, they present a 360 degree view of the reality of Indian business and therefore can be looked at from multiple angles. I would dare to say that they are not just case studies in marketing management but can also be used as case studies in business strategy.

I would like to compliment Dr. Anand Karandikar for bringing out this book and Popular Prakashan for publishing it.

I believe the readers will benefit from these case studies.

— **Ravi Pandit**
Chairman & Group CEO,
KPIT Technologies Ltd.
Jul 23 2020

Foreword

Case studies have been made popular by Harvard Business School. There is a need of case studies based on real life Indian stories. My friend Dr. Anand Karandikar has presented 25 case studies based on real life Indian stories of which he was himself a participant and central figure. Reading these case studies is a thought provoking experience. It leaves a thought in the mind "What if......" and that is the very purpose of case studies which has been admirably fulfilled.

Dr. Karandikar has narrated at length how he could sell more than a hundred Lunas (India's first totally indigenous moped) in Pune when the dealer was selling hardly ten. This was due to his unstinting efforts in formulating a direct marketing strategy and implementing it successfully. The fact that the Luna could be sold by personally interacting with people was experienced by me in Mumbai. Our dealer at Mumbai had a very prestigious show room at Worli but his sales were low. At a dealer conference, Jayantibhai, our dealer told me that the Luna is not a product for Mumbai. I told him that I would spend two full days trying to sell the Luna in Mumbai. We had a breakfast meeting at The Oberoi hotel, where we saw a Luna parked in the basement of Express Towers. The watchman there told us that a peon from the offices situated on the 4th floor used it for taking mail to clients in VT, Flora Fountain, Churchgate, etc. We met the peon who was from Nagpur. He had suggested to his boss to buy a Luna so that he need not walk miles and miles doing the errands. We offered him a commission if got us more clients, to which he happily nodded. Then at lunch we talked to Jayantibhai's cook, Rama, who evinced an interest in buying a Luna because he could then go to more places to cook. We talked to his favourite champi-maalishwala at Chowpatty who was very happy that he would be able to go from house to house and offer his services in the Malabar Hill area. Then the next day we went to Dadar, where there were many cyclists. When they were told about the Luna they showed great interest because it would save them both the effort of peddling and time! Jayantibhai threw me a challenge of selling one in the slums of Dharavi. We went there and met a commuter at the Sion local train station. He told us that he worked at the Godrej Factory at Vikhroli. When we talked about the Luna he was immediately interested because he could bring his daughter home from her school on the way back and also do the vegetable shopping. Jayantibhai finally said that he understood that we needed to approach the customer; the customer may not walk into our showroom. Satisfied that I had done my job, I returned to Pune but Jayantibhai continued to sell only a small number. Then I realized that we needed to set up a direct marketing system and tied up with Dr. Karandikar.

Finally, one of his most successful products is MOSTER. I am glad that the Kinetic group was their initial customer and being satisfied Mr. Ravi Kant took it with him to LML and Tata Motors and greatly benefitted.

I wish the author had given a few initial questions too. For example: ABC Motors:

- Can the tractor business be forward integrated to a tractor rental business? If yes, can a tractor finish tilling an average Indian farm in 24 hours or less? Please work out a business model.
- A tractor owner may want a small air conditioned and noiseless cabin. Can that be provided as an optional extra? Can it be powered by waste heat of the diesel engine?
- Could a 'driverless tractor' be a reality, given that most of the farms are rectangular?
- Would a drone guide the tractor in that case?
- Since diesel is not available in villages but electricity is, can we think of an electric tractor?

Dr. Anand Karandikar is an innovator and a practical person at the same time. He is also an engineer and a marketing consultant. My suggestion to him is to help the start-ups to do proper market research about their innovative ideas. What better person to go to than Dr. Anand Karandikar, an IIT and IIM graduate with 45 years of practical experience?

— **Arun Firodia**

July 26, 2020

Preface

The writings in this book are mainly based on my experiences as a sales and marketing professional practising for 45 years in India. The book is intended primarily for three groups:

- Those who are interested in understanding the working of the market in India.
- Practising sales and marketing managers and teachers of marketing management who would like to get a wider understanding of marketing in India.
- Students who are studying marketing as a part of their MBA program and are keen to know more than the minimum necessary for passing the examinations and giving interviews.

And, oh, yes; the book is also very much for those who like to read for the sake of reading and enjoyment; this book is definitely meant for them.

I am aware that the focussed need of each group is quite different and special. However, I believe that there is a significant overlap of the needs of all the groups when it comes to understanding marketing. My attempt is to engage in the area of this overlap.

How should I describe this book? These are cases; stories; personal narratives; sometimes more of one, sometimes a total absence of the other. My role also keeps on changing. Sometimes I am a young executive, at other times I am the head of a leading consultancy firm, sometimes I am a professor of management sciences and at other times I am just a sceptical observer.

Quantitative data, tables, graphs, quantitative techniques and mathematical equations are kept to a minimum. The engineering and technical terms and management jargon, when used, have been explained briefly in layman's' language. Rarely, references are given, to acknowledge verbatim quotations. I have tried to make the narratives interesting as a story, while ensuring that the facts are also useful as case material for further analysis by the students.

I have intentionally not given questions for discussion at the end of each story; nor have I written guidelines for teachers on how to handle the case. I feel that different approaches are possible to discuss these cases and enjoy the stories about marketing and sales in India in an exploratory way. I am happy that this view is amply supported by Ravi Pandit and Arun Firodia in the Forewords they have written so well. 'Thank you' to both of them.

I could not have raised the questions which Arun Firodia has raised in the context of a new tractor to be launched by ABC motors.

Ravi Pandit has said, "Moreover they present a 360 degree view of the reality of the Indian business and therefore can be looked at from multiple angles. I would dare to say that they are not just case studies in marketing management but can also be used as case studies in business strategy."

I know that what I am trying to do is rather unfocussed and open-ended. Many will raise their eyebrows, but that is how I feel good writing should be and that is what I have done. After you read the book, I hope you feel that the time spent was worthwhile; that is all I am asking for.

The material in this book is not necessarily factual reality, although all the companies which form the basis for the case writing do exist today. However, I have changed names of companies, in most of the cases, as some facts have been changed to make the case more interesting. Sometimes developments in two companies have been combined. At times I have added my own imaginations in a story which appears to be factual. If any researchers are interested in using information in this book as the objective reality, then I request them to approach me to verify the facts from fiction. I would be happy to clarify; to the extent, it is possible to do so.

In the end, I have the happy and privileged task of thanking all those who helped me. I can't really name everybody because the list is too long. None the less I must mention Prof. Sushil Kandalgaokar, Mr. Sundarani and Ms. Sarita Awad who carefully read the first draft of all the cases and made many valuable suggestions. I also thank Mr. Prathamesh Patil and Mr. Gaurav Kalyani for carrying out the boring job of proof-reading so meticulously.

Wishing you a good reading experience.

— **Anand Karandikar**

28th July 2020

Chapter 1

The Luna

The Pioneers

The three Firodia brothers from Ahmadnagar in Western Maharashtra proved to be exceptional contributors to the development of an independent India. Motilal Kundanmal Firodia was the leader of the Cooperative Movement, and became a Member of Parliament in the third Lok Sabha. Navalmal Kundanmal Firodia, who had participated in India's freedom struggle and courted arrest by the British government, joined hands with Bajaj to pioneer automobile manufacturing in India. He made the first auto-rickshaw. He was the one to sign a technical collaboration agreement with Mercedes-Benz - the leading German automobile company - for the manufacture of commercial vehicles in India.

The third brother, Hastimal Kundanmal Firodia became a technocrat entrepreneur industrialist. Mr. H. K. Firodia had obtained his mechanical and electrical engineering degree from the College of Engineering, Pune (COEP) and Master of Science degree in industrial engineering from the USA in 1948. He then started working at the Maharashtra State Road Transport Corporation (MSRTC) workshop to get firsthand experience of servicing commercial vehicles. Later, he joined his brother Navalmal, and guided Bajaj Auto Ltd., from 1960 to 1968 as in-charge of engineering and production. After that, he directed various enterprises in the Kinetic Group.

Mr. Arun Hastimal Firodia is a rare combination of a brilliant engineer and an astute businessman. He inherited the rich tradition of his illustrious father, the late Mr. H. K. Firodia. Born in 1943, Mr. Arun Firodia obtained his B.Tech. with distinction in electrical engineering from IIT, Mumbai in 1965. He later went to the USA and obtained his MS in electrical engineering from MIT (Massachusetts Institute of Technology). He completed his MS in management from Sloan School of Management. Mr. Arun Firodia returned to India. In 1972, along with his father, he started the flagship company, Kinetic Engineering Ltd. Continuing the family tradition of developing vehicles for common people at affordable prices, he developed India's first totally indigenous moped - the 'Luna' which ran on a petrol engine but could also be peddled like a bicycle. Luna became an instant hit with the consumers. It became an all time success story and made Arun Firodia the doyen of the Indian automobile industry. His contribution to trade and industry was recognized by the government with a 'Padma shri' that was awarded to him in the year 2012.

This is a real life case study of the 'Luna' and 'Pioneering of Professional Marketing in India.'

The Two-Wheeler Industry in the 1970s

The two-wheeler industry in India has been in existence since 1955. It consists of three segments, viz., scooters, motorcycles and mopeds. As per the Industrial Policy Resolution of 1948, the automobile industry was controlled and regulated by the government. The production capacity of each firm was determined by the government.

The Monopolistic and Restrictive Trade Practices (MRTP) Act, 1969 and Foreign Exchange Regulation Act (FERA), 1973, were aimed at regulating monopoly and foreign investment respectively. Firms required licenses to open a manufacturing plant. Collaborations with foreign firms were encouraged, but equity participation by foreign firms was not allowed. Consequently, foreign firms were reluctant to share advanced technology.

The impact of the MRTP Act was limited as it only affected large firms like Bajaj Auto Ltd., whose growth rates were curbed as they came under its purview. However, FERA had a more far-reaching effect as it restricted the foreign investment in India. In the motorcycle segment, FERA caused technological stagnation. No new firms entered the motorcycle market during the period from 1970 to 1980, as this segment depended almost entirely on foreign collaborations for technology. The scooter and moped segments on the other hand were technologically more self-sufficient. Thus, there were two new entrants in the scooter segment, and three in the moped segment.

This was the period during which the overall growth rate of the two-wheeler industry was high, at around 15% per annum. The high demand of two-wheeler vehicles was partly a result of the steep hike in the price of oil in 1974 following which two-wheelers became popular as a mode of personal transport. They offered higher fuel efficiency over cars/jeeps. The subsequent increase in sales volume of this industry is proof of its high growth potential. In 1971, sales were around 0.1 million units per annum. But by 1998, this figure had risen to 3 million units per annum. Similarly, production capacity had also increased from about 0.2 million units of annual capacity in the 70s, to more than 4 million units in the late 90s.

Marketing or even systematic selling was conspicuous by its absence during the early 70s in the two-wheeler industry. There was a 10-year waiting period for Bajaj scooters. Distant family friends and members of the Marwari community were generally appointed as dealers. They invested money in real estate by way of a showroom, maintained minimum stocks, and offered the bare minimum service. Dealers adopted a 'take it or leave it' policy. For instance, if a customer complained about scratches on the body of a new scooter, the salesperson would say, "Please give us a complaint note and refuse to accept this scooter. We will forward your complaint to the manufacturer and call you when the new scooter arrives." Arrival of this new scooter would generally take between 3 to 6 months with no guarantee that it would be free of scratches. Meanwhile, the dealer would sell the scooter with scratches to a customer in the waiting line, at a premium.

The Beginning: The Story as Told by Arun Firodia

"My father H. K. Firodia met Vikram Sarabhai during a flight from Delhi to Mumbai. Sarabhai described a lightweight, easy to handle, easy to service, two-wheeler he had seen in Europe, which was a combination of a motorcycle and a scooter. He suggested to my father that such a vehicle

would be good for Indian people, and should be made in India. My father liked the idea very much, but he was busy expanding the business of the Tempo Traveller, so he decided to give me this responsibility and asked for my opinion.

I was planning to return to India after completing my education in the USA. I had no idea about how an automated two-wheeler is manufactured because I was an electronic engineer and a management graduate. At that time, in 1969, the Organisation of Petroleum Exporting Countries (OPEC) had increased fuel prices multifold. Therefore, suddenly there was a great opportunity to make a lightweight, fuel efficient vehicle. I decided to go ahead.

The original Luna of 1972 was a licensed copy of the Piaggio Ciao moped. But we did a lot of new things. We decided to keep the weight down to only 50 kilograms, it had a 50cc engine along with pedals to be used in case of difficulty on a steep incline. Most importantly, this was a totally indigenous product, no foreign collaboration was required. As we were creating a new venture, we were not restricted by MRTP and FERA, the acts which most industrialists feared. The credit for making the first indigenous two-wheeler clearly belongs to us. We wanted to price it such that it was easily affordable to the common man. We planned the price to be around ₹1,000.

However, an increase in oil prices had caused a general escalation in prices which forced us to increase the price to ₹1,600. Even then, it was an affordable buy for a middle class person. Additionally, there was a guarantee that it could go 60 kms in a litre. It was difficult to believe that!

Those were the days of the space race. Neil Armstrong had already landed on the moon. The LUNA missions by the Soviet Union were making repeated trips to the moon, and even unmanned landings on the moon. We felt 'Luna' would suggest a vehicle coming out of space age technology, that was capable of travelling on the rough surface of the moon, hence we named our vehicle Luna.

When you are introducing a new vehicle in the market, you need to do something special and unique. We paid great attention to customers' needs. Prospective customers wanted a vehicle which was easy to drive and easy to maintain. We engineered many things to achieve this. If you need to take the engine out for every maintenance task, then maintenance becomes cumbersome and costly. We found a solution to this problem by separating the engine assembly, gear box assembly and clutch. We made the engine horizontal and located the exhaust on the lower side, which prevented carbon accumulation on the cylinder head and exhaust port. Otherwise, removing the carbon deposits would be a headache, and would have to be done only by a mechanic.

At that time, given the quality of roads and quality of tyres, the tyres got punctured very often. In the European designs, the wheel had to be totally removed to change the tyre. We made the rear wheel such that the tyre and tube could be changed without removing the wheel. We used the technique of Monocoque aircraft frames to make the body very light weight, less than 50 kilograms. We could then use lightweight steel sheets for making the body. We made the petrol tank within the body itself and used plastic parts to reduce the weight. In one injection mould of plastic, we could accommodate a speedometer, power button, headlamp, wire, etc.

Plastic was not well-developed in those days. Bright Brothers made household plastic articles. Their chief engineer Mr. Khan responded to our request, and helped us in making plastic headlights. Sumant Mulgaokar of Telco made dyes for making the chassis on a cost basis. In our Ahmadnagar factory, machines were required for many operations. One machine for making engines, one for making crankcases, another one for making gear boxes, another for making engine blocks, and yet one more for making cylinder heads. We could afford only one machine on our budget. Our chief engineer Mr. Bomra, designed a single machine for all these operations. Dr. S. M. Patil of HMT produced the multipurpose machine.

With all this help, the Luna was totally "Made in India". We had produced the Luna, but it was an uphill task to convince customers that the totally indigenous Luna, would deliver its promise. We tried many schemes, some more successful, some less successful.

To demonstrate that the Luna travelled fast, we raced the Luna with the Deccan Queen train from Pune to Mumbai (obviously not from Mumbai to Pune). To show that the Luna was rugged and could be used over long distances, eight riders went around India in 80 days on the Luna. They travelled from Pune to Kashmir - Nepal - Assam to Kanyakumari and back to Pune. They addressed press conferences in every city on the way. On their return, they did a victory lap in Pune. The famous actor Sunil Dutt also participated.

To show that the Luna was of global quality, we decided to export it. Americans like 'Do It Yourself,' so we produced 'Do It Yourself' kits, we even gave them kits of spare parts. We exported 50,000 Lunas. We advertised the Luna in the famous Time Magazine, with the caption, 'Luna Invades America!'

We tried to popularise the Luna among shopkeepers by pointing out that they could claim 100% depreciation on the Luna within a year. We tried to portray this as a major advantage to the shopkeepers, but did not really succeed.

We went to ladies' clubs and told them that the Luna is easy for women to use. The response was again lukewarm.

Diwali magazines are very popular in Maharashtra in general, and in Pune in particular. We designed covers for these magazines and offered them free of cost to circulating libraries so that the message of the Luna reached a large number of middle class houses.

We distributed T-shirts with pictures of the Luna to college students. We started giving the Luna as gifts to students who came first in the Secondary School Certificate (SSC) examination. We also offered the Luna at a low rent to college students to go for a picnic to Khandala.

After these initial efforts we became a bit more adventurous.

We started giving Man of the Match awards to test cricketers in test matches. I remember giving awards to BS Chandrasekhar for bowling, and to Farooq Engineer for batting. We tried new experiments in advertising. We used ordinary students, sports persons, doctors and lawyers, as models in our advertisements. Simultaneously, we also brought in Sachin Tendulkar and Azharuddin to advertise the fuel saving aspect of the Luna. I think Sachin was only 15 years old then!

All this helped. Sales kept on growing. This resulted in an unexpected problem. We ended up producing more Lunas than our licensed capacity, and we had to pay a fine for this extra production!"

The Two-Wheeler Industry in the 1980s

Two major players, viz. Hero Majestic Mopeds and TVS entered the moped market.

Hero Majestic Mopeds started in the late 1970s, in 1978. Within a few years, Hero Puch became very popular in North India. The Hero Majestic was a household name in the country, and by 1983, Majestic Auto Limited was the country's major manufacturer of mopeds. The Hero Majestic range included: Panther, Student, Hero, Stallion, Gizmo and Ankur.

Hero Puch was one of the largest selling two-wheelers in India. It was the first choice of young men. It had three variants: Automatic, Hero Puch Shakti and Hero Puch 3G (Three Gear). This vehicle was lightweight and sleek with good looking features, and was able to deliver a mileage of about 50 -55 km/litre with a 2-stroke engine.

Sundaram Clayton was founded in 1962 in collaboration with Clayton Dewandre Holdings, in the United Kingdom (UK). It manufactured brakes, exhausts, compressors and various other automotive parts. The company set up a plant at Hosur in 1978 to manufacture mopeds as a part of their new division. In 1980, TVS 50, India's first two-seater moped, rolled out of the factory at Hosur in Tamil Nadu, Southern India. A technical collaboration with the Japanese auto giant Suzuki Ltd., resulted in the joint venture between Sundaram Clayton Ltd. and Suzuki Motor Corporation in 1982. The moped market became highly competitive. TVS used ethnic regional product positioning strategy very creatively and effectively. Tamilians believed that TVS was a Tamil company working for the mobility of an average Tamilian in cities and villages.

Bajaj M80 was launched in 1986. Bajaj M80, was amongst the best-selling step-thru category two wheelers in India during the mid-1980s.

With the initiation of reforms in 1981, foreign collaborations were allowed for all two-wheelers with an engine capacity of up to 100cc. This prompted a spate of new entries in the industry, the majority of which entered the motorcycle segment, bringing with them a new technology that resulted in more efficient production processes and products. The variety in products available also improved after 'broad-banding' was allowed in the industry in 1985. This gave firms the flexibility to choose an optimal product and capacity mix which could better incorporate market demand into their production strategy. This would thereby improve their capacity utilisation and efficiency.

These reforms had two major effects on the industry: First, licensed capacities went up to 1.1 million units per annum, overshooting the 0.675 million units per annum target set in the Sixth Plan. Second, several existing but weaker players closed down giving way to new entrants and superior products.

In response to these changes, the Kinetic group formed Kinetic Honda. Kinetic Honda was a joint venture between Kinetic Engineering Limited, India and Honda Motor Company, Japan. The JV operated during 1984-1998, manufacturing two-stroke scooters in India. The Kinetic Honda scooter had only hand brakes, no brakes to be operated by foot. A child could easily stand between the mother's (rider's) two hands without interfering with foot-brakes. Kinetic Honda was also auto-geared. It became very popular as the 'Ladies Scooter'.

Luna in 1980s

The Luna was continuously updated by Kinetic. New models were launched regularly. Some major models were Luna TFR, Luna TFR Plus, Luna Double Plus, Luna Wings, Luna Magnum and Luna Super.

The dealer network was widened. All such marketing efforts helped propel the Luna brand to the top slot in the initial 12 - 13 years of its existence.

Firodia felt it was time to take the next leap in the field of communication. "We wanted an advertising campaign that wasn't gender or caste-specific. We wanted it to talk to every customer located in any part of the country," he said.

This wasn't easy. Firodia had been working with a few local agencies such as Blaze Advertising in Mumbai and Tom & Bay in Pune to market the Luna. Blaze had produced some of filmmaker Shyam Benegal's feature films, and was also a big name in the cinema advertising space. Blaze was used during the 1970s. In the 1980s, Kinetic used Tom & Bay. But the need for a distinct advertising campaign prompted Firodia to appoint the advertising agency Ogilvy & Mather (around 1984/85) to work on the Luna, and he found a young copywriter named Piyush Pandey. This was Pandey's first assignment; he was very down-to-earth and connected to his roots and wasn't scared to think in Indian terms.

Characters such as Ram Murari, a government employee, Ravi Kumar, a trader and Radha, a medical student, were part of the campaign, and were people viewers could relate to. They had issues of time management, wanted to strike a work-life balance, and at the same time desired to excel in life, business and academics. The Luna was added to their lives, and the advertisements showed how these characters could achieve their dreams with a little help from the moped.

Luna was positioned with the tagline 'Chal Meri Luna' ('Come on, my Luna' in English). It was inspired by the popular children's song 'Chal Mere Ghode Tik Tik Tik' from the 1959 film 'Chirag Kahan Roshni Kahan.' "All the elements fell into place very well – characters were from everyday life, they had problems like any of us, a product that could help them achieve what they wanted, and a tagline that was likeable and connected to our need to position the Luna as a solutions provider," said Firodia.

Before Luna, most advertisements, in print or TV, largely appealed to an elite, English-speaking audience, and were too western in their appeal. In many respects, 'Chal Meri Luna,' broke barriers, making advertising widespread, allowing more people to enjoy it because it was in Hindi and the characters were such that many would easily relate to. Thanks to 'Chal Meri Luna,' the brand extended its reign at the top for another decade.

The 'Chal Meri Luna' campaign, according to advertising experts, was a precursor to the 1990s wave of Indian advertising that used local languages and idioms to the hilt to communicate a brand message. Piyush Pandey and his creative team at O&M were at the centre of this new wave, bringing out advertisements for Fevicol and Asian Paints in the 1990s, that celebrated life, culture and habits the Indian way.

The Two-Wheeler Industry in 1991–1999

The reforms that began in the late seventies underwent their most significant change in 1991 through liberalisation of the economy. The two-wheeler industry was completely deregulated. In the area of trade, several reforms were introduced with the goal of making Indian exports competitive. The two-wheeler industry in the 90s was characterised by:

- An increase in the number of brands available in the market, which caused firms to compete on the basis of product features and price.
- An increase in sales volumes in the motorcycle segment vis-à-vis the scooter segment, reversing the traditional trend.

Luna in the 1990s

The Kinetic group was facing increasing competition in the moped segment, and the size of the moped segment was declining as heavier motorcycles were delivering equally good mileage, more power and a good ground grip. The 'Kinetic Honda' had a unique position as an ideal scooter for women with no competition in the segment, so the Kinetic Group focused their marketing efforts on the Kinetic Honda.

The sales of the Luna were declining. Even in Kinetic's hometown, Pune, the largest dealer of Kinetic Motors, B. U. Bhandari, was selling less than 10 mopeds per month. Arun Firodia was not happy. He felt there was still an untapped market for the Luna. He was exploring possibilities when he met Dr. Anand Karandikar (Anand, hereafter) and together they started direct marketing for Luna.

Direct Marketing for Luna

Anand K. had started a market research and marketing consultancy firm, viz., Marketing and Econometrics Consultancy Services (METRIC). Earlier, after graduating as an engineer, and doing his post-graduation in management, Anand had worked in industrial marketing, rural marketing and market research. He had started the consultancy firm after he was awarded a PhD in management by Pune University. His consultancy firm was in its initial stages. Anand taught management, as a visiting professor on clock-hour basis, at various management institutes in Pune.

Ajit Kale, one of Anand's students, had joined Kinetic in the marketing department. He was assigned the task of canvassing Luna amongst the big traders in Gultekdi Market Yard in Pune. Their pitch was simple: 'buy Luna and give it to your employees, so that they will be able to travel faster to other traders on the various errands that you give them. Employees will be happy, and they will be loyal. You can deduct the instalments towards repayment from the employees' salary, and also claim 100% depreciation in the first year itself.' However, traders were not attracted to the idea.

Ajit felt that he had to do something, but he did not know what. He met Anand and posed the problem to him. Anand said, "This will involve some work, and professional consultancy cannot be given as 'off the cuff' free advice." Ajit suggested to his boss, Mr. Chitale, Manager, Marketing Services, that Anand should be called for a discussion. Mr. Chitale had preliminary discussions with Anand and then introduced him to Arun Firodia.

Anand had no exposure to the automobile industry except for driving an old Lambretta scooter to various management institutes in Pune to conduct lectures. Anand made a very quick qualitative survey. He visited dealers in Pune as a mystery customer for the Luna moped; he talked to users of the Luna and users of M80. He visited large traders with Ajit and observed their transactions. He conducted a group discussion of his MBA students on 'Two-wheelers and the future of the Luna'.

In the meeting with Arun Firodia, in which surprisingly Mr. H.K. Firodia was also present, he shared his very preliminary observations:

- The sale at the dealership counters left much to be desired. The dealers were still operating as if they were running a ration shop for two wheelers.
- Servicing was offered as a favour by the dealers. At one dealership, only the first ten vehicles, waiting at the door of the workshop at 8 a.m. were admitted for the day. The rest had to return. No further appointments were given.
- Customers of the Luna were satisfied with the performance of the vehicle, but it was not an inspiring vehicle any longer. College girls looked down on boys who came to college on a Luna; a boy would be better off if he rode a motorcycle.
- The sales transactions of Ajit Kale with large traders were not creating any impact on the traders' minds.

For Anand, this was the first experience of interacting with very senior industrialists on a one-to-one basis. He was apprehensive. Arun Firodia (and H.K. Firodia) patiently listened to Anand, and Arun Firodia decided to involve Anand in exploring ideas. He made it a routine to take Anand for long rides in his car in the evenings, and bounce his various ideas off on him. Firodia discussed all the sundry issues including the taxation system of Shivaji Maharaj and his experiences as a sales person in a textile shop in Ahmednagar. He took Anand to the Kinetic factory in Ahmednagar in his car and personally walked with him around the shop-floor.

Ajit privately told Anand that his report had created a sensation in the dealership circle. Ajit reported, "HK personally went to the dealership at 8 a.m. and witnessed the situation himself. He fired the dealer left, right and centre. He asked the sales department to issue strict instructions to the dealers asking them to give appointments to the customers for accepting vehicles for servicing. He asked the service department to carry out an audit of the service facilities available with all the dealerships."

All this encouraged Anand. He had not expected such a positive and personal response from these doyens of the automobile industry towards a young person claiming to be a 'marketing consultant'. He felt a great sense of responsibility and challenge in meeting Arun Firodia's expectations.

The traders were the target group visualised by Arun Firodia. On further thought, Anand felt that the traders were a good market segment, but they needed to be further divided into the categories of large and small traders. He felt that the small traders formed an attractive market segment. Large traders would not buy a Luna for themselves as they could easily afford a motorcycle or even a car. Large traders, by and large, were also not 'progressive' employers who would invest in winning the loyalty of their employees by buying Lunas for them.

On the other hand, small traders would buy a Luna for themselves. Small traders included the category of 'mom and pop (kirana)' shops, relatively large panpatti shops, barbers, small laundry owners, large vegetable retailers, etc. Luna would make their travel to work very convenient; it would make it possible for them to go home for lunch in the afternoon, and come back to the shop in good time. There were a very large number of such small traders, and they were easily accessible in their shops.

However, the constraint was that the small shopkeepers would not have sufficient savings to make a full down-payment for puchasing the Luna. Even if they had those funds, they would prefer to invest them in increasing their businesses through more stocks and a larger shop front. Finance agencies would not give them credit because they did not maintain accounts and bank balances that would prove their credit worthiness. Anand felt that the small shopkeepers were credit worthy if they had been in business for more than three years and had enough footfalls in the shop. Their reputation in the market as being credit worthy was very important to them as they regularly received credit from their suppliers for the stock in the shop.

Eureka Forbes had successfully marketed vacuum cleaners through a team of door-to-door salesmen. To Anand, the success of Eureka Forbes demonstrated:

- A dormant need could be activated if the product was made available at the doorstep and its benefits were explained convincingly.

- An individual salesperson acting alone in a big market place can quickly be de-motivated by receiving repeated denials.
- If there was a team of 12 to 15 salespersons operating in a compact market and meeting every day for a review, there was likely to be at least one success story. This would keep the team motivation high, which was critical for success.
- The team had to be trained well in making a product presentation. They would not only answer objections but also convert objections into opportunities by explaining additional benefits.

Based on the above considerations, Anand suggested a comprehensive scheme of direct marketing of the Luna to small shopkeepers, to Mr. Arun Firodia. The salient features of the scheme were:

- Kinetic would recruit a team of 12 boys and girls, graduates with no previous experience so that any damaging habits in 'sales' style acquired by them in earlier jobs would not become a bottleneck.
- Sales persons would be paid salaries on par with the recruited graduates in the commercial department of Kinetic Engineering, and would be offered the same service conditions.
- All the boys and girls would be given a uniform with a Kinetic logo. They would sport a Kinetic cap.
- Each of the salespersons would be given a Luna on loan. The salesperson would visit a prospect, that is a small shopkeeper, on his /her Luna.
- The salesperson would be thoroughly trained in benefits-selling of the Luna. The major theme would be the time saved by the shopkeeper commuting from his home to the shop, including the time saved on the trip home for lunch. The shop could remain open for the extra time that would be saved when a Luna was used. The extra business that could be generated during the extra time would eventually pay for the cost of the Luna. In addition to keeping his shop open for extra time, he also had the benefit of having a healthy

lunch at home. The neighbours would notice that now he was on a Luna and not a bicycle or walking. This would increase his prestige in the eyes of the neighbours and particularly in the eyes of his wife!

- A prospect would be encouraged to feel and touch a Luna; he would be encouraged to sit on the Luna. However, a test ride would be given only if the shopkeeper had a driving licence and experience of driving a two-wheeler.
- Kinetic Engineering, through its collaborative agency - 20th Century Kinetic Leasing - would make credit available to the shopkeeper against post-dated cheques. The criteria for eligibility for credit would be, (a) the shop has been in operation for three years at the same location, (b) that it has a shop licence from the Municipal Corporation and (c) that there were at least 2 footfalls at the shop during the one hour that the salesperson would spend with the shopkeeper.
- All the orders would be handled by one lead dealer, if there was more than one dealer in the town.
- The scheme would break-even if the sales exceeded 45 vehicles per month and dealers were paid only a nominal commission on these vehicles. Anyway, subsequent income through servicing and sale of spare parts would be theirs.

Arun Firodia thought about the scheme only for 15 minutes. He said, "I have my doubts but I don't want to voice them now. Go ahead and implement the scheme in Pune. B. U. Bhandari will be the lead dealer. Let Ajit Kale be the officer in charge of the scheme. I am informing the personnel department, 20th Century Kinetic Leasing and Mr. Chitale to fully support you."

Kinetic Engineering released the recruitment advertisement in the local newspapers. 240 graduates applied. 41 were shortlisted through a written test. 15 persons - 10 boys and 5 girls - were selected for training. They were trained personally by Anand in a three day workshop. A team of 12 persons - 8 boys and 4 girls - was retained at the end of training. The rest of the scheme, including a Luna for individual salespersons, was implemented as planned. Anand attended the daily review meeting for the first 7 days. He then attended 3 review meetings over the following three weeks. At the end of the month, B. U. Bhandari had, under the scheme, delivered 104 vehicles to small shopkeepers.

Meanwhile, the personnel department of Kinetic Engineering raised a serious concern. They said that if the scheme was launched in, say, 25 cities then Kinetic would be recruiting 250 salespersons on its own payroll. Additionally, there would be 25 team managers, around four managers in the head office and one general manager. This was a significant new burden. In case the scheme did not continue, it would not be easy to retrench this staff as they were on the Kinetic payroll and had protection under all the labour laws. The personnel department suggested that the dealers should be persuaded to recruit the sales teams on their own payroll and they should supervise their performance. Kinetic would consider some additional commission to the dealer to share the cost of this team.

The vice president of 20th Century Kinetic Leasing also pointed out, “Today, we are implementing the scheme in the town where our head office is situated. We can closely supervise the performance of the team and do recovery follow-up with the customers. But we do not have any comparable administrative support structure in other cities. Citibank has already burnt its fingers by giving two-wheeler loans to persons without strict credit rating checks. We are not sure that the shopkeepers will keep on repaying the loan. They are the dadas in their own galli. In case they default, who could take possession of their vehicles? We should proceed very slowly and cautiously.”

Arun Firodia decided to try alternative options. He asked Anand to implement the scheme, exactly as it was, in Aurangabad. He asked the dealer in Kolhapur, who was a relative of his, to advertise the scheme on his own in Kolhapur, recruit salespersons on his payroll, and supervise their functioning. He asked a local advertising agency to implement the scheme in Bhopal on their own, in exchange for a Kinetic account for advertising in Madhya Pradesh.

The review meeting at the end of three months revealed the following:

In Pune, the team had sold 104, 102 and 109 Lunas respectively in the first three months. So far five cheques had bounced, but the team had been able to collect payment in cash from all the defaulting customers. The sales team was stable, and only one salesperson had left who had already been replaced.

The response to the advertisement for salepersons by the Kolhapur dealer and the advertising agency in Bhopal was rather poor. In Kolhapur, only 20 people applied. In Bhopal 47 people applied. In Pune, the passing percentage for written tests was set at 70%. In Kolhapur, only two people could clear with this percentage. In Bhopal, five applicants cleared the passing percentage. In effect, the quality of the recruited salespersons was below par in Kolhapur and Bhopal. The respective agencies carried out their own training because they found the fees quoted by Marketing and Econometric Consultancy Services (METRIC – consultancy service of Anand) rather high. In each city, only six vehicles could be sold under the scheme in the third month.

In Aurangabad, METRIC implemented the scheme as per the original design. The scheme worked well. 203 persons applied for jobs with Kinetic. A team of 12 persons was recruited. They sold 85 Lunas in the first month itself.

The following aspects became very clear to everybody:

Good salespeople could not be attracted on a dealer's payroll or on the payroll of a small advertising firm. Dealers or advertising agencies could not effectively supervise the sales teams. It was necessary to have a manager on the Kinetic payroll to supervise the team. Training had to be given in a very systematic and professional way by experienced and skilled trainers. The percentage of bounced cheques was low, but cheques issued by customers did bounce. The sales team had to be on its toes to quickly follow up with the customers to recover the money.

Arun Firodia and Anand discussed the issues meticulously. It was very clear that Kinetic would have to take a high risk if the scheme was to be implemented aggressively in at least 25 cities. It was true that sales of mopeds were declining. It could not be ruled out that aggressive competitors like Hero and TVS would start similar direct marketing schemes quickly.

Small shopkeepers presented an untapped market: they were large in number, perhaps more than a million. But risks were high. Anand said, 'There is no method in management sciences which guides on how to find an optimum risk return pay off. It is ultimately the investors' gut level feeling'. Thus, Anand finally threw the ball in Arun Firodia's court.

Arun Firodia kept the issue under consideration for a fortnight. He eventually decided not to proceed with the scheme. One reason behind the decision could have been his ongoing tussle with Honda Motor Company, Japan, over the future of Kinetic Honda. His mental and financial resources had, perhaps, a more important claim from Kinetic Honda Scooters.

Postscript 1: The moped market continued to decline. Kinetic stopped production of the Luna in the year 2000. Kinetic Motors sold the two-wheeler business to the Mahindra Group in 2008. M&M formed a new company - Mahindra Kinetic Scooters & Motorcycles Ltd.

Postscript 2: Kinetic and Honda separated in 1998. The Firodias bought Honda shares and acquired full control over Kinetic Honda Scooters. Honda Motorcycle and Scooter India (Private Limited) (HMSI) was founded in 1999, as the wholly owned Indian subsidiary of Honda Motor Company Limited, Japan. HMSI became the market leader in auto-geared scooters.

Postscript 3: Anand and his company continued to be consultants to the Firodia group. They continued to be consultants to Kinetic Honda Scooters for whom they conducted customer satisfaction surveys. They were retained as consultants by Force Motors, a company in the Firodia group managed by Abhay Firodia, Arun Firodia's cousin.

Postscript 4: Mr. Ravi Kant who was the marketing manager of Kinetic Honda during this period of direct marketing of the Luna, later went to LML scooters. He invited METRIC to work for LML. Subsequently Ravi Kant became the vice president at Tata Motors and eventually its Managing

Director. He invited METRIC to be consultants for Tata Motors. When Tata Motors took over Jaguar Land Rover in the UK, Ravi Kant invited Metric Consultants to work for Jaguar Land Rover in UK.

Postscript 5: Mr. Hiroshe, the then Managing Director of Kinetic Honda, later referred METRIC to HMSI and HMSI retained METRIC as consultants for locating all new dealerships.

Postscript 6: Marketing and Econometric Consultancy Services, a partnership firm, became Metric Consultancy Ltd., a public limited company in the year 2000. From the small beginning with Kinetic Engineering and Arun Firodia, METRIC grew to become the largest research based marketing consultancy firm in India.

Acknowledgements

- The story as told by Arun Firodia is based on 'गोष्ट 'लुना'च्याजन्माचीआणिवाढीची', (The Story of Luna's Birth and Growth). Loksatta, Chaturanga, Saturday, 7th February 2015.
- The write-up on the two-wheeler industry is based on: 'The Evolution and Structure of the Two-wheeler Industry in India.' Sunila George, Raghbendra Jha, Hari K. Nagarajan https://crawford.anu.edu.au/acde/asarc/pdf/papers/2002/WP2002_02.pdf
- The story 'Chal Meri Luna,' is based on the article in Business Standard Saturday, February 23, 2019 https://www.business-standard.com/article/companies/luna-is-dead-long-live-chal-meri-luna-114120300487_1.html

Chapter 2

Gone with the Wind

Anand Karandikar completed his B.Tech. in metallurgy from IIT, Mumbai in the year 1972. He got admission in IIM, Kolkata and completed his postgraduate studies in management with specialisation in marketing and econometrics. He was interested in pursuing a career in market research. He got a coveted job in Tata Economic Consultancy Services as an economist. His initial assignments included a research based project formulation for a dairy and for the manufacture of Phthalic Anhydride.

Anand did not have any background in dairy or in chemical manufacturing. Although, Anand completed these assignments to the satisfaction of his boss and the clients, he was not very happy. He felt his work was becoming esoteric with no understanding of the ground realities. He came to know that Mukand Iron and Steel (Mukand for short, hereafter) was looking for a market research officer in their foundry division. Anand saw this as an ideal opportunity for combining his basic knowledge of metallurgy with his professional interest in market research. He applied for the job and got selected.

Anand started working in the foundry division of Mukand located at Kurla in North Mumbai.

Mukand, was then the largest steel foundry in the country. Mukand also had a plant for continuous casting of steel bars by melting iron scrap. This new plant was in Kalwe, north of Mumbai. The continuous casting plant of manufacturing constructional steel, which was in short supply. It was the flagship division of the company. The foundry unit was an old manufacturing plant, struggling to break even. It was in competition with many small foundries that had much lower fixed overheads and paid much lower wages as they were situated in distant, semi-urban places like villages around Kolhapur.

Market research was an absolutely new activity at Mukand. Anand had a very loosely defined job description, "Find new clients; Find out new requirements of existing clients; Find out how profitability per kilogram of casting can go up; Do whatever, but contribute to earning profits for the foundry."

Anand became the blue-eyed boy of Mr. Lokur, the marketing manager, because of his initial successes, described below.

Anand's first success was during his orientation program itself. While walking around the factory shop floor, Anand came across castings meant to be used as jaws of the stone crusher. The front surface of the jaws was being machined on a lathe. Anand wondered as to why the jaws needed to have a smooth front surface as stones of different sizes were going to be crushed between the jaws.

These jaws were made of manganese steel because it is work-hardening steel; so that these jaws become harder and harder as they are subjected to impact while crushing stones. This work of hardening manganese steel hardens during the process of machining, and therefore machining the surfaces of the jaws was time-consuming and costly. Why did the surfaces which were going to impact stones need to be smooth?

Anand made enquiries with Mukand's 'methods' department. An engineer in the department took out a drawing of these jaws and said, "There is a triangle mark on these surfaces, it means the client wants this surface to be machined. We work as per clients' requirements; therefore, we are machining the job."

Anand was not convinced. He went to the nearest stone crushing quarry and saw the operation of these machines. The crushing surfaces of the jaws had sufficiently worn out because of the continuous impact, but the jaws were functional and working well. Anand went to the company who made these crushing machines and met their design engineer and asked him as to why the jaws required to be machined? The design engineer was baffled.

He opened the drawing and saw a triangular mark on the surface. He took Anand to his boss. Within a few minutes, the boss circled the triangle, marked it 'cancelled', signed the drawing and gave it back to Anand. Elimination of the machining meant that the cost came down significantly. Anand suggested that half of the savings should be shared with the customer. The commercial manager did not like this cost-sharing suggestion. "The client has not asked for a reduction in price, why offer it to him?" was his question. Anand said, "This order will be completed in two months. The next time the customer floats the enquiry it will be with a drawing without the requirement of machining. Our competitors will quote a lower price. After looking at that price, the client will feel cheated. We will make a short term gain but lose the account permanently." Mr Lokur fully supported Anand. The customer was very happy that the procurement cost was reduced by 25%. Within two months, the customer placed an open order on Mukand, without inviting competitive quotations.

Anand's second early achievement was in the context of castings made for battle tanks. The defence equipment enquiry was initially for the American Society for Testing and Materials (ASTM), class 3 radiographic quality castings. Mukand won the order through a competitive tender process. After the order was received, the defence quality assurance department raised the quality standard to ASTM class 2. The dealing sales clerk issued an 'order amendment' mentioning this new specification to the production department. It was by accident that Anand came to notice this order amendment. Anand went to Mr. Bhate, technical manager foundry, and said, "As I understand, moving from ASTM class 3 to ASTM class 2 is going to involve a significantly higher cost; we cannot supply ASTM class 2 castings at the price of ASTM class 3 castings. Am I right?" Mr. Bhate agreed with Anand.

Anand then spent time with foundry engineers working out details of what was needed to be done so that the casting quality was raised to ASTM class 2 from ASTM class 3. It was clear that the risers, which carry extra metal to compensate for shrinkage and absorb impurities, would have to be much bigger. Even then, the rejection percentage would go up from about 5% to about 15%. Anand discussed these issues with Mr. Lokur.

Mr. Lokur said, "I will have to go to Delhi and explain this to the seniors in defence procurement. I need a good presentation in a language which commercial people from defence procurement will understand." Anand made charts showing how the micro defects permitted in ASTM class 3 castings are 10 times more than those permitted in class 2 castings, how the extra metal required for larger risers would mean the use of 40% extra liquid metal and how radiographic inspection costs would go up. Mr. Lokur rehearsed this presentation with Anand and flew to Delhi to meet the defence procurement people. He came back very happy because he had managed to get an increase of 80% over the original price.

Because of these initial successes, Mr. Lokur decided to give Anand, who was still only an officer on probation with four months experience, a freehand to go anywhere and explore the market.

The problem was how to find new clients? Castings were an industrial product, procured by purchase departments and manned by professionals. Mukand was an old established foundry, therefore, if any user required steel castings, it was expected that he would send an enquiry to Mukand - being the best-known name in the foundry industry. It was therefore worth finding out whether in the past, Mukand had received enquiries for steel castings which had not been converted into orders, and explore whether these castings could now be considered by Mukand. Anand carefully studied the list of enquiries received in the past five years. However, this effort did not yield any positive results, as most of the enquiries were mainly for very small quantities of very simple castings, which any Tom, Dick and Harry foundry could make, and for which Mukand could not compete on price.

Anand then decided to adopt another approach. He compiled statistics of the growth of various possible end-user industries for steel castings. One of the industries, which was then growing fast and was likely to grow faster, was about production of electricity through thermal power stations.

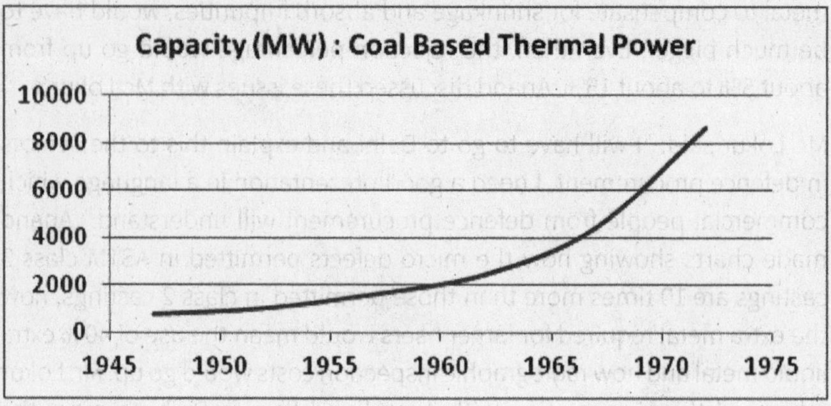

Anand noticed that there were no enquiries for steel castings from thermal power stations, electricity boards, or large boiler manufacturers. He was rather curious to know why such a big industry did not require any steel castings at all. He decided to study operations of thermal power stations and visited the large thermal power station at Koradi near Nagpur.

He explained the purpose of his visit to the officer in charge of the thermal power station, who welcomed Anand and said, "If you find something, tell me. I am also interested in it." Anand visited the thermal power station but everything was encased within large steel shells. The coal was getting into the system, generating power and emitting smoke. What was happening inside the steel shell was not visible at all; it was a big black box. In frustration, Anand decided to visit the scrap yard and he unexpectedly found large rings, apparently of steel, broken in places, lying in the scrap yard. These rings had a groove. Obviously, the best process for manufacturing these rings was casting. Anand found that these rings were made of a material called Ni-Hard.

On further enquiries, Anand collected the following facts:

- The Ni-Hard rings came with the original boilers imported by electricity boards.
- The Ni-Hard rings were a consumable item, they wore off grinding coal and required regular replacements.

- These rings were not being made in India but were being imported.
- Ni-Hard is white cast iron with 3% to 4% nickel and is extremely wear-resistant.
- Mukand had a licence for making cast iron castings as well as alloy steel castings in addition to a license for making steel castings.
- Mukand had never in the past made castings out of Ni-Hard.
- Making Ni-Hard castings was difficult for a cast iron foundry, even though Ni-Hard is a cast iron, because the cupola furnaces used for making cast iron are not suitable for making Ni-Hard.
- Making Ni-Hard rings was difficult for an alloy steel foundry because the induction furnaces used for making alloy steel castings are small in size in comparison with the size of Ni-Hard rings.
- The electric arc furnaces, used by Mukand, were good enough for making Ni-Hard.
- Mukand had sufficiently large furnaces to make castings of the size of Ni-Hard rings.
- The price of the imported rings was very high - the prices looked attractive by simple thumb rule estimates.

Anand approached Mr. Lokur and suggested, “We should get drawings made of these rings and make a ring on a development basis, investing our own resources. We should approach the Maharashtra State Electricity Board (MSEB) for a trial order.” Mr. Lokur had a detailed discussion with Mr. Bhate and decided to take the risk. Mr. Lokur issued a work-order for the manufacture of the Ni-Hard ring as per the drawings to be made by Mukand engineers using new imported Ni-Hard rings as the basis.

Anand meanwhile approached the central procurement cell of the MSEB in Mumbai to seek a developmental order. That was the time when import substitution was a very much talked about topic, and promoted by the government. The chief stores manager of the MSEB was happy to issue a trial development order. The price was the same as the price of the imported ring.

In a sand mould, cast iron flows more easily than steel. Consequently, it was not at all difficult for the production department to make the rings exactly as per the specifications. The Mukand-made Ni-Hard ring was sent to Koradi to be used on a trial basis. The good news was received after three months. The Mukand-made ring was functioning well; while the imported ring installed at the same time in another boiler had to be replaced because of high wear.

Everybody was very happy with this development. The cost accountant approached Mr. Lokur to enquire whether there was a mistake in the price, as his calculations showed that the contribution per kilogram on this ring was three times the normal contribution!

The MSEB stores department was very proud of their contribution to import substitution. They sent an annual contract for the supply of Ni-Hard rings. They added an additional item, viz., Ni-Hard balls. These balls were used between two Ni-Hard rings of the crusher. They were of relatively small size and a bit more difficult to cast because they were hollow balls. However, the methods department accepted the challenge and decided to manufacture the hollow balls. Mr. Lokur asked Anand why the initial developmental order did not include these hollow balls. Anand said that these hollow balls were already being made by some local alloy steel foundries because their smaller induction furnaces could be used and therefore the price for these balls was not very attractive. Mr. Lokur said, "Nonetheless, let us quote for these balls also so that the customer gets the rings and the balls from one and the same source."

After about a month Anand received a call from Mr. Vishwanath Kedia, Chairman of Nitin Castings. Nitin Castings was a much smaller alloy steel foundry specialising in reformer tubes for fertilizer plants. They were also the largest suppliers of Ni-Hard balls. Mr. Kedia told Anand that he wanted to exchange professional notes and invited him for dinner at the Taj Mahal Hotel in Mumbai.

Dining at the Taj Mahal Hotel was a new experience for Anand. Mr. Kedia discussed the general situation in the steel foundry industry with Anand and then asked, "How many persons are working with you in the marketing of Ni-Hard?" After a week, Mr. Kedia invited Anand to the Cricket

Club of India. He offered Anand a job in Nitin Castings at a salary which was roughly two and a half times the salary that Mukand was paying; his designation would be 'All India Marketing Manager.' Suddenly Anand had an opportunity to head a marketing department and become the highest-paid executive at his age in Mumbai. Anand could not refuse this attractive offer.

Postscript 1: After about 20 years, in the year 1995, Anand casually dropped in to the sales department of Mukand to meet old colleagues after a long time. He was surprised that everybody remembered him. After exchanging news for 10-15 minutes, Anand was surprised when five senior workers from the shop floor walked in with a bouquet of flowers. They said, "We have our jobs because of the work we do with the Ni-Hard ring. Your story is often told. At that time, we could not give you a proper send-off, so we decided to come and express our appreciation and gratitude." Anand could not control the tears in his eyes!

Postscript 2: Anand was sad after reading the following news:

The Hindu: Our Bureau: Mumbai, June 18, 2000

Mukund Ltd., has decided to close down its foundry unit at Kurla in Mumbai.

In a notice to the Bombay Stock Exchange, the company said it has "effected a complete production cutback at the plant" from June 16th. There are around 1,200 employees at the plant and the management had recently offered them VRS.

According to the company, the foundry's output accounts for only 7% of the company's turnover. Company sources said the management had taken a decision as the unit has been making losses due to lack of orders.

A union official, however, said the management's plan is to develop and sell the 25-acre plot where the foundry unit is situated. The union official said the foundry unit is economically viable and alleged that the management was intentionally closing down the foundry.

Source: https://www.thehindubusinessline.com/2000/06/19/stories/14191803.htm

Chapter 3

Handloom Terry-Cot

Background

Anand K. had resigned his highly paid job as a marketing manager in an engineering company in Mumbai and had gone to Udgir to do full-time social work. Udgir is a small town in Latur district of the Marathwada region of Maharashtra state in western India. Udgir is located at a place very close to where the three states of Andhra Pradesh, Karnataka and Maharashtra meet.

Anand started many activities in Udgir amongst the socially and economically weaker sections. This is the story of one of his activities.

Anand had noticed that a large number of young men in Udgir wore safari suits. The safari suits made of terry-cotton fabric were expensive and were generally worn by senior executives and rich traders in cities like Mumbai and Delhi on special occasions. He wondered how some of his friends could afford costly safari suits for daily wear.

He posed this question to Suresh, the unemployed son of a small farmer and a diploma holder in textiles. Suresh laughed and explained, "This is not the safari suit you get in Mumbai. This is our local safari made of Nanded terry-cotton. The fabric is woven on handlooms in the city of Nanded and surrounding areas and it is made from short lengths of yarn leftover by the Mumbai textile mills. This short length cannot be woven in a large automatic loom or even in a small power loom. This leftover yarn is available as waste material at throw-away prices. Traders buy it as waste and sell it to handloom weavers. Terry-cotton yarn from waste is woven into fabric on handlooms. This is a cottage industry flourishing around Nanded. The cloth is sold in many small towns in this region. It is available in almost every textile retail store in Udgir. There are at least ten retail stores selling this cloth. This is quite cheap, in fact, cheaper than a lot of good quality cotton cloth. We buy this terry-cot and get safari suits stitched from local tailors. The tailoring is also fairly cheap because in Udgir we have many more tailors in comparison to the population of the city. Tailoring is a traditional occupation of a sub-caste of Muslims - Darji and a sub-caste of Hindus – Shimpi. They are backward castes. Since they are generally not well educated they cannot take up any other occupation. I paid only ₹50 as stitching charges for this safari suit; I know in Mumbai you pay ₹400 to 500 as stitching charges for a safari suit. The terry-cotton woven on handlooms is available for anything between ₹20 to ₹25 per metre, compare this to the terry-cotton which sells at a price of more than ₹100 per metre in Mumbai. Here again the backward castes, Julaha, Netkani, Koshti and Ansari work on handlooms with low incomes. Now you can understand why we can afford to wear 'executive suits' for daily use in Udgir."

Anand was surprised. He asked, "Does this cloth last long enough? Are the colours permanent? Is there any other problem?" Suresh said, "Colours do not fade, the cloth is long-lasting, but there is only one problem - the cloth shrinks substantially. So, don't buy the cloth and give it for stitching. Wash it well, let it dry, wash it again, dry it again, get it ironed, and then give it to the tailor. The tailor knows Nanded terry-cot. He will stitch your safari slightly oversize. The initial two washes will ensure that the subsequent shrinkage is not very significant. As you keep on using the safari suit, the fitting will improve! Try it for yourself!"

Anand did try a Nanded terry-cot safari suit and found that the suit was very comfortable to wear because it was somewhat lighter in weight compared to the suit made of terry-cotton available in Mumbai, and therefore more suitable for the hot and humid climate of Maharashtra.

Anand was already exploring ways and means of providing more gainful employment to artisans working in Udgir. An idea dawned upon him - Why not stitch safari suits in Udgir and sell them in Pune and Mumbai?

A quick field check revealed that two handloom weavers in Udgir were already making Nanded terry-cot and ten more were willing to do this if the raw material was available and finished products could be sold in the market. Weavers had no difficulty in making the handloom terry-cot from waste Terylene yarn and cotton yarn.

Anand realised that there was more money to be made in selling readymade suits than selling only the handloom terry-cot fabric. A very careful search in the Pune market revealed that only two small shops on Laxmi Road were selling Nanded terry-cot suits, but they were not selling well.

Was taking measurements to stitch a safari suit a very skilled job? Anand wondered, because he had noticed what the tailor did while taking his measurements for stitching a safari suit. He discussed it with the tailor and found that only eight critical measurements were needed, none of them were difficult to measure with a tape.

The next time Anand went to Pune, he wore his safari suit made in Udgir. He also carried a spare suit in his bag. He met ten to twelve relatives and friends. Everywhere, he eventually brought the conversation around to the topic of the safari suit he was wearing. He would ask, "How does it look? Am I looking smart?" Almost everybody agreed that the safari suit was looking good. Were they saying it out of politeness? Anand wondered! But he decided to press on.

He said, "Look if you give me an order now, I will take the measurements. I have samples of shades for you to select. After 15 days when I come back, I will deliver your safari suit to you. The price is only ₹200, instead of ₹500 or more, which you would have to spend to get a safari suit stitched in Pune. Incidentally, this will also help the rural artisans to have gainful employment, their earnings per day will almost double."

Maybe because of the relationship, maybe out of genuine interest, maybe out of curiosity or maybe because of the thought that the loss would be only ₹200, almost everybody placed an order. In fact, some friends placed an order for two suits. Anand went back with measurements for 14 suits. He purchased the necessary cloth from retailers in Udgir. He got the fabric washed and pressed twice from the local washer man. He gave the fabric for stitching to 14 different tailors. He told the tailors to keep the usual extra margin for possible shrinkage over the next 10 washes.

He told the tailors that he would pay them normal stitching charges now and if they did the job well, they would get a 20% bonus after he delivered the suits to the customers. After 15 days, Anand carried a bag full of safari suits to Pune and delivered them to all his friends and relatives. He asked them to try the suits on so that if any alterations were required, he could take them back. He was happy that no suits required any alteration. After coming home, he made a quick calculation. He had collected ₹2,800 by selling 14 suits at ₹200 per suit. He had paid ₹900 for the cloth and ₹700 for stitching to the tailors. This left a surplus of ₹1,200. After deducting a bonus of ₹140 to be paid to the tailors, the surplus was ₹1,060. Wow!! Anand had invested almost no capital. He had not even invested in buying the cloth as the traders had given it to him on credit of one month.

Anand decided to set this up as a systematic business venture. He titled his proprietary company 'Handloom Terry-cot.' He eventually wanted to form a cooperative of weavers and tailors. But initially, he did not want to burden the cooperative with the risks involved in a new venture. He also wanted a free hand for making all the decisions. The branch manager of the State Bank of India in Udgir became curious when Anand went to open an account in the name of 'Handloom Terry-cot'. He was impressed by what Anand told him and offered a working capital facility of ₹10,000, even though Anand had not requested it.

The weaving and washing of the fabric, and stitching the safari suits were all manageable activities. The real crux was the sales channel. Anand did not want to sell 'Handloom Terry-cot' safari suits, door to door in Pune, for the rest of his life. He met Jayant Joshi, a friend who was a commercial artist. Together they explored methods to make an attractive display folder, which would not cost much, and would display the 'Handloom Terry-cot' safari suit worn by a smart young man.

Jayant Joshi creatively designed an album where the front side was a cut out on cardboard paper showing a smart man, with a piece of Handloom Terry-cot cloth at the back, so that the display looked as if the man was wearing a safari suit of Handloom Terry-cot. The idea was that the salesman would carry about 12 samples of cloth. However, as and when a new shade became available, only the cloth needed to be replaced and you had the man wearing a safari suit in this new shade in the album!

Anand decided that one of his target market segments would be college students who had a limited amount of money but would like to wear a safari suit to impress employers at the time of an interview (and girlfriends!). He approached Professor Ranganekar, then in charge of the student's cooperative store in a leading commerce college in Pune. He suggested to Professor Ranganekar that the student's cooperative store should become the central point for selling safari suits in Pune. Prof. Ranganekar felt that the college would contribute to providing gainful employment to rural artisans on one hand and salesmanship training to college students, under the expert guidance of Anand, on the other hand!

Anand selected ten students as salespersons for Handloom Terry-cot. This was a team of part-time salespeople, with each student generally working for 2 to 3 hours a day. The key characteristics of the sales team were:

- Salespersons were trained in sales talk and answering objections, in a two-day workshop; they practised a lot amongst themselves and freely criticized each other as to how to improve their performance, during the training workshop.
- All of them were given uniforms of a safari suit made out of Handloom Terry-cot.
- They were trained how to take the correct measurements and how to fill up the order form.
- They became proficient in the use of the specially designed album.
- They learned the technique of getting references of new prospects from existing customers.
- A salesperson earned a remuneration of ₹10 per suit sold by him.

In the first month, Anand was stationed in Pune. The sales team met every day to review performance. Customers came up with all kind of objections, some of the objections were:

- I do not want a safari suit I want only a pair of trousers, or I want a kurta, stitch it for me.
- You say the cloth will shrink. Will you return the money if I can't wear the suit because of shrinkage?
- You say this is for the benefit of rural artisans. You are college students from Pune. How do I know that the profits will really be shared with the rural artisans?

Each objection was discussed in the sales meeting and a standardised response was evolved. Efficacy of the response was analysed in a subsequent sales meeting and improvements were suggested, if necessary. Each salesperson maintained a detailed log of the prospect visited, his age, occupation and his response. This was discussed threadbare in the meeting.

In the second month, the sales review meetings became less frequent - once a week. Only eight salesmen remained operational during the second month. They booked orders for 190 safari suits worth ₹38,000. There were no rejections, no customer complaints. In the third month, the team sold 225 suits. The sales team was stable.

Anand knew that this business could not become a large business as waste yarn available from textile mills would prove to be an eventual constraint. His rough enquiries in the Mumbai market indicated that there was enough waste available to provide year-round work for 2,000 looms and at least 250 tailors. This was good enough for a small town, the size of Udgir, having a total population of 80,000. Anand handed over Handloom Terry-cot to a cooperative formed of weavers and tailors from Udgir.

Postscript: After two years, the Khadi and Village Industries Commission (KVIC) launched Polywastra. This was also Terylene and cotton yarn woven on handlooms and the fabric had a texture and shades similar to Handloom Terry-cot. However, KVIC had no system of delivering stitched to size safari suits at the doorsteps of customers. Consequently, Polywastra did not have much of an adverse impact on Handloom Terry-cot.

Chapter 4

Camlin

Camlin Ltd., (Hindi: कैम्लिनलिमिटेड) is an Indian stationery manufacturing company based in Mumbai, India. Camlin manufactures art materials, marker pens, fountain pens, inks, pencils, and other stationery products. Camlin started its operations as 'Dandekar & Co.' with 'Camel Brand' ink powders and tablets back in 1931 and shortly afterwards started producing 'Camel ink' for fountain pens. The company became well-known for its 'Camel' fountain pen ink and 'Camlin' fountain pens in India.

It was incorporated as a private company in 1946 and was converted into a public limited company in 1988.*

Camlin systematically promoted the brand through many innovative programs implemented consistently over many years. The 'Camlin Art Plaza,' maintained outside the famous Jehangir Art Gallery in Mumbai, has provided a low cost exhibition space at a very strategic location to many upcoming artists. The 'Camlin Painting Competition' for school children, became a major annual event in western India in which thousands of students participated.

Mr. Madhav, financial advisor to Camlin, felt that the value of the Camlin brand was not being fully realized. The sales growth was slow, while the overall market was growing faster. Moreover, though the company was never in the red, the bottom line was under severe pressure. Despite strong opposition from line sale managers, Madhav convinced the Dandekars that an outside expert agency should be appointed to have a look at the sales and marketing operations. A firm called 'Metric' was invited to take on this task.

*(In May 2011, the Japanese stationery major Kokuyo S&T, acquired a 50.74% stake in Camlin and the firm was renamed Kokuyo Camlin Ltd.)

Metric Consultants decided to begin their work by concentrating on one product line so that the efforts became focused, cost effective and results were quick so that a 'buy in' by line managers could make further work easier.

Pencils for school children were chosen as the product, and the markets of Mumbai and Pune were selected as the study area. The choice was based on the following considerations:

- Pencils for school children constituted a major share of the total sales (about 15%).
- The competition (Natraj, Apsara, etc.,) had gained substantial ground against Camlin's 'Flora' branded pencils.
- Mumbai and Pune, the 'leading' markets for consumer trends, was the single largest geographic market segment for Camlin pencils.
- Mumbai and Pune were Camlin's home ground too. From top to bottom, everybody in Camlin thought that they knew this market. If Metric could find something useful from this market, then 'buy in' would be easier.
- Metric, since it is based in Pune, could work efficiently in the Mumbai–Pune market. The implementation of the recommendations and the evaluation of the results too, would be easier in the home base.

Questions to be Answered

Metric Consultants held detailed, exploratory discussions with Madhav and the managers of Camlin. They studied the available historical data on sales and prices. They carefully read the field sales supervisors' reports on the market situation and market share. They visited a few retail shops and observed some retail transactions. The consultants drew up a list of questions:

- How often is the decision maker a child? How often is it the parent?
- What is the trigger for the purchase? Mother's monthly purchase basket? Ran out of stock? Examinations?

- What factors govern a child's choice of pencil to be purchased? What is the relative importance of each factor?
- What factors govern a father's choice of pencil to be purchased? What is the relative importance of each factor?
- What factors govern a mother's choice of pencil to be purchased? What is the relative importance of each factor?
- What is the 'brand awareness'? What is the 'brand position'?
- What is the availability at the retailer's counters? What share do Flora pencils get in a retailer's window display?
- What is the brand pushed by retailers? Why?
- How do children judge the quality of pencils?
- How does the quality of Camlin pencils compare with that of its competitors?
- What is the comparative quality perceived by children?

This was the initial list of questions. Additional questions were to be added as they arose with the progress of the work.

The Investigations

Metric Consultants used a variety of research tools and techniques:

- Observations of sales transactions at the sales counters.
- Focused Group Discussions (FGDs) of children, parents and teachers.
- Action research in children's playgroups.
- Interviews of children, parents and retailers.
- Interviews of distributors and their sales persons.

All the techniques were used in multi-layered, open-ended formats. In this approach, the methodology keeps on evolving as the research proceeds. The advantages of this approach become clear from the following experiences.

Topics to be discussed in a focus group were decided on the basis of findings from the previous focus group and the Focus Group Discussion (FGD) guidelines kept on evolving. The number of focus groups was only approximately estimated at the beginning of the assignment. These FGDs stopped only when nothing significantly new was discovered from the latest two FGDs.

One of the aspects to be investigated was whether children liked the designs on the pencil's body. Discussions and interactions with 6- to 10-year-olds were not very productive, so a simple experiment was designed. In a playgroup, pencils were offered as prizes. When a child was a winner, he/she was asked to take one pencil as a prize from a box full of assorted pencils of all designs.

The research officer noted the code number of the chosen pencil and demographics of the child. The preferences of more than 200 children were tabulated, which helped in finding not only the most preferred surface designs, but also the change in the preferences with age and sex. The tentative findings were presented to Dr. Ameeta Deshmukh, managing director of Metric. Ameeta was an art connoisseur and collector of paintings. She was deeply disturbed. "Children cannot have such a poor sense of colour and design," she said. "Something has gone wrong," she insisted. Ameeta told the research officers to repeat the exercise with one difference. "Ask the child the reason for choosing the particular pencil," she instructed.

The preference pattern emerging from the second exercise was similar to the one found in the first exercise. But the reason for the preference in 87% cases was, "This is a new pencil, I have never seen it before!" So, the children had opted for novelty, not for an appealing design.

Another area in which this sequential, multi-layered approach proved quite useful was in the context of the 'display' by retailers. Camlin had designed a very eye catching, dangler pouch for their pencils. The field investigators in Pune, during their first phase of observations, reported that these dangler pouches were conspicuous at retailers' counters by their total absence!

So, an investigation was initiated to find out the reasons for the retailers' reluctance to display the sling pouches. The retailers showed ignorance. The field investigator, tracing the issue back to the distributors' warehouse, found that the distribution van loaders were taking out the pencils from pouches and repacking them in bunches of 50 in simple polythene bags. The van loader said, "This new fancy packing by the company takes too much space, I can't carry half the load. You are from the company? Tell them to stop this nuisance."

Metric Consultants collected the comparative quality data from the R&D department of Camlin. The data showed that Camlin pencils had a longer life, smoother flow on the paper and a more uniform darkness of the line. However, the data were from laboratory tests, which did not accurately mimic the actual use of pencils by children. Metric therefore launched an observational study of use of pencils by children. The findings were:

- If the sharpener is not in the best condition (rusted blade, misaligned blade, loosely fitted blade, etc.), which is often the case, then the lead breaks frequently, while sharpening. This is a major nuisance and also results in a significantly shorter life for the pencil. When a not-so-good sharpener is used by children, in actual use observations, Camlin pencil lead broke more often than that of the leading competitors.
- If the pencil had an eraser, it did not erase properly. Black stains were visible, causing the child to apply more pressure and in the end spoiling or even tearing the paper.
- Camlin pencils last longer for the same amount of writing, 'if' there is no breaking of lead while sharpening.

Some of these findings emerging from the actual usage study were not captured in the Camlin laboratory tests.

Findings and Recommendations

- Two aspects of quality needed the attention of R&D: (a) breaking of the lead while sharpening and (b) the quality of the erasers.

- The brand awareness for Camlin is very high. The brand is associated with 'high quality art material.' However, 'Flora' pencils were not being associated with Camlin. Camlin is not known as a pencil brand. Neither children, nor parents bother much about the brand of the pencil. It is a low involvement product. All leading brands are treated as more or less equal, with Nataraj having a slight edge. Special advertising support is required to position pencils as, 'Pencils that write better and last longer.'
- Separate prizes were recommended to be sponsored for 'pencil drawings' in the annual Camlin painting competition.
- Almost all retailers stock Camlin and other major competing brands. But retailers seemed to push new and unknown brands because of the higher profit margins on them. Distributors' personnel must understand the importance of window display. Their Key Result Area (KRA) should be linked to the dangler pouch display and incentives should be linked to reports from independent audits. Retailers should be given special incentives linked to their total annual off-take of pencils and not the off-take of all art material and stationery as one single group.
- Giving small presents to all children attending a birthday is an established practice. Pencils are a popular gift among middle class and lower middle class families. Camlin should launch a special hamper of birthday gift pencils with distinctive and unique designs.

Chapter 5

Building Metric Consultancy Ltd. (Metric)

Part A: Building the Organization

Entrepreneur

After doing his B. Tech from IIT Mumbai, Dr. Anand Karandikar majored in marketing and econometrics from IIM Kolkata, in 1974, where he studied economics and econometrics under Prof. Jati Sengupta, Prof. Ranjit Sahu, Prof. N. Chandra and Prof. Paresh Chatopdhya.

Dr. Karandikar held salaried jobs for a decade carrying out market research and social sciences research. He started work with Tata Economic Consultancy Services (TECS), in 1974, mainly on projects related to demand estimation. He felt his work in TECS was very esoteric, with hardly any context of ground reality. Being a graduate in metallurgy from IIT Mumbai, he chose to work in Mukand Iron (1975-77) and in Nitin Casting (1977) in the area of market research for foundry products. For a couple of years, he worked as a full-time youth activist in the rural areas, but after realizing that he had no solution to the problem of risks faced by farmers, he came back to Pune and developed the research activity at Indsearch (1978-89) with a specialized focus on risk aversion by farmers.

Dr. Ameeta Deshmukh was Dr. Karandikar's colleague at Indsearch; together they formed 'Marketing and Econometric Consultancy Services' (METRIC), a partnership firm in Pune, to undertake market research and socio-economic research in 1989, (later, in the year 2000, METRIC Consultancy Ltd. – a closely held public limited company – was formed.)

Market Research Service Providers on the Scene

In 1989, when METRIC was established, there were nine relatively well-known Indian agencies in the areas of market research and marketing consultancy. Additionally, market research was offered as a service by many teachers at management institutes. Most of the nine relatively well-known Indian agencies had tie-ups with international agencies for borrowing technologies. Some of them were owned by large business houses. Market research and marketing consultancy were considered to be the apex applied intellectual activities in the discipline of business management.

Market research agencies which were then operating in India were mainly staffed by statisticians and economists. They employed hardly any marketing or sales professionals. The research agencies sold research based on methodologies bought from foreign collaborators and worked mainly for multinational corporations selling FMCG and pharmaceutical products in large cities.

Many of these nine Indian agencies do not exist today; they are either closed or have been taken over by international agencies. All major international agencies now operate in India. METRIC survived, grew and became an international agency! This is the story of how this was achieved.

METRIC – A Success Story

The major reasons for Anand Karandikar to start on his own and establish 'Marketing and Econometric Consultancy Services' were:

- The need to develop research methodologies to solve real-life 'marketing' problems in India – with the widest possible understanding of 'marketing'.
- The need for a real integrated approach of combining market research methodologies with in-depth understanding of 'technology' and 'social reality' at the grass-roots level.
- The freedom to commit mistakes and to learn from them.

Metric is Unique in Many Ways:

- Market research models, developed by METRIC in India, are used in 30 countries.
- It offers a synergistically organized bouquet of services under one roof: research, consulting, training, making educational short films, facilities for managers' training, call centre and recruitment services.
- It is an organization totally owned by its employees. There are no outside financial interests. Seven senior employees own the entire company.
- It is an organization run by professionals. All senior METRIC consultants are well experienced in handling line management responsibilities in reputed organizations. They also have the best formal professional qualifications.
- The company has the capability of innovating new methodologies to solve difficult problems. It is an organization where the practice is not of finding a fit of available readymade solutions to a client's problems but generating innovative solutions.
- It has a live network with 40 management professors for fruitful industry-academic collaboration.
- More than 110 full-time, permanent employees are engaged in the work of collecting primary data. Each of these employees receives more than 35 days of training in a year. The quality of primary data is guaranteed.
- It is an organization of substance. METRIC has developed ten new research and consulting processes, formalized as models, in the past 24 years. Perhaps, it is a world record of creating intellectual property in the field of management research and consultancy. All these models are now used by large blue-chip companies.
- It is an organization with style. The office is an art gallery. The surroundings are developed into a garden having a global variety of flora and fauna.

The success of METRIC is mainly due to the management practices followed by Dr. Karandikar and his team in three areas:

- Human resource development
- New product development
- Financial management

These practices evolved in the first five years, based on early experiences, and are summarized in the following paragraphs.

Human Resource Development

Recruitment

- Recruit good students from 'second- tier' institutions - METRIC could not afford the high salaries of IIM graduates; moreover, good students from 'other' institutes are keen to learn because they want to prove themselves.
- Do not recruit from competitors – they have acquired serious bad habits and have an 'I am always right' attitude because they come from big companies.
- At least 50% of the staff at all levels should be women, at least 30% should belong to SC/ST, (no reservation quota is legally compulsory for METRIC). These policies were followed because social surveys require understanding the problems of various sections of society. Chances of a better understanding of a group are higher if you belong to the group. METRIC's management made this policy loud and clear to all its staff so as to create confidence amongst employees belonging to special groups. For instance, METRIC is perhaps the only private sector commercial organization which prominently displays photographs of Mahatma Phule and Dr. Ambedkar and has a large number of their books in their library, although none of the owners belongs to scheduled castes or tribes.
- Recruit from different disciplines - The largest group was always MBA degree holders specializing in marketing, but they constitute

less than 30%. Engineers with primary interest in appropriate technology, students of politics and sociology, people who had resigned from the Indian Forest Service, geographers and statisticians – all were systematically head hunted. METRIC's management believed that the complexity and diversity of today's world could only be absorbed by an equally diverse staff.

Rural Call Centre

- Computer Aided Telephonic Interviews (CATI) became a common method of data collection through primary interviews. The cost of getting work done through call centres in urban areas was high because of the high real estate cost of a seat in a multi storied, air-conditioned building with extravagant interiors.
- METRIC established the first real rural call centre in India at village Bopordi, Wai- Mandhardewi Road, District Satara, Maharashtra.
- About 80 young women from the neighbouring villages, were recruited and trained to use state of the art hardware and software. They handled telephonic interviews for many reputed national and international organizations.
- A steady and well-paid, white-collar job at the METRIC call centre made a huge contribution to improving the quality of life of these young rural women. The Indian Express came out with a special story on this call centre titled, "Rural Girls Find a Calling - How a Call Centre Changed the Lives of Women in Wai and Nearby Villages- Written by Swasti Chatterjee | Published: March 4, 2012 available at:https://indianexpress.com/article/news-archive/print/rural-girls-find-a-calling/

Training

- Considerable investment is continuously made in human resource development. Even in the small-sized initial office, there was a training room. The area devoted to training grew at a faster pace than other office infrastructure. Today, METRIC is proud to have a full-fledged, fully equipped residential training centre where 40 employees can stay at a time in air-conditioned double-occupancy rooms.

- Staff members are encouraged to organize their own learning programs on subjects of their choice. Every staff member undergoes at least 25 days of structured training in a year. Staff members from all over India attend at least two residential training workshops, on METRIC's campus, every year.
- The competence and confidence of staff members increased substantially. Competitors have come to acknowledge the quality of training. METRIC employees are in demand and METRIC cannot provide enough growth opportunities to all. Hence there is a problem of high attrition rates. None the less, METRIC's management has not fallen prey to the myopic view of 'not being the trainers for the competitors' and has continued its investment in training the staff.

Compensation

- METRIC introduced almost all employee benefits like a provident fund, gratuity, long service bonus, grants and leave for improving qualifications, leave travel and medical reimbursement, even when they were not statutorily compulsory.
- Although Ameeta was junior in terms of age, qualification and experience, she was offered a 50% share in equity and management by Dr. Karandikar, at the time of forming the company. Later, other select employees, at all levels, were given an exgratia share in equity. This has significantly contributed to 'entrepreneurship within the organization' by many staff members.

Development of New Products

METRIC continuously developed new products and services. In fact, this is the main reason why METRIC has survived and grown. These developments are in the areas of market research, marketing consultancy, direct marketing and training of customer interface staff.

The story of how the most used model, nationally and internationally, 'MOSTER' was developed at METRIC is told in 'Part B' of this case study.

The need for new products primarily originated from clients. It was the client organizations which posed the problems in their own terms. All the successful new models developed by METRIC are in response to specific needs expressed by clients, as can be seen from Table 1.

Table 1: Models Developed in Response to Customer Needs

Model Name	Brief Purpose	Developed in response to
RIRA	To measure and manage risk aversion by farmers	ICAR, GOI, New Delhi
MOSTER	Measure customer satisfaction and improve customer retention	Kinetic Honda, Pune
DeMatrix	Dealership loyalty evaluation and classification of dealers	BPL, Banglore
CRIDA	Credit rating of market dealers stocking competing brands	SPIC, Chennai
M-Price	Price sensitivity of demand and optimum price brand	Research Solutions, Nairobi
MetriQuity	Consultancy in brand management	CVBU, Aftermarket, Tata Motors, Mumbai
Mods20 degrees	Consultancy for measuring and improving employee engagement	Tata Auto Comp, Pune
TCIS	Training for customer interface staff	LML, New Delhi
Insitu Training	On the job training for sales counter staff	Bharat Petroleum Corp. Ltd. Mumbai
LOCATE	Best locations for single-brand retail outlets	Honda Scooters & Motorcycles Ltd. N. Delhi

Quantity and Quality

As seen from the table, over the span of the last 24 years, METRIC successfully developed six new models in market research, two new models of training, and two original processes of marketing consultancy. Volume-wise, this performance is, perhaps, unmatched by any competing agency or institution, small or large, anywhere in the world. Quality-wise, the models, processes and systems have been purchased by large and reputed organizations the world over; and subsequently, these organizations have been repeat clients of METRIC.

Learning from Mistakes

The temptation to develop products because 'We want to do it' or 'We can do it' – could not always be avoided. For instance, METRIC developed a Data Envelopment Analysis (DEA) package for comparative dealership evaluation. The reasons for doing so were, firstly, DEA was in fashion amongst academicians and secondly, 'we could do it'. It flopped - there were no buyers. However, they learned from this experience and mostly avoided such temptations.

Continuing Ongoing Process

Product development is seen as a continuing process. Every problem stated by the customer, every new need of the customer, is taken seriously. The model is improved as a whole system. Piecemeal solutions confined to sectors to meet immediate contingencies are not permitted. For instance, the most popular model of METRIC, MOSTER, launched in the year 2000, is now in its 8th editi on.

Financial Management

Transparency and Credibility

METRIC started with an initial capital of only ₹5,000, one portable typewriter and an office in a 10'x 10' space demarked in the 1BHK residential flat of

Dr. Anand Karandikar. It was absolutely necessary that the working capital required to do fieldwork was provided by the clients. In effect, clients were required to pay almost half of the project cost as advance, without any guarantees and any visible signs of financial prosperity or credibility of METRIC. METRIC adopted a policy of total truth and transparency. The information on cost structure, including the expected profits, was fully and honestly shared with the client. Clients were welcome to ask for explanations and make suggestions for cost reduction. This often resulted in a client negotiating only with METRIC without having competing quotations and paying in time to avoid delays in the project execution.

To further build client confidence, METRIC adopted a policy of never asking for a price rise on account of cost over-runs; and not to compromise on quality to achieve cost reduction. In some cases, to communicate this policy to the client, the cost over-run data was shared with the client, without comment, and surprisingly, in response, sometimes clients increased the fees!

Risk-taking

Dr. Anand Karandikar and Dr. Ameeta Deshmukh continuously and daringly kept on investing all surpluses generated through the business, and the loans that could be obtained through maximum capital gearing, in development of new products and services. They did this even when a few of the new products and related diversifications were not successful. (In fact, surpluses parked in shares and mutual funds, because there was no immediate opportunity for investing in new products, caused problems when the stock market crashed in 2008.)

Accountability

At the earliest opportunity, METRIC became a public limited company (though investment from the public was not asked for), so that all the statutory requirements regarding governance, including external audit and outside directors had to be compulsorily followed.

Succession

Dr. Anand Karandikar retired from METRIC in the year 2014 on attaining the age of 65. Dr. Ameeta Deshmukh took over as chairman and managing director. METRIC continues to flourish as the leading research-based marketing consultancy organization.

Part B: Developing 'MOSTER' Model

1990

METRIC was one year old. Paul Mascerhenus, a student of Anand Karandikar, was the market research officer at Kinetic Honda. There was a job vacancy for canvassing customer satisfaction questionnaires designed by Honda, Japan to 100 customers for each of 110 dealerships. Paul offered the job to METRIC. The client wanted only the filled questionnaires to be analyzed in Japan. METRIC analyzed the data on its own initiative and reported to Mr. Hiroshe, mananging director of Kinetic Honda that many aspects causing dissatisfaction to Indian customers were not covered; aspects like low ground clearance of the scooter, less mileage and a narrow time slot in which dealers' workshops accepted the scooter for servicing. Mr. Hiroshe asked METRIC to present the findings to H.K. Firodia, chairman of Kinetic Honda. It was decided that METRIC should improve the questionnaire and research methodology.

1991 to 1994

METRIC researched the best methodologies from around the globe, improved questionnaires, and repeated four annual rounds of customer satisfaction surveys for Kinetic Honda. Mr. Abhay Firodia, Mr. Arun Firodia, Mr. Hirose and Mr. Ravi Kant - then general manager of marketing, Kinetic Honda, all took great interest in the research process, forming research-based strategies and implementation. METRICwas requested to conduct a training program for company staff, dealers and dealers' staff for implementing a research-based strategy.

1995

Mr. Dharmadhikari (Dharma), who joined METRIC, had spent 15 years in international marketing. He reviewed the international scene and pointed out that customer satisfaction surveys were increasingly being discredited. In the USA, the fashionable slogan was, 'customer satisfaction is dead'. The two major problems were:

- Importance of attributes emerging from the research was contrary to the obvious.
- There was no empirical correspondence between customer satisfaction and customer retention.

Dharma said that if METRIC could develop a radically new and valid approach, a large market, nationally and internationally, was ready for it. Ameeta Deshmukh reviewed the research experience in India in the context of international controversies. She said, "Hey guys, read Noriaki Kano. His theory of two-dimensional quality is well established for new product development. It has great potential for being the basis for quantitative measurement of customer satisfaction."

Dr. Anand Karandikar started working on the nuts and bolts to build a systematic tool. The methodology and the tool were christened MOSTER, an acronym derived from Monitoring Satisfaction To Ensure Retention.

1996 to 1997

Mr. Ravi Kant, who had now become marketing director of LML, New Delhi, invited METRIC to work with him and decided to support the development of the new MOSTER method. Mr. Kant involved METRIC in forming research-based strategies and implementations. The results were a phenomenal success. Sales went up by 300%, and the company's net worth, which had become negative, was fully restored.

1997 to 1999

- MOSTER was improved, particularly by incorporating the use of the Serv-qual model of Dr. Parshuramn for qualitative research.

- International brands like Mercedes and Babcock-Wilcox opted for the use of MOSTER in India after getting approval from their head offices.
- MOSTER was chosen by clients for products as diverse as oil engines, mixers, pesticides and housing.

2000

METRIC's management decided to globally market MOSTER. "We must bet on our own intellectual creations," said Dr. Anil Gore, statistical advisor.

Dharma was designated as the director of international operations. Dharma started marketing on the web, sitting at his computer. He contacted hundreds of the first generation market research companies. His sales pitch was simple, "Like us, you also find it difficult to compete with the big five, particularly in the area of customer satisfaction research. You know that they are doing a bad job, their customers are unhappy. But you do not know what better to offer. We have a better product; a tested and proven product. Are you interested?"

2001

Thirty (yes thirty!) international agencies showed interest. They included, to name a few, Dr. Lima Pichat form Bangkok, Thailand; Dr. Frank Chain of Diagaid from Shanghai, China; Mr. Edward Newton from City Research, London, UK; and Mr. Fernando Krasovitzky from Mexico.

They were invited in batches of five/six for a three-day workshop in Pune. Twenty-five of them attended the workshops in that year. They paid an entrance fee of US$ 5,000 and agreed to pay a fee of 15% of the project value.

2002

Tata Motors appointed a special committee to recommend an appropriate methodology to track customer satisfaction. MOSTER was selected.

2003

- Tata Steel managers suggested to Dharma that METRIC should explore the possibility of doing relative value analysis proposed by Ray Korduplesky, using data from MOSTER to enhance value functionalities of the MOSTER system.

- Dharma and his team worked on reverse-engineering of the relative value maps. The relative value maps drawn using MOSTER data were found to be very useful by Tata Steel managers.

- Relative value maps, showing the relative position of market players on two dimensions of satisfaction regarding quality and satisfaction regarding price became the standard additional deliverable of the MOSTER system.

2004 to 2009

- New international agencies and international and Indian clients continued to join the MOSTER family.

- Notable international agencies were Psyma Research with its head office in Nuremberg, Germany and a presence in eight countries, Consulmark in Lisbon, Portugal, Research Solutions in Nairobi, Kenya and MMR in Atlanta, USA.

- Dr. Anand was invited to conduct staff training workshops by the following agencies.

No	Origination	Country	Duration	City	Year
1	Psyma Int. Medical Marketing Research GmbH	Germany	2 days	Nuremberg	2005
2	Consulmark	Portugal	2 days	Lisbon	2005
3	Logic Market Research	Egypt	1 day	Cairo	2006
4	MMR Research Associates, Inc	USA	3 days	Atlanta	2008
5	Pan-African Research Services Ltd (PARS)	Kenya	2 days	Nairobi	2010

Small but significant improvements kept on happening with MOSTER. For instance, Fernando in Mexico developed a very cute animated presentation; Jose Constantino in Portugal developed a Computer Aided Telephonic Interview (CATI) tool. All these improvements became part of standard MOSTER.

A few of the 'Big Five' agencies started offering 'Kano based satisfaction studies' on a 'me too' basis.

2010

- Spurred on by the 'me too' competition, Dharma and his team developed an analysis of drivers of loyalty. This development involved using an overall loyalty score as a dependent variable and positions in dissatisfaction – satisfaction – delight space on various attributes as independent variables.
- Anand developed a dummy variable econometric regression model to predict the contribution of each product/service attribute in generating customer loyalty.

2011

- Mr. Ravi Kant, now the vice chairman of Tata Motors, suggested to Mr. Ralf Speth, M.D., Jaguar Land Rover, (JLR) UK that JLR might benefit from the services of METRIC Consultancy. After due diligence spanning a time of four months and six meetings, Jaguar Land Rover, UK appointed METRIC Consultancy (UK) to study customer satisfaction in the aftermarket using MOSTER.

2012

- "We have MOSTER data for all brands, ours and competitors, for wristwatches; can it be used to find white spaces?" This question was asked by Mr. Harish Bhat of Titan Watches.
- Dharma and his team had already developed expertise in using the technique of correspondence analysis.

- Anand used the expertise to find correspondence between demographic variable and delight status of the customers.
- Ameeta liked the findings. She suggested a few changes.
- The senior manager from Titan said that they got new, significant and useful insights.
- The process of making correspondence analysis was integrated as a standard deliverable of MOSTER.

2014

- Dr. Anand Karandikar retired from METRIC on attaining the age of 65.

After 2014

- METRIC continues.

Chapter 5

Situating Dealerships for Honda Motorcycles and Scooters in India

Preamble

A retail location is considered to be one of the most important elements in retail marketing strategy. It is a long-term decision associated with long-term capital commitment. In store-based retailing, good locations are one of the key elements for attracting customers to the outlets and sometimes can even compensate for a mediocre retail strategy mix. Location is considered one of the elements of the retail marketing mix that is unique and cannot be imitated by competitors.

Over the years, the importance of the location of retail shops has been highlighted by many researchers, academicians and practitioners to understand the importance of retail location in achieving success. In today's highly competitive environment, choosing the correct site for a retail outlet ranks amongst the top factors in determining the outlet's success or failure.

In the case of the brand-specific exclusive retail outlets, the retail outlet boldly carries the name of the brand and principal company, for instance, 'Shubham Honda'. In case the retail outlet closes down because of its bad location, it creates an impression amongst people that the brand is not selling. This ill-will can affect the sales at the retail counters at other locations. Location of the retail outlet is, therefore, very important to the principal company.

Background

Honda Motorcycles and Scooters India (HMSI) was a company formed by Honda Japan in 1998 after they had withdrawn from Kinetic Honda

Motors. HMSI had started manufacturing auto-geared, battery-start scooters, an advanced version of the scooters manufactured by Kinetic Honda.

HMSI opened its first 25 dealerships all over the country. None of these dealerships was earlier a dealer of Kinetic Honda. HMSI had an understanding with Kinetic Honda that the new company would not offer dealerships to the dealers of Kinetic Honda.

HMSI followed the same procedure for situating a dealership in a particular town, as was practiced by all automobile manufacturers in India. The automobile manufacturer would first select a dealer based on his financial strength, antecedents and familiarity with the automobile business. Once the dealer was selected, he would be given specifications for the showroom in terms of the space required for the display of the vehicles and the workshop for servicing the vehicles, generally adjoining each other. The dealers usually had real estate property of commercial retail value. A dealer would search for properties which according to him, were reasonably priced and were likely to increase in value in the next five years. He would shortlist two or three sites, generally owned by him or by his business associates, and show them to the sales executive of the automobile company. Together, they would select one of the sites for locating the showroom.

Mr. Ashok Sen, sales director of HMSI, had followed a similar procedure while deciding the location for the first 25 dealerships in 25 towns. These 25 towns had not been selected on any clear criterion as HMSI dealerships were soon to be opened in 300 towns. The average sales of HMSI scooters from these first 25 dealerships were just 20% lower than the average sale of scooters in the first year by a new dealership in the town.

Mr. Hirose, Asia Pacific Manager for Honda Motors, had visited about ten of these dealerships during his tour of India. He was uncomfortable with the locations of the dealerships. He felt the dealerships were situated at locations where the real estate property was likely to have the maximum appreciation. They were generally on the outskirts of town, in an area which was getting urbanised at a fast pace. Consequently, these dealerships were at one end of the town. The density of prospective customers in the neighbourhood catchment area was low.

Mr. Hirose discussed the issue with Mr. Sen, and also with some of the dealers. All were unanimous in their opinion that a motorcycle dealership could not be located in the crowded heart of the town, off generally old traditional commercial streets or the main streets. In these crowded old central parts of the city, access was difficult for motorised vehicles, parking was a big problem, and commercial space was very costly. Consequently, showrooms for scooters had to be away from the central business area.

Mr. Hirose agreed that the central crowded old city areas were to be avoided. But he was not convinced that the dealerships had to be located on the outskirts of the town in areas which were yet to be sufficiently developed. He felt that the procedure of asking the dealers to shortlist the places, and then selecting one of them was inherently flawed. The dealers had a relatively myopic view. A dealer thought that if the dealership succeeded, well and good. But if, for whatever reasons, the company's vehicles did not sell, he should be able to close the dealership and sell the real estate at a much-appreciated price, thereby not only cutting losses but also possibly making a profit. According to Mr. Hirose, this way of thinking on the part of the dealers was not acceptable to Honda Company. Honda wanted each dealer to be wedded to the future of the parent company.

Mr. Hirose had earlier worked as the managing director of Kinetic Honda. At that time, Hirose had retained Dr. Anand Karandikar and his team for the task of measuring customer satisfaction and improving service at the dealerships. He was also familiar with the work Dr. Anand and his team had done for a sister company - Kinetic Motors - to improve the sales of Luna mopeds. He suggested to Mr. Sen that Dr. Anand should be invited as a consultant to advise on the locations in the next 40 cities where Honda had plans to open dealerships within the next 6 months. Mr. Sen felt that there would be resistance from the new dealers because they were used to deciding the location themselves. Hirose told

Mr. Sen that these dealers should be told that they would be selected as dealers only if they were willing to start the dealership in their towns at the location specified by HMSI. As a compromise, HMSI should promise the dealers that if, after two years of operation, the dealer found that the location was not good and he wanted to relocate, then HMSI would bear the cost of shifting.

Mr. Hirose then personally telephoned Dr. Anand K., and invited him and his company to work on the consultancy assignment of suggesting appropriate locations for dealerships in the 40 towns specified by HMSI.

Anand had specialised in econometrics, along with marketing, while doing his two-year, full time, residential, Post Graduate Diploma in Management from IIM Kolkata. Specialising in econometrics, from IIM was very exceptional. The main reason why Anand specialised in the subject was due to the faculty. At that time, IIM Kolkata had the best faculty in economics and econometrics comprising Professors Barun De, Nirmal Kumar Chandra, Ranjit Sahu and Jati Sengupta. In his professional career, Anand had taught econometrics to MBA students at the University of Pune, and had used econometric methods in the field of marketing, mainly for risk analysis and demand forecasting, with good results. In the invitation from Mr. Hirose of HMSI, Anand saw an opportunity to apply econometric methods to solve managerial decision-making problems in an entirely new and perhaps virgin field.

Building an Econometric Model

The objectives of the assignment were penned as:

- To develop a standardised methodology for making informed decisions about the locations of HMSI dealerships in various cities. The methodology should be objective, purposive, reliable and cost-effective.

- To use the developed methodology so that the branches situated at the recommended locations would have the highest benefit-cost ratio and a very high chance of success.

The research process was planned in two main stages:

Stage 1: Developing and testing a model using data from the first 25 dealerships.

Stage 2: Using the model to find suitable locations for the next 40 dealerships in 40 specified cities.

Stage 1

The research process is illustrated in Flowchart 1.

Flowchart 1: The schematic research process

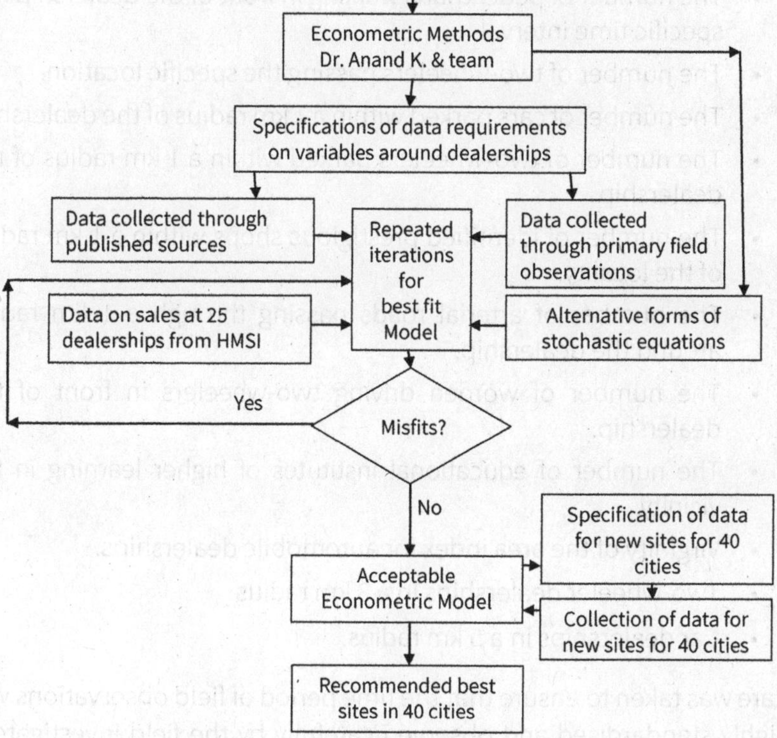

The 25 dealerships for which HMSI had the sales data were located in 25 different cities. HMSI supplied information on the sales in their first year of operation.

Some normalising variables were also used in the model to eliminate the effect of the total market size and isolate the effect of the dealership location. For this purpose, some major city-level variables, for which data were available from secondary sources, were identified. These variables were:

- Size of the population in the city.
- The number of cars in the city.
- Number of two-wheelers in the city.

A number of location-specific variables were thought of through brainstorming. These variables included:

- The number of pedestrians walking in front of the dealership in a specific time interval.
- The number of two-wheelers passing the specific location.
- The number of cars parked within a 1 km radius of the dealership.
- The number of two-wheelers parked within a 1 km radius of the dealership.
- The number of identified prestigious shops within a 1 km radius of the locality.
- The number of arterial roads passing through a 1 km radius around the dealership.
- The number of women driving two-wheelers in front of the dealership.
- The number of educational institutes of higher learning in the vicinity.
- Virginity of the area index for automobile dealerships.
- Two-wheeler dealerships in a 3 km radius.
- Car dealerships in a 5 km radius.

Care was taken to ensure that the time period of field observations was highly standardised and observed carefully by the field investigators. For instance, the number of two-wheelers passing in front of dealerships had to be observed when passing from left to right between 10 a.m. to 11 a.m., and when passing from right to left between 11 a.m. to 12 noon on a weekday, which was a working day and not a festive day.

Linear, as well as non-linear models were tried. An attempt was made to keep the variables at the city level to a maximum of 2, and those at locality level to a maximum of 5 in number, so that the degrees of freedom, that is 25 data points minus the number of variables, was high.

The best model had the ratio of the explained variation to total variation, i.e., R2 of 0.81. The model used six variables. All the parameters had correct signs and low standard errors. Graph 1 shows the number of actual sales with the predicted sales by the best model.

Graph 1: Actual Versus Predicted Sales of HMSI Scooters at 25 Dealerships

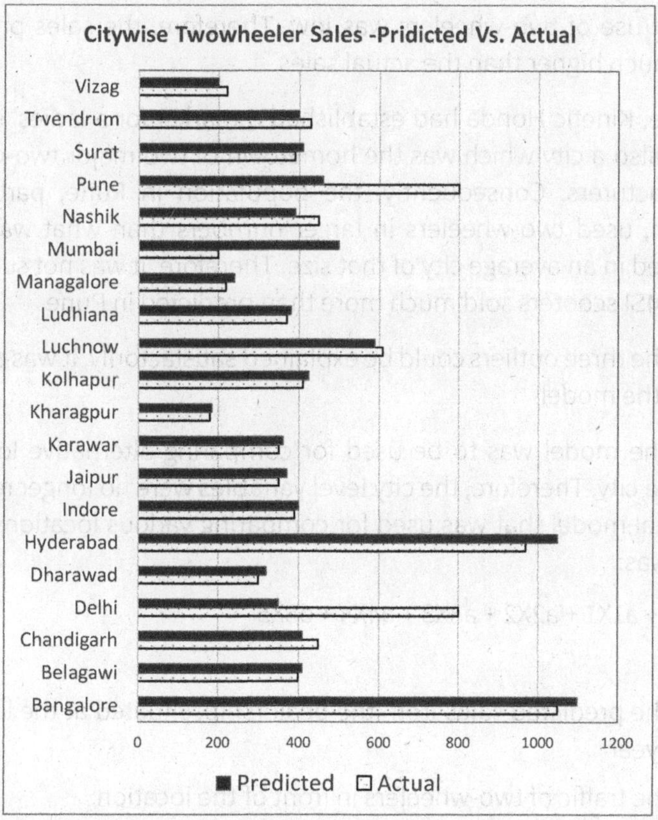

The model was analysed qualitatively by Dr. Anand K. and the HMSI sales team, to check that the mathematically derived relationships were not contrary to logical and intuitive theories.

The three outlier cities were Delhi, Mumbai and Pune (marked by black arrows in the graph). The outliers were explained well through qualitative analysis.

In Delhi, women driving scooters often faced harassment on roads. Honda was considered a ladies' scooter. Delhi women did not use a scooter, or any two-wheeler for that matter, as far as possible. Consequently, the sales of HMSI scooters were bound to be much lower than predicted by the model.

In the case of Mumbai, given the north-south geography of the city, and availability of three railway lines and an efficient public bus service, the general use of two-wheelers was low. Therefore, the sales predicted were much higher than the actual sales.

In Pune, Kinetic Honda had established a market for a ladies' scooter. It was also a city which was the hometown of two major two-wheeler manufacturers. Consequently, the population in Pune, particularly women, used two-wheelers in larger numbers than what was to be expected in an average city of that size. Therefore, it was not surprising that HMSI scooters sold much more than predicted in Pune.

Since the three outliers could be explained satisfactorily, it was decided to use the model.

Now, the model was to be used for comparing alternative locations within a city. Therefore, the city level variables were no longer relevant. The final model that was used for comparing various locations within a city was:

$$Y = a0 + a1X1 + a2X2 + a3X3 + a4X4 + a5X5$$

where,

Y = The predicted sales from the dealership, situated at the location, after 1 year

X1 = The traffic of two-wheelers in front of the location

X2 = The movement of women pedestrians in front of the location

X3 = The number of two-wheeler dealerships within a 3 km radius of the location

X4 = Number of arterial roads within 1 km radius of the location

X5 = Virginity index of the location

The virginity index was calculated as:

100/(1+ number of automobile dealerships in a 3 km radius)

Stage 2: Using the Model to Find the Best Locations in Specified Cities

Once the model was approved, ten possible good sites were identified in each city. This was done through:

- Discussion with the dealer.
- Discussion with the field sales officer of HMSI.
- Discussions with three or four prospective customers.
- Discussion with the town planning official in the municipal corporation.
- A quick look-see tour of the city by field investigators working with Anand K.

If there was a difference of opinion regarding a site, it was generally included for further study.

Data were painstakingly collected for each of the possible sites in the city. A schematic map was prepared to show the location and the value of the variable.

A typical map is seen in Figure 1. below:

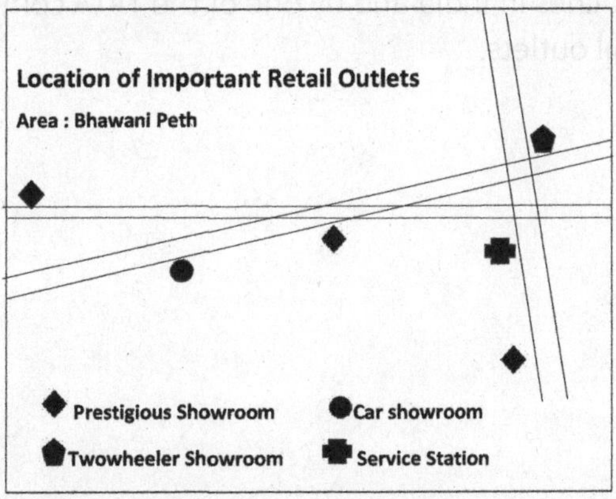

These data were then fed into the model to determine the predicted sales at each possible location in a city. The locations were ranked in decreasing order of likely sales. One great inherent advantage of the method was that in case the most preferred location could not be chosen the model output also indicated the loss in sales that would be incurred by choosing the second-best location.

The entire exercise took ten weeks to complete. The next 40 dealerships in 40 cities were located at the first priority locations emerging out of this exercise.

A review after one year showed that the average sales at these 40 dealerships were 15% more than the average sales achieved in the second year of operation by the first 25 dealerships.

HMSI used this methodology to situate the next 280 dealerships in the next two years. The company did not receive even a single request from any dealer to shift the location of the dealership due to sales not being good at the existing location.

HMSI became the market leader in non-geared scooters within a span of three years. Although the major credit for this success was attributable to a good product, the credit was also partly due to the correct location of the dealerships.

Postscript: The method developed by Anand K. and his team was subsequently used, equally successfully, by an international bank to locate its branches in India and by one of the TATA companies running exclusive retail outlets.

Chapter 7

Atlanta City

Jignesh Mehta, an MBA from an autonomous management college in Pune, Maharashtra, India, was already a successful businessman at the young age of 35. His father owned a medium-sized textile shop on Laxmi Road, the main commercial street in Pune. Jignesh joined his father's business immediately after his MBA, though he had received several placement offers on campus. Jignesh took it upon himself to expand his father's business. He converted his father's shop into a speciality sari shop and renamed it 'Shubha Mangal'. He focused on specialising in high value silk saris, which were famous for their place of origin, like Paithani silk, Kanjivaram silk, Dhaka Jamdani silk, Kashmiri silk and Banaras Shalu. He visited the places of production himself and developed direct relationships with the weavers there. He placed orders in advance with them for saris which would match the taste of upper, middle class women in and around Pune. 'Shubha Mangal' became 'the' place for women to purchase their saris for social gatherings and events like marriages. Within ten years, Jignesh had expanded to two more outlets, one in Kothrud and another one in Aundh, which were both burgeoning areas of Pune at that time. Jignesh also got elected as a managing committee member of the Mahavir Cooperative Bank, which mainly financed businesses belonging to the Gujarati trader community in Pune.

Having tasted early success, Jignesh was now exploring possibilities of business expansion or diversification. This was when Subhan Mohite, a schoolmate of Jignesh, met Jignesh and proposed to him a diversification in the housing and real estate sector.

Subhan Mohite was a lawyer by profession. He belonged to a farmer family from Hadapsar area near Pune. His father was active in the co-operative sugar movement and was also a member of the managing committee of a co-operative sugar factory. His uncle too, was active in politics and was a member of the local council. Subhan had entered into the real estate business in partnership with two other school friends.

Subhan mainly handled land deals. His expertise was in buying agricultural lands from farmers on the periphery of Pune city, getting them converted into non-agricultural lands, and acquiring approvals for plans from all the authorities. His partners used to look after construction and marketing activities. Recently, the other two partners had fought with each other and the partnership had been dissolved. As his share, Subhan received all the rights on a residential scheme, which was a project under construction, on a three-acre plot of land on the outskirts of Pune, about half a kilometre from the Pune-Ahmednagar highway. Subhan had already got the plans sanctioned for eight, six storied buildings with four flats on each floor.

Additionally, there would be a small garden, a clubhouse with a swimming pool, jogging tracks and tennis courts. The construction had already begun and the RCC structure of four buildings was almost ready. A sample flat, fully furnished, was also ready. In the recent finance bill, the finance minister had announced a special scheme for all developers of residential properties in India. If a housing project was completed within the next twelve months, then the developers could claim benefits of a substantially low, almost nil tax payment on the income they generated.

The purpose of the scheme was to give an incentive to construction of housing properties. This announcement had created a sense of urgency in Subhan to complete the project on hand. So far, just 10 flats out of 192 had been sold. Subhan was short on funds to complete the construction. He had to get a substantial down payment from customers who booked the flats for delivery within the year.

Subhan approached Jignesh with a proposal, saying, “Jignesh, I know everything about land purchase, I know something about getting quality construction done at a reasonable cost, but I know nothing about marketing. You are the only person in my knowledge, who has marketing expertise. Join me. This is an excellent opportunity. Yes, in addition to your talent, you will have to invest money; but the returns are as high as 30% within the next 12 months, and almost tax free. You can't beat the offer. All you have to do is to sell residential housing."

Jignesh replied that he would let Subhan know his decision within a fortnight. Jignesh completed the minimum due diligence quickly. He investigated and found out that Subhan's partners had fought because they had fallen in love with the same girl and it had nothing to do with the problems in business. He got the papers for the scheme checked from another lawyer and found them to be in good order. He went to the site with an experienced civil engineer; the civil engineer opined that the construction carried out so far was of a good quality.

Officially, the project site was outside the Pune Municipal Corporation limits and therefore, the local council taxes were much lower than taxes of the Pune Municipal Corporation. The approach road from Pune city to the site went through a village which was rather crowded for about one kilometre. The project was serviced by the municipal bus service and had water supply from the municipal corporation.

The question was, should Jignesh enter the real estate business? Jignesh had a friend, who was a professor at the National Institute of Construction Management and Research (NICMAR), a premier institute of construction management located in Pune. He discussed the general situation in real estate with the professor and asked him how the housing sector was doing. The professor said a student of his had recently written a note on the housing industry, and gave the note to Jignesh. The highlights of this note were:

- The real estate sector occupies a significant place in the Indian economy, second to agriculture.
- 80% of the real estate developed in India is residential; the rest comprises offices, shopping malls, hotels and hospitals.
- Once known as the pensioner's city, Pune has now become an industrial hub. The last decade has made Pune a promising city, growing in dimensions on all fronts. Kothrud, one of the fastest

growing residential suburbs in Pune, found a mention in the Guinness Book of World Records!

- Builders constructing houses, always think alike and hence create 'me too' templates. Most of the schemes lack an innovative approach.

Jignesh Mehta consulted his father, who said, "In the hierarchy of roti, kapda, makaan (food, clothing, shelter) you are already at kapda (clothing). You can now surely move to makaan (shelter)".

After due consideration and discussion with his co-directors in the cooperative bank, Jignesh decided to join Subhan Mohite in the real estate business. They formed a new company, Sahyadri Real Estates Private Limited.

Jignesh immediately began thinking about marketing. The last line in the report written by the young student was still ringing in his mind. He did not want to be a 'me too' real estate developer. He wanted the project to be unique, satisfying specific needs of a clearly identified market segment.

The location of the project was towards the east of the city. This area of the city was generally considered as a cosmopolitan area in which traditional Marathi people did not prefer to stay. The area was treated as an extension of the military cantonment. This gave Jignesh an idea, that of considering Army officers, serving and retired, as the special market segment for this project. Jignesh made a quick list of major defence establishments in and around Pune. He was surprised to find more than a hundred such establishments including well-known establishments like the National Defence Academy, Southern Command Headquarters, the Explosives Factory at Khadki, Bharat Electronics, which produced mainly defence related electronic equipment, Armed Forces Medical College, Air Force Base Station and the College of Military Engineering. Even a naval establishment, namely INS Shivaji, was based at Khandala near Pune. Almost every army officer had been trained at the National Defence Academy and would have fond memories of their alma mater.

Jignesh made a quick, rough estimate of the armed forces officers currently serving in Pune, the armed forces officers who had stayed in Pune sometime in the past and the armed forces officers who had been staying in Pune after retirement. He came to a number which was definitely more than 10,000 and could even be 25,000. He found a contact in the Rajendra Sinhji Institute (RSI), which is basically a club of army officers. He hosted a small tea party for about fifteen army officers who regularly came to the Rajendra Sinhji Institute and discussed with them the idea of promoting a special residential real estate scheme for armed forces officers in relative proximity to the Rajendra Sinhji Institute. He received a very enthusiastic response. Some residential schemes for army officers had already come up in Pune, like the 'Rakshak Society' but now they were fully sold out. There was currently no new housing scheme which was aimed at army officers in Pune and they were eager to move into such a project if there were to be one.

Jignesh finally decided to focus on army officers. In consultation with Subhan, he decided to offer them a lower price – a discount of almost ₹400 per sq. ft. The base rate of ₹8000 /sq. ft. was already very competitive.

The project was originally named 'Balaji Housing' by Subhan in consultation with his astrologer. Jignesh did not like the name. He wanted the name to be cosmopolitan, free of any religion, caste, creed or region in India because it had to appeal to officers from the armed forces, who belonged to various religions and castes, and came from varied regions of India. It was also necessary, according to Jignesh, that the name sounded upmarket and prestigious. Subhan consulted his astrologer and reported to Jignesh that the new name must have at least two 'A's and two 'T's, the more the 'A's and 'T's the merrier! Finally, after considering a lot of options, the project was renamed 'Atlanta City'.

On a piece of paper, Jignesh jotted down the salient aspects that he must keep in mind in deciding the marketing and sales strategy for Atlanta City. These points were:

- The project is well designed, and competitively priced.
- The location is future ready, roads need to be developed, may not appeal to people who want immediate possession to move in.

- Army officers are a viable target group: it is large, Pune is a desired retirement location, and Pune has large army establishments.
- The target group is selectively reachable.
- A discount of ₹400/sq.ft. is an attractive incentive.
- Army officers mistrust 'civilians,' particularly 'builders.'
- The target group needs to be broadened to include all armed forces (army, air force, navy) and other defence establishments.
- The sales must begin with a bang and continue at a very fast pace. If the project is seen as 'not selling' then it will not sell.

Sales Management

Jignesh asked Subhan to increase the height of the compound wall from the current 4 feet to 6 feet, with wire mesh on the top. He also asked Subhan to install a number of security cameras on the compound wall. He told Subhan that this was essential, as often the army officer's wife and children would be staying at home, when the officer himself would be away at the place where he was posted. The officers would be particular about the security. Closed circuit cameras were also to be an essential part of every lobby in the building. All these cameras were to be monitored through a central security office near the entry gates of Atlanta City. Jignesh and all the sales people introduced this security system to the visiting officers - the prospective customers.

Army hospitals in Pune were well equipped with all the modern amenities. However, it was clear to Jignesh, from his discussions with the army officers, that the officers from the armed forces wanted general practitioners, both male and female, close at hand to give advice, and if necessary, emergency assistance. Jignesh identified two doctors, male and female, who had recently retired from the AFMC. He made a special offer to both of them to buy flats in Atlanta City. Jignesh told them, "First, you will get a 10% discount instead of the usual 5%. Secondly, after three or more years, if you decide to sell the flat, I guarantee you a repurchase at a 30% higher price." Neither of them could refuse such an attractive offer.

Jignesh then approached General Kale who had a great reputation for being a judicious buyer and drove hard bargains for imported army equipment. He made the same offer to the General that he had made to the medical professionals. General Kale also accepted the offer as he realised this was really a good, risk free investment. Jignesh was very happy because he knew that a casual mention of General Kale as having bought a flat would substantially eliminate the problem of credibility of Sahyadri Builders.

Jignesh put up a notice in the Rajendra Sinhji Institute and announced that every day officers would be picked up from the institute at 4 p.m. for a site visit to Atlanta City and dropped back by 7 p.m. for a drink at the institute.

Jignesh hired a mini-bus for the purpose of personally escorting the army offices. On the way to the site, Jignesh would wait till the minibus was about to enter the crowded village road. He would begin his sales speech when the crowded patch began, so that the army officers did not notice the crowd as they were listening to the presentation being made. On the way back, the route would be different. Jignesh would say, "Now we will show you how close we are to the airport and to the railway station. This road was very wide and well maintained, although longer by about three kilometres.

Jignesh had recruited six retired army jawans as security guards. They were positioned at strategic locations in Atlanta City. They would smartly salute the visiting army officers. 117 officers visited the site in the first month. Three officers booked flats in the first month. During this period Jignesh was busy putting together all the nuts and bolts of his 'grand sales strategy' which he named Sales Chakra. The implementation of the Sales Chakra started after 45 days and involved the following:

- One retired brigadier, three colonel level retired officers from the three services and the wife of an army officer were recruited as the sales team. They were designated as Atlanta Sales Managers (ASM).

- The team was trained in benefit selling and Customer Relationship Management (CRM) through a week long training program.
- The team members travelled to major defence establishments in the country and recruited local 'Camp Sales Representatives' (CSRs). A CSR was generally the wife of the senior-most officer in the establishment.
- All CSRs were invited to Pune, all expenses paid. A two-day residential program was held for them. CSRs were equipped with a handy and classy presentation kit.
- CSRs were promised a commission of 1% of the sales value.
- The army canteen establishment was approached to display posters of price discounts at all the counters.
- A 'customer gets customer' scheme was announced: an existing customer got a further reduction of ₹250/sq. ft on his price when he got a new customer.
- The sales process stopped at the Brigadier. The promoter-builder did not meet the prospect.
- All events in the armed forces establishments, like the navy ball, in which Atlanta City could participate with sponsorship, were identified. Twenty events were short listed for participation.
- More than 200 establishments were identified where personal presentations by Atlanta Sales Managers (ASMs) were desirable. These establishments were allocated as Key Result Areas (KRAs) to individual ASMs.
- The list of customers was updated every week, and the list was circulated to all CSRs. It was circulated to all the customers and was also boldly displayed in the sales office.

Results

All 192 flats were sold within 10 months.

Chapter 8

Click Photo Printing Systems Pvt. Ltd.

This is a story from an era in which there were no mobile phones and of course, no mobile phone photography. One had to buy a film roll, load it in a camera, click the photographs, take out the exposed roll and get it developed and printed.

P. Balachandran (Chandra, from here on) started the company, CLICK Photo Printing Systems Pvt., Ltd (hereafter referred to as CLICK), in Bengaluru, immediately after graduating with an MBA in the year 1990. This is the story of how Chandra made CLICK the most recognised photo printing laboratory in the city of Bengaluru (then Bangalore). The story also touches upon the initial teething problems and the eventual inevitable decline of the business.

Chandra's father was an engineer working as a senior manager in a private sector company in Bengaluru. He bought a Yashica camera on one of his trips to Japan and presented it to Chandra when he was 15 years old. Chandra was an avid amateur photographer by the age of 21. He decided to enter the business of developing and printing photographs at the age of 24.

Konica had revolutionised the photo printing system in the 1980s. Before that, there used to be only a manual colour photo printing service, in which the delivery usually took around seven or more days. Konica's 'minilab', was a small photograph developing and printing system, as opposed to a large centralized photo developing lab. The minilab consisted of two machines, a film processor and a paper printer/processor. The minilab did the job of developing the negatives and printing on paper automatically within one hour. With this, the cost of colour photography also came down drastically.

Most amateur photographers could now afford colour photography and could have their prints quickly and conveniently developed. The market for photo printing boomed.

Chandra purchased the Konica Nice Print System and set up shop (hereafter referred to as a lab!) at a very good location on 'Commercial Street' in Bengaluru. He also set up a manual processing and enlargement lab in a small place on the first floor of a nearby building.

Chandra recruited a staff of ten employees. One manager, who was a general-purpose assistant to Chandra and in charge of the lab when Chandra was not around; four sales girls who managed the counter from 8 a.m. to 9 p.m. in two shifts, four lab operators, two in the day shift and two in the night shift and one operator for the manual lab.

The major aspects of the CLICK photo system business in the first year are described in the following paragraphs.

Customers

There were three types of customers: amateurs, professionals and collection agents.

Amateurs were greater in number, but generally brought only one roll for developing at a time. They did not know much about how to judge the quality of the photo prints. Often a large number of their exposures were wastages.

Professionals were less in number. They brought in, on an average, five rolls at a time. Professionals had a certain understanding about quality. They were very price conscious.

The collection agents ran collection centres in areas where there were no photo printing labs. They collected the negatives from the customers, brought them to the lab every day, or more or less frequently, depending on the number of rolls collected; and took prints from the lab and delivered them to the customers. They charged up to 15% in commission from the lab and 5% to 10% service charges from the customer.

The initial business for CLICK was 65% from amateurs, 20% from collection agents and 15% from professionals.

Printing Paper

There were two types of photo printing paper, commonly known as glossy print and matte print. The cost of both papers was similar.

Customers generally preferred the glossy print. Matte prints took longer because the lab had to wait utill they got sufficient orders to start a print-run on the matte paper. The price charged for a matte print was 20% higher than the price charged for a glossy print because of the short production runs.

However, the matte print resulted in double the profit margin compared to the glossy print.

Enlargements

Enlargement of prints was a very profitable business. The profit margins per square centimetre of paper printed were almost twice the margins obtained on prints in the standard postcard size.

Amateur customers seldom ordered enlargements, and even professional photographers rarely did so. Enlargements contributed to only 2% of the total sales. The manual enlargements lab was mostly idle.

Transactions at the Sales Counter

Chandra often observed the interactions at the sales counter; his major observations were:

The transactions with the amateur customers were quick and to the point. The customers were asked whether they wanted matte prints or glossy prints. Most of the customers were quick to choose glossy prints. Some customers asked for an explanation. The salesperson's standard response was, "Glossy prints will be available in two hours, matte prints will be available tomorrow; glossy prints are cheaper." Customers generally chose the glossy print.

The information about the price was exchanged, that is, the development cost was fixed and the printing cost would depend on the number of good prints. The customers were told the total cost estimate based on an assumption that all the prints would be good. When customers came in to collect the prints, they were given the developed roll and printed photographs. Many amateur customers showed disappointment because some of their exposures were not printed. If they asked the salesman for an explanation, the salesman said, "Bad exposure is not worth printing, we saved your money." The customer paid the amount and left.

The professional photographers came in and met the manager. They bargained and bargained for discounts. They often insisted on meeting Chandra. If the discounts were not perceived to be sufficient, some even walked away without depositing the rolls. Chandra felt that it was a standard practice of professional photographers to hammer down the price and make labs drop the price to the absolute minimum.

The photo printing business was very competitive. There were at least 10 competing shops offering the same service in Central Bengaluru, although many of them did not offer large enlargements through manual processing.

Chandra was also exasperated by the continuous bargaining by professional photographers. He felt helpless with the amateur customers when entire rolls of 36 exposures could not be developed into even a few good prints. He was puzzled when collection agents switched from his lab to another competing lab for no apparent reason that he could see, the other lab was neither offering higher commission nor was it nearer to the collection centre; apparently, the agent wanted to keep his eggs in more than one basket.

Even after a year, CLICK was having insufficient business, much below the breakeven level. Against the capacity to process 150 rolls per day, CLICK lab was receiving only 50 rolls per day. Chandra had borrowed money from banks to set up the business. He was not able to repay the loan instalments. Chandra did not want to borrow money from his father. He was worried.

T. Rajan had been Chandra's classmate when they were doing their MBA and was also an enthusiastic photographer. Rajan had joined his family business of wholesale trading in grocery after doing his MBA. Rajan was finding it difficult to adjust to the working style of his father and two uncles. Rajan asked Chandra whether he could come in as a partner in the CLICK business.

Chandra considered this a god-sent gift. Rajan's investment would take care of the loan instalments for some time. Funds would also become available for market development activities which Chandra was thinking about. Chandra consulted his chartered accountant about converting CLICK Photo Systems from a proprietary firm into a partnership. The chartered accountant advised Chandra to form a private limited company as partnerships were prone to break up and it was difficult to continue the business in the same name and style after a break up. Private limited companies were more sustainable. Additionally, the words 'Private Limited' added prestige in the eyes of onlookers. Of course, there would be a requirement of more shareholders, holding annual general meetings and completion of legal formalities on a regular basis. "But they are worth the trouble," said the chartered accountant.

Chandra discussed the issue with Rajan. Both of them decided to form a private limited company and to offer shares to all the ten employees. All the employees accepted the offer of becoming partial owners of the company. The new company became CLICK Photo Printing Systems, Private Limited. (The ten employees together owned 10% of the shares, Rajan owned 39% of the shares, and the balance 51% of the shares were with Chandra.)

Chandra and Rajan involved all the employees in planning strategies and tactics to make CLICK not only a viable business, but a very reputed and highly profitable business. The CLICK team introduced a number of innovative practices over the next three years. Some of these practices were introduced simultaneously. At the end of the third year all the new practices were in force.

The initiatives by the CLICK team are described, in the chronological order in which they were introduced, in the following paragraphs.

Promoting Matte Prints

The matte print was to be promoted because the net profit margins on the matte print were 100% more, although the price of the matte print was only 20% more.

The entire CLICK team studied and understood the features of glossy and matte prints.

"So, in the glossy vs. matte finish debate, which print type is the right one for you?"

Glossy Photo Finish

Glossy photos do just what their name implies — they gloss over the photograph, giving it a nice shine. The paper and the coating behind that glossy photograph are actually made up of the same material as a matte image, except that more of the final coating is used. That extra layer of shine tends to give the image an apparent boost in colour and, well, like anything with a bit of shine to it, glossy photos look good. The problem with the glossy photo finish is that it creates glare. You'll see light reflecting off the photo itself, making it hard to view it equally under different lighting scenarios. One of the issues many photographers have with glossy photos is also the fingerprints they tend to attract. The finish of a glossy photo leaves the print more susceptible to fingerprints, which means photos that will see a good deal of handling aren't the ideal shots to use with a glossy finish.

Bottom line: Glossy photos are good for colourful shots — but only if you don't mind the glare or the fingerprints.

Matte Photo Finish

With less of that final shiny layer, matte prints offer a similar lifespan, but without that glossy sheen. Matte photographs don't have quite the same colour boost as the glossy ones — though if you shoot and process the photo right, you can still get a good deal of colour from a matte print. Matte photos tend to be better for less vibrant colour schemes or monochrome shots, particularly if you are trying to imitate a film effect. Where the glossy finish tends to emphasize colour, matte prints tend to play up the texture in an image.

Without that extra gloss, the matte photo is not as susceptible to shine and fingerprints. In general, though it is not always the case, professional photographers tend to choose matte over glossy because of the lower likelihood of glare and fingerprinting. While matte tends to play up texture, the image may look a bit grainy because of that enhanced texture.

The bottom line: Favoured more by pros, the matte finish doesn't reflect glare or retain fingerprints, but the tendency to highlight texture could also bring out unwanted texture.

A matte photograph's anti-reflective qualities often makes it a better choice for framing large prints, while the enhanced colour may help snapshots stand out more with a glossy finish. While there is no right or wrong answer when choosing your photo finish, there are pros and cons of each type that are important to understand in order to get the most from your prints." (Source:https://www.photodirect.com.au/glossy-vs-matte-finish-what-print-type-is-best/)

At the CLICK counter, the nomenclature of glossy print and matte print was changed to 'quick prints' and 'long-lasting prints' for all transactions with amateur customers. Every amateur customer was explained the advantages of long-lasting prints before being asked to make a choice of paper. As far as possible, the finger print proof quality of matte paper was demonstrated to the customer. He was also shown the same photograph printed as a matte print and glossy print where the matte print photograph, looked much better. If the customer was still in doubt, the salesperson used hints like "these are your memories, they are for lifetime; you will not be able to shoot these photographs again. You don't want them to be spoiled by fingerprints." This was done softly without acting pushy.

If the customer showed even the slightest but definite inclination towards quick prints, the salesperson quickly accepted the order for glossy, nay, 'quick', prints.

Consoling an Amateur Photographer

If only a few photographs could be printed from a roll of negatives, then, the lab operator would attach a note explaining the reasons for not printing. The note would also tell the customers that they are welcome to meet and discuss the problem with the supervisor, so that next time, there will be a much higher rate of success. If the customer approached the supervisor and during the discussions the supervisor felt that the person was really keen on knowing more, the supervisor would give two complimentary passes to the person, inviting him to attend two lectures in the 'Good Photography' course run by Chandra and Rajan.

Promoting Enlargements

The customer might need enlargements for any of the following reasons:

- To sell the prints as part of a business model.
- To give them as gifts, these are perfect as presents.
- To display them on their own walls at home.
- To have a portfolio of their work.
- The images might need to be bigger than their initial resolution.
- To enhance the quality of low-resolution images.

The supervisor would identify the photographs which would look much better when enlarged. A separate note would advise the customer as to which specific photographs would look much better on enlargement. They would be given to customers in a separate envelope. The customers would again be invited for a discussion with the supervisor. If a customer went in for 4" x 6" prints instead of postcard (3" x 4") size then the market doubled. If the customer could be persuaded to go in for 5" x 7" prints instead of the postcard size then the market increased by 300%. If the customer opted for enlargements, the profitability per square inch increased by 80%.

Fixed Prices Practice

Prices for bulk orders by professional photographers were finalised after a careful study and analysis of pricing practices and bargains offered by competing labs. The prices at CLICK were 5% more than the lowest price available in the market. A price schedule was printed for various quantities of print.

Loyalty Program for Professional Photographers

A loyalty program for professional photographers was started where the last 10 prints out of every hundred prints were offered at the bare minimum variable costs and the last 50 prints out of every 1,000 prints were completely free of cost. Price negotiations were totally stopped.

Collection from Your Counters

Chandra realised that some of the collection agents spent as much as three hours, coming and going from their counters to the CLICK lab in Commercial Street. They could not afford to make the trip if they had collected only one or two rolls. Some of them made the trip only when they had collected four or more rolls. This meant that the collecting agents could not promise a firm delivery schedule to the customer who gave the first or the second roll; and sometimes the agent could not deliver at the promised time. He then blamed the delay on the lab to save his skin. Consequently, the reputation of the lab was also damaged.

The CLICK team plotted the locations of all the collection centres which were using their services. They then designed routes such that a CLICK collector, travelling on a two-wheeler on the route could visit each of them in a day. The four routes so designed covered 90% of the collection centres. There were some routes on which there were less than 20 collection centres.

Chandra and Rajan went to these areas and located a few stationery shops and persuaded them to become roll collection centres.

A team of five collection boys with four mopeds was set up. The collection centres were offered a 10% discount on prices charged at the CLICK sales counter, which was 5% less than the 15% discount given to the collection agent if he personally brought the rolls to the CLICK sales counter. The collection service operated six days a week. Despite having one extra person in the collection team, it sometimes happened that there was no boy to collect the rolls on one of the routes. In such an eventuality, Chandra would himself go on the route collecting the rolls. Collection agents were highly impressed when they saw Chandra at their counter!

Loyalty Program for Amateur Photographers

A data bank of customers' names, the date on which they deposited the roll, how many good prints were delivered, along with customer's address and phone numbers was created and continuously updated. With the first repeat order the customer got a free postcard size print of the photo of Dodda Ganesh Deity. With the fourth repeat order, the customer received a complimentary coupon to a three-hour workshop on good photography conducted by Chandra and Rajan.

With the eighth repeat order, the customer received an invitation to a 'one day nature photography trek' - all expenses paid by CLICK Photo Systems. From the 11th roll onwards, the customer received an honorary membership to the CLICK Photo Club. As a member of the CLICK Photo Club, they were entitled to a 10% discount on all their orders and the right to exhibit one of their photographs in the Annual Photographic Exhibition organised by CLICK Photo Systems.

Rescue Your Old Photo Albums

The appeal of the scheme, drafted by Rajan, said,

"You probably have some old photo albums that are not in such great shape, maybe many of your old photos are in danger. If sticky pages have been used then your photos might already be in rough shape. Photos on old black paper pages, even with photo corners, might not be faring well, either your photos might be yellowing, or even breaking into pieces. This is bad news. Is there anything you can do to rescue these precious memories?

We are happy to say that there is a solution!

CLICK Photo Systems offers 'Rescue Old Photo Albums' service. Come to CLICK with your old albums. We do the rest. You can continue to enjoy viewing the heritage photos in an album, sharing them with family, and preserving them for generations to come."

The scheme was displayed prominently on the sales counter. All customers were given a nicely printed pamphlet. However, the response was almost nil. Then, an advertisement was released in the local newspaper. Even then, only five old albums were received in a month. Recovering those albums proved to be much more difficult and complicated than what was anticipated, so this scheme was discontinued.

Photography Classes

The classes were started to help amateur photographers whose rolls resulted in only a few prints and who were given complimentary passes for photography classes. These classes were run either by Chandra or by Rajan in a 150 square-foot room adjoining the manual photo processing laboratory. Initially they were held on the first Saturday of every month. The capacity was ten seats. Slowly the reputation of the classes spread through word of mouth. Even those who did not receive complimentary passes at the CLICK counter wanted to join the class. The frequency increased to every Saturday by the end of the third year.

Annual Exhibition of Photography

CLICK organised an annual exhibition of photography at a small, centrally located art gallery in Bengaluru for a week in the month of May. Initially, Chandra and Rajan had to put in a lot of effort to ensure participation by reputed photographers from all over the country. Though there was no formal competition, they paid participation fees running into thousands of Rupees, to reputed photographers. They also canvassed amongst reporters on the 'art beat' and art critics for good and prominent coverage of the exhibition in their newspapers and TV channels. Within three years, the exhibition became a recognised part of the art scene in Bengaluru. The lifetime members of the CLICK Photo Club were entitled to exhibit one of their photographs in the exhibition. It became a major attraction to amateur photographers to become a life member of the CLICK Photo Club.

CLICK Treks

Rajan was very impressed by the following announcement about a photography nature tour on the Internet, "Travelling is all about seeing new places and storing them in your memories to cherish forever. And since photography plays such a major role in our travels today, there is no better way to enjoy a memorable trip than by heading out on one of the many photography tours in India. There are many styles of photography tours in India which complement the many diverse sights to be seen in the country. From wildlife photography tours to cultural photography tours to tribal photography tours, there is a vast range of choice for you to pick from."

Source: https://www.thrillophilia.com/photography-tours-india)

Rajan felt that most of his middle-class customers could not really afford to spend time and money on photography tours extending over weeks and costing thousands of Rupees. Nonetheless, they would appreciate a compact version giving them a similar experience. Rajan thought of one day treks around Bengaluru. Chandra liked the idea too. The first trek was organised to the Nandi Hills as a complimentary gift to loyal customers, customers who had got their eighth roll developed at CLICK. On their return, many of the participants said that they would like to join another trek within a couple of months and they were willing to pay the costs. Soon CLICK photography treks became a regular monthly feature. The CLICK team had to organise additional treks during the summer and winter holidays. Youngsters requested monsoon treks, even though they knew that good outdoor photography had little chance when the sky was cloudy and that it could rain any time.

The Results

By the end of 1995, that is five years after starting the business; four years after Rajan joining the business and CLICK becoming a private limited company, the results were unbelievably good:

- The number of amateur customers doubled.
- The ratio of the number of matte prints ordered by amateur customers went up to 45%.
- Enlargement orders by amateur customers went up to 10% of the total prints.
- The business from professional photographers increased by 25%.
- The business from collection agents increased by 20%.
- In effect, the sales increased by 100% and the profitability increased by 200%.

CLICK Photo Printing Systems Private Limited opened a new Branch on M. G. Road in February 1996. Within six months this branch was operating at full capacity.

Further Expansion

Three mini lab owners in Bengaluru approached Chandra and Rajan to explore whether CLICK would buy their businesses. Both Chandra and Rajan were very happy with these developments. They were now recognised as the leaders of the photo printing business, not only in Bengaluru, but throughout southern India. They decided to cash in on their reputation to expand outside Bengaluru rather than buy sick laboratories in Bengaluru itself.

CLICK Photo Printing Systems offered advice and training to the labs from other towns, which did not compete with CLICK. Workshops were organised on new sales strategy for photo printing labs in Dharwad, Hubli, Chikmagalur, Mangalore, Mysore, Gulbarga and going as far as Hyderabad and Nagpur.

A cartel of these labs was then formed under the leadership of CLICK to purchase paper and chemicals at lower prices, by offering to buy much larger volumes. This not only reduced the costs but also made CLICK a recognised leader in the field.

Chandra and Rajan knew that successfully running a photo printing lab required the personal involvement of the owner in day-to-day operations. They knew that running a lab by remote control was very difficult, if not impossible. They therefore developed a franchising model. The investor was to be a local photography enthusiast. He was to start his own mini lab, and would use CLICK as the brand name for immediate credibility. The head office would provide all the support for setting up marketing systems as well as for purchasing raw materials at discounted prices. The franchisee would pay a 5% royalty to CLICK photo systems for the services rendered.

By 1999, there were 12 franchisee CLICK photo operators in medium-sized cities in Karnataka, Andhra Pradesh and Maharashtra.

Postscript: The arrival of digital photography in India was somewhat slow. In 1986, The Japanese company Nikon introduced the first Digital Single-Lens Reflex (DSLR) camera, the Nikon SVC. In the mid-to-late 1990s, DSLR cameras became common among consumers in the developed world but many amateur middle-class photographers in India continued to use 'aim and shoot' cameras with film rolls till about 2000. However, by 2005 digital cameras largely replaced film camera cameras.

Mobile phone cameras arrived in India unexpectedly fast. In 2000, Sharp introduced the world's first digital camera phone in Japan. By 2005, the higher-end cell phones had an integrated digital camera. By the beginning of 2010, almost all smart phones had an integrated digital camera. By 2010-2015 everybody was using a mobile camera phone to point and click.

Chandra and Rajan saw the writing on the wall as early as 2000. They realised that photographs would no longer always be a physical product; photographs would often exist only as megabytes on a smart phone or files on social media. While the number of photos snapped daily would go on increasing manifold, the number of photos being printed on paper would decline. The printing industry would shift towards total digital dominance.

Chandra and Rajan closed both the labs in Bengaluru in 2005, when operations had declined to just above the break-even level. They advised their franchisees to do the same, in good time, and cut back the losses.

Chandra and Rajan continued to organise the Annual Photography Exhibition and it continues to be an important event on the Bengaluru art scene.

Chapter 9

Integrated Diverse Educational Analytical Systems (Ideas) University

Navin Choksi was a self-made man. His father had come to Mumbai from Vadodara (then Baroda) in the year 1940 and had started a stationery shop. Navin was born in 1945 and was the only son. Navin had started finding institutional buyers for stationery while he was studying at the Poddar Commerce College in Vadodara. He graduated with an average academic performance. He soon started dealing in shares outside the Bombay Stock Exchange and slowly acquired a small clientele which trusted his judgment.

Navin accidentally met Dhirubhai Ambani in 1975 and was greatly impressed by him. Navin invested a significant portion of the money that he had saved, in shares of Ambani's Reliance. He advised his clientele to fully invest in Reliance. This investment paid off very well. By 1980, at the age of 35, Navin was already recognized as a serious broker for doing curb deals outside the Bombay Stock Exchange. (Curb trading occurs outside of general market operations, commonly through face to face, computers or telephones after the official exchanges have closed). Navin's clientele grew larger and larger; by 1985 Navin Choksi became an official stockbroker with an office in the Bombay Stock Exchange and by 2005, he had become one of the largest and most reputed stockbrokers on the Bombay Stock Exchange.

Navin was married, but did not have any children; neither did he have any close surviving relatives. He had been regularly donating to various charities and had donated almost two crore Rupees without asking for any credit or any role in managing the charities to which he donated.

Navin was now actively considering setting up a charitable trust, to which he could donate a large portion of his property. He wanted the trust to make a significant contribution to the Indian society on one hand and be a good memorial for himself, after his death, on the other. He wanted the activities sponsored by the trust to become self-sustained within a few years; at least before his support to the trust stopped.

So far, Navin had mainly donated for purely charitable causes like temples, orphanages and feeding stray animals. Such activities could never become self-sustainable. Navin now wanted to donate for a major activity which would eventually become self-sustainable. Two major fields in which such activities were possible were education and health. The government was progressively withdrawing from both these activities and private organizations were playing an increasingly important role. Navin decided that his new charitable venture would be either in the field of education or health. He asked a business analyst from his company to prepare brief notes on the scope for private charitable institutions in each of these fields. His assistant quickly put up a note, as the leading international consultancy firm, Pricewaterhouse Coopers, had recently published reports, advising private sector investment, in these two sectors in India.

(Future of India: The Winning Leap – PwC www.pwc.in › assets › pdfs › future-of-india-the-winni

Healthcare - Healthcare Industry & Sector in India | PwC--www.pwc.in › industries › healthcare)

The salient features of the notes are given below.

Education Sector

- The market size of the higher education segment in India stood at around ₹15.30 billion in the FY 2010 and is expected to grow at a CAGR of over 11% over the next three years.
- Presently about 11 million students are in the higher education system. This represents just 11% of the 17-23-year-old population.

The government hopes to increase this to at least 21% by 2017 - a target which still falls short of the world average.

- With the emergence of India as a knowledge-based economy, human capital has now become its major strength. This has put the spotlight on the severe inadequacies of India's infrastructure for delivery of education, particularly higher and vocational education.
- India's public expenditure on education (centre plus state expenditure) has ranged between 3.26% and 3.85% of the Gross Domestic Product (GDP) from 2004-05 till 2009-10 and this needs to increase if it is to come at par with the expenditure incurred by the developed economies.
- The allocation for technical and higher education in the Eleventh Five Year Plan (2007-12) has been raised almost nine-fold to US$ 18.8 billion from US$ 2.1 billion in the Tenth Plan. However, this was still a fraction of the estimated requirements necessary to achieve the targets.
- While there has been some private investment in setting up educational institutions, there remains a glaring mismatch in demand and supply, particularly in high-quality institutions. Example - only 1 out of approximately 150 applicants gets admission into the elite Indian Institute of Management (IIMs) compared with the ratio of 1:10 for Massachusetts Institute of Technology (MIT).
- A high-powered advisory body - National Knowledge Commission (NKC) has recommended that the number of universities increases from the present 370 to 1500 by 2015.
- All India Council of Technical Education (AICTE) establishes, maintains and regulates the norms and standards in technical education. Its purview includes training and research in engineering, technology, architecture, town planning, management, pharmacy, applied arts and crafts, hotel management and catering technology. The AICTE has permitted

Section 8 Company to act as a sponsoring body of a technical institute with the clause that no foreign investment (directly or indirectly) will be permitted in such a company.

- The University Grants Commission (UGC) is the major regulatory body for higher education in India. The UGC is responsible for the coordination, determination and maintenance of standards of teaching, examination and research in universities.

- Key issues and challenges for foreign participation are: (a) The "Not-for-Profit" entry barrier for private capital. (b) The regulatory framework, which is a major barrier. Multiple approvals are required. Policies are also inconsistent. For instance, though the FDI policy permits 100% FDI through automatic approval route in the education sector, AICTE prohibits foreign participation - direct and indirect, in JVs in Indian institutions. (c) The UGC is not open to recognizing foreign universities.

The Health Sector

- The Indian healthcare delivery system is categorized into two major components - public and private. The government, i.e., the public healthcare system comprises limited secondary and tertiary care institutions in key cities and focuses on providing basic healthcare facilities in the form of Primary Healthcare Centres (PHCs) in rural areas. The private sector provides a majority of the secondary, tertiary and quaternary care institutions with a major concentration in metros, tier-I and tier-II cities.

- The Indian healthcare sector is diversifying and opportunities are emerging in every segment, be it providers, players or medical technology. With growing competition, organizations are cognizant of new challenges and are looking to explore the latest business dynamics and trends impacting their segment. New players are building their entry strategy and domestic players are exploring new care models to stay ahead.

- The hospital industry in India, accounting for 80% of the total healthcare market, is witnessing a huge investor demand from both global as well as domestic investors. The hospital industry is expected to reach US$ 50 billion in 2015; growing at a CAGR of 16-17%.
- Home-based care services will gain popularity as average life expectancy will cross 70 years by 2022.
- India is experiencing 22-25% growth in medical tourism. The medical tourism industry in India is expected to double its value to become a US$ 2 billion market in 2015. Medical tourist arrivals in India are expected to reach 130,000 in 2015.
- The diagnostics industry in India is currently valued at US$ 3 billion. The share of the organized sector is almost 25% in this segment (15% in labs and 10% in radiology).
- The primary care industry is currently valued at US$ 10 billion. The share of the organized sector is practically negligible in this case.
- The hospital and diagnostic centres attracted Foreign Direct Investment (FDI) worth US$ 1.25 billion between April 2000 and June 2000, according to data released by the Department of Industrial Policy and Promotion (DIPP).
- The significant demand-supply mismatch has led healthcare to emerge as an attractive sector for PE investments.

Navin Choksi chose education. He decided to choose the educational sector for two reasons:

- Foreign direct investment was more difficult in the educational field as the University Grants Commission did not accept it and the All India Council for Technical Education did not accord its approval to institutions in which there was foreign equity participation. Therefore, there would be less danger of well-known multinational universities entering India and capturing the market; making it difficult for the Indian institutions to survive.

- In 2009, the Gujarat government had passed an act allowing private universities in the state of Gujarat. These private universities could be started either by a charitable trust for public purposes or a Section 8 company registered as a not-for-profit public limited company.

Navin decided to start the educational institute in the city of Vadodara where he had ancestral linkages and ancestral land measuring about 20 acres north of Vadodara. The land could be very useful to start a university.

Navin decided to study this field of his new venture in some greater detail. He knew that the city of Pune, known as the Ox-Bridge (a combination of Oxford and Cambridge) of the East, had a number of educational entrepreneurs who had successfully established educational institutes which had been given 'Deemed to be University' status by the University Grants Commission.

These institutions were doing well and were self-sufficient. He met some of these educational entrepreneurs to seek their advice and learn from their experience. He also had a detailed discussion with some educationists as to what the new educational institution should focus on. He found that a medical college required a large hospital with patients, which was costly to set up and difficult to run.

An engineering college required workshops, and engineers from not so reputed colleges were already finding it difficult to get jobs. It was also clear that the students, who did not get admission to either engineering or medicine, opted for graduation in science or arts or commerce.

The future for these BSc, BCom and BA graduates was not very bright. Many of them applied to MBA courses with limited success, because there again they competed with graduate engineers who were doing their MBA, as employers preferred MBAs with an engineering degree for better-paid jobs. A number of academicians also noted that the real problem was with BA courses - the quality was rather poor. There was a widely felt need to integrate BSc, BCom, BA syllabi and offer a wide choice for students at the graduate level.

It was necessary to develop an attitude of scientific enquiry amongst the students. If a graduate course could be designed with a good combination of the science and arts streams with some job-oriented skills from commerce courses, then it could be a good basic graduation course. After which, post-graduation could be pursued either in management or in communication or in social work or in human relations. Navin also realized that such a course would require a relatively low investment as no hospital beds or workshops or laboratories would be required, and it could be started with a much lower gestation period.

Navin decided to name the new institution Integrated Diverse Educational Analytical Systems (IDEAS) University. He registered it as a Section 8 company with his wife as the second director and ₹1 million as the initial equity capital.

The main objective of the IDEAS university was: 'To provide learning, teaching, capacity, capability and skills development and research and development in higher and technical education, covering liberal arts, humanities, social sciences, life sciences and biotechnologies, nano sciences and technologies, professional disciplines such as engineering, technology, management, business and commerce, applied and creative arts, vocational education, media, information and communication technology and education per se and their inter-disciplinary studies and development.'

Navin knew that all the initial work would be in constructing buildings; only then could the university start functioning. Navin had met Mayank Dave, a young builder from Vadodara when he had bought a posh residential bungalow in a gated community there. He knew that Mayank Dave was a management graduate with academic inclinations, despite being a successful builder. Mayank used to teach as a visiting professor of marketing in a management college in Vadodara. Navin invited Mayank for a business meeting in Mumbai and explained his concept of IDEAS University to him, in detail. He told Mayank that he would have a free hand in constructing the university, staffing it and running it for the first five years. He told Mayank, "I am only a commerce graduate with a second class, you are a management graduate and I understand you are pursuing your PhD on a part-time basis. You will head the university as the president. You will have a minority shareholding in the holding company. We will hand over this university to academicians after you make an initial success of it. You will, of course, continue with the holding company for a lifetime. You will become chairman of the holding company after I retire. This need not be a full-time job for you. You can continue your building activities. However, your first priority, if you accept, must be to set up IDEAS University." Mayank found this a challenging and satisfying opportunity and accepted it.

Mayank proceeded with the construction of the IDEAS University with full zeal. He appointed a leading architect to design the campus. The special feature of the architectural design was that almost all the classrooms were underground. The concept was that the students and staff should enjoy the open air as much as possible without the clutter of buildings. Only the library building, the canteen and a small administrative block were above the ground. When the students entered the classrooms, they had no distraction of nature, of birds and bees; they could fully concentrate on the blackboard/whiteboard and the teacher. The university buildings measuring more than 2,00,000 square feet were ready within two years, by December 2011.

Meanwhile, Mayank and Navin were also busy in creating the human resource infrastructure. They invited some of the leading academicians, artists and scientists to be on the governing council of IDEAS University. The composition of the governing council was very impressive. They approached a senior professor from the Indian Institute of Management, who was about to retire and asked him to become the first director of IDEAS University management school. Very well-known persons were also recruited to head the school of communications and the school of philosophy. They appointed a team of 31 teachers. The faculty was cosmopolitan with a good composition of age, gender and specialization. The faculty of IDEAS University had more than a hundred and fifty papers published in international research journals.

Mayank appointed recruitment agents in all the major cities of India. These recruitment agents were educational advisors running career guidance centres for undergraduate and graduate students.

IDEAS University was planned as a fully residential institution, both for students and faculty. The university was to begin with four courses:

- Undergraduate BBA course of three years after 12th standard.
- Postgraduate MBA of 2 years.
- Postgraduate diploma in communications of 1 year.
- Pre-PhD, MPhil in philosophy of 1 year

IDEAS University opened its doors to students in June 2012. Navin and Mayank were surprised that the response of students was not good. IDEAS University had a capacity of 180 students in the undergraduate BBA course, 80 students for the MBA program, 80 students in the school of communication and 20 students in the school of philosophy. The enrolment was less than 50% in all the courses. The major shortfall was for the BBA course where 100 seats were vacant in the classroom.

The academic program began with full gusto. Mayank hoped that after completing one year, the admissions would improve, primarily because by then he would have received all the sanctions from the statutory authorities and also because the existing students would become good word-of-mouth canvassers as they would be very happy with the quality of education they were receiving.

IDEAS University received recognition as a 'private university" from the Government of Gujarat and the UGC. It was rated as "A" by AICTE. The BBA course was also recognized by three American universities for admission to their MBA program.

After the first year, however, the admissions did not improve (BBA 95 against 180, MBA 50 against 80, school of communications 45 against 80, M Phil in philosophy five against 20). Mayank and Navin were seriously worried. They knew that the employers' response would depend on the admissions to applications ratio. Employers give a lot of importance to the quality of incoming students as judged by the percentage of rejection at the stage of admission; rather than the quality of education imparted to the students during their studies in the college. And eventually, the prospective students looked at the employment potential.

Navin and Mayank decided to involve faculty and students in designing a marketing plan for popularizing IDEAS University among prospective students. They had brainstorming sessions with the faculty; all members were asked to submit their plans for improving admissions. Prof. Dr. Abhay Bajaj, who was a faculty member in marketing, suggested a scheme which was quite novel and appealing. The note submitted by Prof. Dr. Abhay Bajaj is reproduced below:

Improving Admissions to IDEAS University

(A note submitted by Prof. Dr. Abhay Bajaj on 1st August 2013)

- The primary task should be to improve admissions to the undergraduate BBA course. Once the BBA course is full, that would itself be a recruiting ground for MBA and communications diploma. The seats for M. Phil philosophy are not the main issue. Incidentally, some of the BBA students may be attracted to doing M. Phil philosophy. This note primary deals with improving admissions to the three year BBA course.
- IDEAS University must attract the attention and imagination of 12th standard students as they are the prospects for admissions to the BBA course.
- 12th standard is a crucial examination in the career of a student as the performance in the 12th standard decides admission to engineering and medical courses. Students, therefore concentrate on studies in the 12th standard. They use all the available resources; they screen and select the best teaching aids which will help them in learning and performing better in the 12th standard examination.
- YouTube is the new social media that is increasingly being used by students. Currently, the best teaching material is available on

YouTube. The films by the Khan Academy have pioneered this frontier of education. However, most of the video films available on YouTube have been made in the USA; the speakers talk with an American accent and refer to situations and problems in the USA. This makes it difficult for Indian students to grasp and use these educational films.

- IDEAS University should take a lead in making educational short films, say of 12 to 15 minutes duration, which would be useful to 12th standard students as a quick revision of important topics. These films should use a good number of pictures, cartoons, photographs and animations; including animated graphs and mathematical equations; to make the film visually interesting and easy to understand.
- Generally, integrated education is understood as making courses from different disciplines available as a wide choice for students. This we are already doing for the BBA course at IDEAS University. In the 1st year, the student can take any two subjects from physics, chemistry, zoology, botany; any two languages from English, Hindi, German and Gujarati and any two subjects from a wide variety of subjects offered in commerce and the performing arts. This is good. However, in the educational films on YouTube, we must integrate different disciplines in each lecture; so that, our approach of integrated learning becomes clear, unique and attractive to the students.
- Some illustrations, I feel, are in order, for making clear this method of integrated education in each lecture.
- While teaching the planetary system we must also teach the life of Galileo and also briefly mention the Renaissance movement in history.
- While teaching the theory of light, when it comes to, 'Is light a particle or is it a wave?' the film must also bring in the philosophy of science and the theory of competing paradigms.

- Even in history, if the story of re-capture of Kondhana fort by Shivaji's soldiers is being told, then we must briefly mention the science behind why the Monitor Lizard (**घोरपड**) is able to cling to a stone surface with such a great strength that a Maratha soldier could climb up using the rope tied to the Monitor Lizard, without it losing its hold on the stone.
- These are some of the instances I collected by talking to teachers of the subject at IDEAS University. We can definitely ensure that most of our films are intrinsically multidisciplinary.
- These films should not be, I repeat, should not be, made by the faculty of our university. We must identify very popular 12th standard teachers from the upmarket English medium schools in major cities of Ahmedabad, Vadodara, New Delhi, Mumbai, Pune, Bengaluru, etc. We can take the help of students already in IDEAS University to nominate teachers.
- These popular 12th standard junior college teachers should be invited to our campus to be the anchor-persons for these films. Our faculty should help these teachers to make the content of the film intrinsically multidisciplinary.
- The idea of inviting teachers from these A-grade schools to our campus for making films is two-fold: firstly, a popular teacher knows how to communicate with the students. Each subject requires a style of its own, secondly, and more importantly, these teachers will see our campus, interact with our faculty and would become our ambassadors in their schools.
- The effort should be done on a sufficiently large scale, say 200 films made by a hundred teachers in the next 200 days, so that it has an impact on the student community.
- We should create our own channel on YouTube and use social media to popularize our channel.
- We should design attractive posters showing films produced by IDEAS University in the last fortnight. This poster should be sent

to a select thousand schools every fortnight for display on their notice boards.

- We have a full-fledged studio for making short films in our communications department. This studio can be used by selected students under the guidance of faculty members, to shoot and edit films anchored by the best school teachers. I have found that there are at least eight students who are good at making cartoons and doing computer-aided animation. Their team can participate to make the films visually very interesting.
- I have not suggested any specific name for this scheme or for our channel on YouTube. That needs to be decided.

Navin and Mayank were both impressed by the scheme suggested by Prof. Bajaj. They decided to launch the scheme under the leadership of Prof. Bajaj, exactly as he had suggested it.

The scheme was named 'Ideas Edu-Films' and was launched in full swing. 97 teachers from 64 schools came to IDEAS University campus and acted as anchorpersons in 201 films. The films became very popular. The minimum hits where 10,000, and the maximum hits exceeded 300,000. There were more than 250,000 subscribers at the end of the year.

Mayank also continued his other promotional programs through educational advisors and by holding roadshows about IDEAS University in seven major cities. The second-year students of BBA and MBA courses were encouraged to go to their junior colleges during the vacation and make a small presentation, prepared by the school of communication, about learning in the IDEAS University and the campus life in IDEAS University.

All this helped. The applications for admissions in the year 2013 were 700 for BBA, 400 for MBA, 450 for the communications diploma course. Even the applications for 20 M. Phil seats increased to 15 in number.

Postscript 1: In the year 2015, in a faculty meeting, a number of faculty members suggested to Mayank that 'Ideas Edu-Films' should be withdrawn from the YouTube channel as they were creating two major difficulties: (1) Many students thought that these anchor teachers were teaching at IDEAS University, although the school in which they were teaching was mentioned in the credit line at the end, and were disappointed when they found that these teachers were not teaching at IDEAS University. (2) Some enthusiastic, aggressive students were demanding that the teachers in the IDEAS University follow, in every lecture, the integrated approach that was shown in the films. It was good to make one or two films like this but for a faculty member it was not possible to use this approach in each and every lecture. A large number of lectures in mathematics or history had to be only the core subject.

Mayank and Navin felt that the 'Ideas Edu-Films' had served their purpose, as evidenced by the flood of applications. They withdrew the films from the YouTube channel and put them in the university library as CDs for reference of those who might be interested.

Postscript 2: Mr. Navin Choksi requested Mayank Dave to retire as president of the IDEAS University in December 2015. In his place a senior professor recruited after retirement from a reputed American University was appointed by Mr. Navin Choksi.

Chapter 10

Indhan - Do It Again?

The date is 1st January 2019. Mrs. Hetal Somani has to take a major decision in her career at the age of 38. When Hetal was younger, she had worked very hard for three years to make 'Project Indhan' a success. Then she had to abandon it. Now, after 10 years she has many options. She can start the project Indhan again, she can join her husband's business, she can take up a job or she can continue to be a housewife. She knows that her heart demands that she pursues her old dream of becoming a social entrepreneur. She is wondering whether Project Indhan is still a possible and viable option.

Project Indhan

Hetal graduated as an engineer in chemical technology at the age of 22 from the Gujarat Institute of Technology, Ahmadabad, in 2005. In her final year of engineering, she was attracted by two very different things. First, she accidentally read about the achievements of Ranchhodlal Chhotalal, (Rai Bahadur CIE) (April 1823 – October 1898). As the first Indian president of the Ahmadabad Municipality in 1885, he carried out one of the pioneering works of an underground drainage system in British India. He stood against the conservative society and was able to implement an underground drainage line. Second, she read a term paper by her fellow classmate Kalpana, on how to convert household food waste into cooking gas in the house itself. Hetal felt that converting waste into cooking gas at home was a natural extension of the pioneering work done by the great Ranchhodlal Chhotalal.

Hetal and Kalpana decided to do their final year engineering project work on building a small viable working model of a mini chemical plant to convert household waste into cooking gas. Both of them studied the models that were in the experimental stage. They succeeded in building a small plant which they installed in the canteen of the chemical engineering department. This became a path-breaking project in the engineering college and was appreciated by everybody. There was some media coverage about this device in the newspapers. Hetal and Kalpana received a special prize for a socially relevant innovation instituted by the Society for Green Cities.

Hetal and Kalpana decided to make their mini chemical plant on a commercial scale, immediately after graduating from college. Within a year they made a commercial prototype which had the following features and benefits.

Features of Indhan

- The plant was named 'Indhan' (meaning fuel).
- The plant could supply cooking gas by digesting household food waste.
- The food waste of a family of two or three adults and two to three children was sufficient to generate cooking gas to run a single gas stove for 30 to 45 minutes.
- The bacteria in the digester break down the organic matter and convert it into biogas and fertilizer.
- This process produced a mixture of gases – primarily methane, some carbon dioxide and tiny portions of other gases such as hydrogen sulphide. The biogas was filtered to remove the hydrogen sulphide. It looked, smelled, and burned just like any LPG/piped gas. (Methane burns with a blue flame without producing any smoke or soot).
- One kilogram of kitchen waste produced 0.5 cubic meters of biogas. For a typical urban household, biogas (having a calorific value of almost 6600 kCal/kg) saved about 100 kg of LPG or 250 litres of kerosene per year.

- Biogas did not present an increase in health risks when compared to the domestic use of natural gas.
- The plant size was 1.00m x .075m x 1.00m.
- The plant had an easy, top-loading design.
- The kitchen waste was not required to be crushed to feed the plant.
- The plant required zero electrical power.
- The plant was priced at ₹15,000 including all taxes.
- The installation was done free of cost.

Social Benefits

- The primary benefit of biogas is that it is renewable. When you choose to cook using biogas that is made from your waste food, you are reducing the demand for fossil fuels, which are non-renewable resources. Mining, processing and transporting fossil fuels take a lot of energy and resources, which is harmful to the environment and is a leading contributor to climate change.
- Biogas has zero net greenhouse emissions.
- The organic matter used in biogas digesters is typically a waste product. By using biogas, we can reduce the amount of food waste and other organic materials being sent to landfills.
- Furthermore, biogas systems produce a nutrient-rich sludge which is a high-quality liquid fertilizer. There is no mess and no work is needed. The fertilizer flows from the user-friendly pouring sleeve straight into your fertilizer can.
- Home biogas is widely produced in developing regions of the world. The World Bank and the United Nations actively encourage its use as a cheap, clean energy source.
- China has 27 million home biogas plants.
- Indhan is a socially-oriented company that cares about spreading biogas technology to all. During the promotion campaign, you can get involved too!

Promotion of Indhan

Hetal and Kalpana got married at the same time the prototype was ready. Kalpana married a medical doctor in Mumbai and Hetal married into the family of a medium scale industry owner. Hetal's father-in-law had a factory making automobile parts. Her husband was a mechanical engineer working in his father's factory. They supported Hetal in pursuing her, according to them, 'hobby', of making Indhan plants for producing cooking gas at home. In fact, the factory of her father-in-law was available to her as an R&D centre and a production facility. Kalpana remained in touch with Hetal for almost a year and even met her three times during the year. Kalpana delivered her first baby boy within 12 months of her marriage, so she could not devote any significant attention to Project Indhan any longer. Luckily, Hetal did not have to work alone for long. Her sister-in-law, Pooja, joined Project Indhan after getting her MBA degree.

Hetal and Pooja worked hard, and on many fronts, to promote Indhan amongst upper-middle-class households of Ahmedabad city:

- They got small write-ups published in newspapers and magazines.
- They gave lectures at various ladies' clubs.
- They invited prospects to see the working of Indhan at their own house, which was a three-bedroom apartment on the seventh floor of a prestigious housing complex.
- Prospects could also visit the Institute of Chemical Technology where they had now installed the advanced commercial version of Indhan.
- They printed small pamphlets which they gave to the boys who delivered LPG cylinders.
- They aggressively canvassed amongst relatives and friends of the Somani family and business associates of the Somani factory. They also canvassed amongst their friends.

The Unexpected Difficulty

In the first 12 months of the commercial promotion of Indhan, Hetal and Pooja installed 28 Indhan plants. They were installed in the houses of relatives and friends. If there were any complaints, normally regarding choking of slurry passage or smell of gas, then Hetal personally attended to them. In the next 10 months, there were only 10 installations. There was no installation in the last two months. Hetal had thought that the first few installations would create highly positive word-of-mouth promotion and enquiries would flow in. However, that was not happening at all. Hetal and Pooja discussed the problem amongst themselves and with Hetal's husband and father-in-law. They couldn't see a solution. Hetal's father-in-law and Pooja's father, jestingly said, "Running a hobby workshop is one thing, a woman can be good at it. Making a chemical plant and selling it to a large number of households is an industrial-commercial activity which should be left to men." Hetal and Pooja were hurt but kept quiet.

Pooja suggested to Hetal that they should consult Professor Mrs. Gautami Makwana in Pooja's management institute. Pooja said, "Professor Gautami Makwana is a very popular and brilliant teacher of sales and marketing with good experience of working in consumer durable companies like BPL and Whirlpool."

Hetal and Pooja met Prof. Gautami Makwana and shared with her the history and current situation of Project Indhan. Prof Makwana said, "I'm really happy that two young women are working on this innovative engineering product which is socially relevant. I will charge a fee, no doubt because our institute insists on it; but the fee will be nominal. I will involve my students in doing fieldwork, mainly to contact your 32 customers to get their feedback. Give me a list of your customers and meet me after a month. Till then, continue your efforts"

Prof. Gautami Makwana's Advice

- I had taken a list of your first 32 customers. My students spoke with 30 of them. The remaining two could not be contacted. We asked them simple questions like, 'How satisfied are you with Indhan? (Give marks out of 10.) Would you recommend this plant to your friends, relatives and neighbours? (Options: definitely yes, maybe yes, can't say, maybe not, definitely not.) Did you have any problem with the working of the plant? What was the problem? How soon corrected?

- Hetal and Pooja, I am sorry but the overall situation is not good; in fact, to say it bluntly, it is rather bad. Your customers were surprised that somebody was talking with them and asking them for their feedback. Five of them had serious complaints about the working of the plant. The two major complaints are blockage of the slurry pipe and suspected leakage of gas indicated by a foul smell. They said that generally when they tried to contact you, you were not reachable. Moreover, they also said "How can we call on the daughter or daughter-in-law of Somani Seth to do repairs of the plant which processes dirt from my house? That will be insulting the Somani family." They hired local plumbers who used their general knowledge to attempt repairs. Three of them said that the plant got repaired but the plumber charged a high price because he had to work with the foul-smelling dirt. The other two plants are lying unrepaired and unused!

- Only two of the customers said that they were very happy and they would recommend the plant. 26 of them were in the 'can't say' category. Two said that they will not recommend the plant. Generally, in customer satisfaction research we subtract the percentage of people who will not recommend the plant from the percentage of customers who will definitely recommend it; the net score is called the Net Promoter Score (NPS). For a good product backed by good service, the NPS should be above 80%. You have a zero NPS. This just will not do.

- You have to set up a good service organization which is responsive to customer complaints. The response time must be less than a few hours as customers feel panicky if they suspect poisonous gases are leaking and polluting their house.

- Secondly, you mentioned that the slurry is a good fertilizer. Most of your customers stay in large flats in tall multi-storey buildings. They do not have a garden to maintain; so they have no use of the slurry and its disposal is problematic for them. Most of them drain it through their toilet drainage. This means they do not get any benefit of the by-product but in fact, it becomes a nuisance to them. You should collect the slurry from the customers by paying them at least a nominal price.
- The economic benefit is very precariously balanced. The customer is expected to pay ₹15,000 upfront for installing the plant. He will get cooking gas for about 30 minutes burning of a single burner. This represents a monetary benefit of roughly ₹4 per day and about ₹1460 per year: a slightly less than 10% return on the capital invested while the capital keeps on getting depreciated. Guajaratis are continuously investing in the share market. This rate of return is not that attractive. You must bring down the cost of manufacture and the selling price should be no more than ₹12,000; then the benefit of ₹1460 will be a 12.6% return and the payback period will be eight years. If customers get some income from the slurry, that would be a bonus.
- I had personal discussions with about ten customers. Your customers installed your plant not because they were convinced about the economic benefits or because they are very socially conscious. They bought the plant because they could not say 'no' to members of Somani family.
- But I will go a step further. Even if you were to reduce prices; set up a good responsive service organization and you were to collect slurry from the customer by paying them at least a nominal price - your problems will not be over. Hetal, you told me that you were inspired by the work of Shri Ranchhodlal Chhotalal and his contribution to building an underground drainage system in the city. Are you aware that Ranchhodlal Chhotalal was opposed by Brahmins from Ahmedabad, who said, 'In the underground drainage system our excreta and their excreta will mix, this will

pollute our purity.' They even stoned Ranchhodlal Chhotalal at a public meeting. Now the situation has improved, yes, but only to some extent. Even now most of the upper caste, upper-income group people think that taking care of dirt is polluting. It is the job of the other lowly castes. I should dump the dirt and forget about it; others should take care of it. This attitude of upper caste, upper-class people is going to be your major hurdle. It will not change quickly. You have to be ready for a long struggle before you taste the fruits of your labour. Good luck to both of you.

Hetal and Pooja returned from the meeting with Prof. Gautami Makwana in low spirits. Pooja was now engaged to a businessman in Vadodara and was likely to part company from Project Indhan in another two months. Hetal was pregnant. Both of them decided to find a buyer for Project Indhan. There was no buyer. Hetal decided to close down Project Indhan with a heavy heart on 1st of January 2008.

By January 2019, Hetal had a son and daughter, who were both in primary school. Hetal's father-in-law had expired in 2015 and her mother-in-law, who was living with her, was very happy to look after her grandchildren, so now Hetal had time on her hands. She felt that with the Swachh Bharat Abhiyan launched by the Prime Minister, people living in Ahmadabad would have become more conscious about their responsibility regarding the healthy disposal of kitchen waste. There is a good chance that the state government or the central government will sanction a 50% subsidy for Indhan installations. Hetal has discussed this changed situation with Kalpana, Pooja, her husband and her mother-in-law. All of them said that they would support Hetal to the maximum possible extent. But ultimately Hetal knows that this is her call.

Chapter 11

Selling a Drug for De-Worming Cattle to Indian Dairy Farmers

Background

De-worming of animals is a major area of concern worldwide. Especially, when the productivity of animals is at the receiving end due to the influence of the worms, the concern becomes grave. From the World Health Organization to pharmaceutical companies, resources have been invested to develop a drug that would prove effective in deworming the animals. But will such a drug find its own market? In the context of Indian farmers, will the drug be preferred over traditional practices? How do veterinary doctors prescribe a drug? Can a drug that cures a recurring problem require promotion?

Deworming involves treating the animal with an anthelmintic drug (a drug capable of causing the evacuation of intestinal worms) infected with parasites, such as roundworm and tapeworm. Purge de-wormers for the use in livestock are often formulated as a liquid that is squirted into the back of the animal's mouth, as an injectable, or as a pour-on which can be applied to the animal's top line.

Ivermectin is a broad-spectrum anti parasitic medication, which falls under a class of medications called anthelmintics, which treat the parasites by killing the worms in the intestines.

Ivermectin is sold under brand names Stromectol in the United States, Mectizan in Canada by Merck and Ivexterm in Mexico by Valeant Pharmaceuticals International.

Though India is poised to become the world's number one milk-producing country, with a population of 193 million cattle and 78.8

million buffaloes, the per capita productivity of the dairy stock is very low due to the influence of gastrointestinal nematodiasis, caused by endo-parasites (parasites residing inside the body of the cattle) and ecto-parasites (the parasites on the skin of the cattle).

The annual losses due to worm infection are around ₹30 lakhs in the Kheda district of Gujarat alone. In spite of significant production loss, the problem is neglected due to its chronic and insidious nature. Effective control strategies against bovine parasitic gastroenteritis in India have not been formulated due to the paucity of information on parasite epidemiology in various agro-climatic conditions.

Mr. Goyal, marketing director of Ratan Lab, had convened a meeting of his regional sales managers at his office in New Delhi. In the meeting, Mr. Goyal came directly to the main question bothering him, "Ivermectin, the largest selling drug the world over for de-worming cattle, is offered by an MNC in India. It will be out of the patent regime very soon. We can make the molecule without a problem. Should we market it? I am surprised that the global trend is not evident in India. Ivermectin does not sell much in India. Why?" He expected his regional sales managers for Maharashtra, Gujarat and Punjab, Sanjay, Ajay and Avatar respectively, to provide a convincing explanation, as the MNC had a very strong presence in these large veterinary medicine markets in the three states.

Mr. Goyal continued with the supplementary questions, "I know the MNC has priced the drug very high at ₹250 a dose, but are the low sales entirely due to the high price? What is the market size? Is it grossly overestimated? Is the efficacy of the drug less for Indian cattle and Indian worms? Or is it that the awareness levels of the farmers are so low? Given the fact that farmers have their own way of deciding preventive and curative treatments; does this drug not fit strongly in their consideration set? Are there several other contributory factors?"

All the regional sales managers were taken aback by this unexpected barrage of questions coming from the big boss. Avatar began with a response, "The highly fragmented cattle population in the country is a sales manager's distribution nightmare. Spread over a very wide geographic area, the cattle population is extremely difficult to reach through a good retail network. Small farm-holdings tucked away in every nook and corner of the country make it impossible for any marketer to reach a substantial proportion of the market. Besides, the costs of sales promotion and transportation raise the end price substantially."

"Don't give me the general and standard excuses for not achieving the sales, I know them by heart," barked Mr. Goyal. He continued, "I want specific information and analysis. Please tell me what to do to grab this opportunity, if it is an opportunity."

There was an eloquent silence.

Mr. Goyal continued, "I know you are not prepared; it is not your fault. Sanjay and Ajay, you are from the Institute of Rural Management, Anand (IRMA), you are experts in selling products to farmers, yes? And the major markets are in your states. You will make an in-depth investigation and help me understand the root cause of the problem. Also, I want your well-reasoned recommendation on what to do... And yes, do it within 15 days. I have to report to the MD, before the board meeting."

Sanjay and Ajay looked at each other, dismayed by the daunting task given to them and the short time available. Avatar's face brightened, he could not hide his relief!

Sanjay and Ajay worked hard for the next 14 days (and nights), compiled a lot of information from secondary sources, talked with their field personnel, talked with some veterinary doctors on their panel and even found time to talk with a few progressive dairy farmers. The summary report, as prepared by them, is reproduced in the following paragraphs.

The Market for De-worming Drugs in General and Ivermectins in Particular

Prepared by

Sanjay Patil – Regional Manager, Maharashtra

Ajay Vora - Regional Manager, Gujarat

For

Mr. V. K. Goyal – Marketing Director

Background

Milk production in India, which more or less remained stagnant from 1950 to 1970 with a very low growth rate of 1% per year, increased exponentially thereafter as a result of the White Revolution. India has emerged as the largest producer of milk in the world. The per capita availability of milk has increased from 112 gm per day in 1970-71 to more than 225 gm per day by the year 2000.

Integrated animal healthcare takes into consideration the diversity of livestock and the environment. It combines animal treatment with disease prevention through vaccination, improved management, feeding, sanitation, and clean water. One of the major reasons for the low per animal productivity of milk is the parasitic infestation.

IvermectinIn

In the mid-1980s, ivermectin was introduced as probably the most broad-spectrum, anti-parasite medication. It is effective against parasites within the body (endo-parasites) and parasites residing on the skin outside the body (ecto-parasites). It is effective against most common intestinal worms (except tapeworms), most mites, and some lice. It is not effective against fleas, ticks, flies, or flukes. It is effective against larval heartworms (the "microfilariae" that circulate in the blood) but not against adult heartworms (that live in the heart and pulmonary arteries), though technically it can shorten their lifespan.

The most common uses in small animal practice for ivermectin would include:

- Monthly prevention of heartworm infection.
- Treatment of ear mite situations.
- Clearing heartworm larvae in active heartworm infection.
- Treatment of sarcoptic, notoedric or demodectic mange.

Ivermectin is the largest selling drug the world over for removing endo and ecto parasites in cattle. While in development, it was assigned the code MK-933 by Merck. It is available in tablets / chewables for heartworm prevention, topical solution for ear mite treatment or as an oral or injectable solution for other parasite problems.

Ivermectin is sold under brand names Heartgard, Sklice, and Stromectol in the United States, Ivomec in Europe by Merial Animal Health, Mectizan in Canada by Merck, and Ivexterm in Mexico by Valeant. In Southeast Asian countries, it is marketed by Delta Pharma Ltd. under the trade name Scabo 6.

Ivermectin was introduced in India around 1985 by the MNC. The current annual sales of Ivermectin are estimated to be about half a million doses valued at ₹125million.

(Source: The life and times of ivermectin - a success story by S Õmura @courses.umass.edu/mic590s/2009/Reading/Omura2004.pdf - makes interesting reading)

Incidence of endo parasites in Indian cattle faecal sample data on parasitic infestation in cattle and buffaloes are collected by government veterinary dispensaries in Pune district on a routine basis. This information, collected by four dispensaries, has been compiled specifically for the present report.

Table: Incidence of Endo Parasites in Cattle and Buffaloes in Pune District

Name of Centre	Faecal samples tested				% Fecal samples found positive			
	Total samples tested	Cross breed-cows	Local cows	Buffa-loes	Total positive samples	Cross breed-cows	Local cows	buffa-loes
Daund	90	32	9	49	47	47	67	53
Bhigwan	88	45	26	17	25	40	15	30
Kedgaon	25	13	-	12	7	31	-	25
Khed	93	93	-	-	33	35	-	-
Total	296	183	35	78	35	38	29	41

Studies on Parasitic Infestation

The study for parasitic infestation covered 177 dairy farmers, 31 veterinary doctors and 7 researchers in the field of veterinary parasitology, through focus group discussions and structured interviews. The discussions revealed the following status for the incidences of endo-parasites and ecto-parasites.

Incidences of Endo-Parasites

Data from primary and secondary sources indicate that 25 per cent to 50 per cent of dairy cattle (both cows and buffaloes) suffer from a sub-clinical infestation of endo-parasites.

Faecal samples collected from four veterinary dispensaries in Pune district for the year 1997-98, show incidence ranging from 31 per cent to 47 per cent in crossbred cows and 25 per cent to 53 per cent in she buffaloes.

A 1983 in-house research paper from Mumbai Veterinary College showed the incidence of parasites in cattle is low (17 to 20 per cent) during the dry season and reaches a high (50 per cent) during the monsoon season.

A 1992 study by Sanyal on month-wise variation in egg count of endo-parasites shows a progressive increase in egg output reaching its peak in October. Similar results were collected by Mathur in the study of cattle, conducted in Eastern India

Incidence of Ecto Parasites

The incidence of ecto-parasites has not been quantified mainly because the veterinary dispensaries do not maintain any data on the subject. However, Dr. Salve of Government Veterinary College, who is an authority on the subject, has furnished the following guesstimates of ecto-parasite incidence.

- Cattle and buffaloes 55%
- Pet dogs 30%
- Scabies (mites), all animals 20%

A study conducted by Mumbai Veterinary College has revealed that from the categories of ecto-parasites, incidence of visible parasites in cattle and buffaloes is 53.33 per cent, while the incidence of scabies is 21.9 per cent.

Losses Due to Parasitic Infestation in Cattle

The effect of parasitic infestation in case of dairy cattle was measured in terms of three parameters – (1) Loss in milk yield (2) Increase in lactation period (3) Delay in oestrus (sexual arousal or activity).

Data from the results reveal that the productivity of the cattle is indeed affected by the parasitic infestation. De-worming of the cattle increases the milk yield and the lactation period, and reduces the time of the first oestrus.

A study conducted by Mumbai Veterinary College on the buffaloes at Aarey Milk Colony in 1995 showed untreated buffaloes for parasitic gastritis gave 10 per cent reduced milk yield over the lactation period, whereas the treated group of buffaloes showed an increase of 10 per cent milk yield per lactation period.

A study conducted by NDDB (National Dairy Development Board) showed an increase in the milk yield by 11.26 per cent with a gain of 1.42 litres per cow per day. The study also revealed that there is an increase in the length of lactation by 27.2 days while there is a reduction in time of the first oestrus by 8.2 days. A similar study conducted on buffaloes showed that treated buffaloes had an increased yield of 13.2 per cent.

Benefits of De-worming

A veterinary college in Gujarat is currently studying the impact of de-worming drugs on a more long term basis. They have shared their interim findings on an assurance that their name will not be disclosed.

Table: De-worming Benefits: Treatment and Control Groups for Cows

Description	Control (%)	Treatment (%)	Variation (%)
Milk yields from previous lactation (liters/head/day)	13.32	13.49	NS
Milk yields from experimental lactation (liters/head/day)	12.61	14.03	1.42
Lactation length (days)	290.60	317.80	27.20
Time to first oestrus (days)	41.10	32.90	8.20

The above analysis clearly indicates that the treatment of gastrointestinal parasitic infection leads to (a) Increase in milk by 11.26% per lactation (b) Increase in length of lactation by 27.2 days (c) Reduction in time to the first oestrus by 8.2 days.

A very similar impact was observed in the case of buffaloes as well.

Benefit-Cost Analysis

Benefit-Cost Ratio When Drugs Other Than Ivermectin Are Used for De-worming

The National Dairy Development Board (NDDB) team from Anand worked on the subject for both dairy cows and buffaloes and have given figures of net profits for the period of observation, i.e., 100 days when de-worming drugs (other than Ivermectin) are used. Their key findings: "At the prevailing prices of milk and anthelmintic, a net profit of Indian ₹844/- above the cost of anthelmintic would be obtained from the additional milk produced by each treated cow in the first 100 days of lactation." "The production of additional milk per treated buffalo in the 100 days observation period resulted in an additional income of ₹672 per buffalo. The cost of treatment was ₹136 per animal."

Benefit-Cost Analysis When Ivermectin is Used
(Based on the estimates given by Mumbai Veterinary College)

No	Description	Cows	Buffaloes
1.	Milk yield per lactation	3000 ltrs.	2000 ltrs.
2.	Incremental yield at 10%	300 ltrs.	200 ltrs.
3.	Rupee value of increased yield	₹4500	₹5500
4.	Incidence of parasites	30%	30%
5.	Benefit	₹1350	₹1650
6.	Cost of using 1 dose of ivermectin	₹250	₹250
7.	Benefit to cost ratio That is	₹1350: ₹250 5.5 is to 1	₹1650: ₹250 6.6 is to 1

De-worming Practices of Indian Farmers

We requested the regular market research agency of the company, 'Fact Finders" to help us understand the de-worming practices of the farmers. The agency covered 15 respondents in Mumbai, 80 farmers in rest of Maharashtra and 70 farmers in Gujarat. The relevant summary of their findings is as below:

Table: Summary of a Report from Farmers Dip Stick Survey

No	Aspect	Mumbai	Rest of Maharashtra	Gujarat
1	Estimated incidence by farmers of endo-parasites in			
	% of Crossbreed cows	30%	54%	43%
	% of local cows	NA	60%	65%
	% of buffaloes	45%	50%	55%
2	Estimated incidence by farmers of ectoparasites in			
	% of crossbreed cows	20%	40%	35%
	% of local cows	NA	72%	53%
	% of buffaloes	60%	68%	45%

No	Aspect	Mumbai	Rest of Maharashtra	Gujarat
3	% who practice preventive de-worming	55%	5%	9%
	% who use only allopathic medicines for preventive de-worming	45%	1%	5%
	% who use only traditional medicines for preventive de-worming	Nil	4%	3%
	% who use both type of medicines for preventive de-worming	10%	Nil	1%
4	% who practice curative de-worming	95%	35%	55%
	% who use allopathic medicines for curative de-worming	55%	25%	40%
	% who use traditional medicines for curative de-worming	34%	8%	9%
	% who use both types of medicines for curative de-worming	6%	2%	6%
5	% who use Ivermectin for preventive de-worming	12%	Nil	Nil
6	% who use Ivermectin for curative de-worming	15%	2%	3%

Health care practice of milk animals is found to be most developed amongst stable owners in north Mumbai suburbs. The dairy owners in Mumbai are more professional in their approach and each dairy has a contracted veterinarian who visits their dairy farm twice a week. These farmers totally depend on the doctor's advice and hence do not resort to the use of any traditional remedies for their herds.

The practice of de-worming of animals in Gujarat is more developed in comparison to Maharashtra, because of the dairy co-operative societies which are very active in the state. The doctors appointed by dairies visit the villages regularly for check-up of animals. The doctors very often supply the drugs free of cost.

Use of Traditional Medicines for De-worming

The dip-stick research by fact finders has indicated that a majority of farmers in Maharashtra and Gujarat use only traditional medicines for preventive de-worming. We, therefore, carried out a quick qualitative investigation in this practice of dairy farmers. 20 of the 25 participants in the two focus group discussions in Baramati (agriculturally very advanced area near Pune) mentioned the use of traditional remedies for the treatment of parasitic infections.

Farmers closely observe their animals and the environment. They know when an animal is sick. They have names for the different animal diseases and know animals of which age and sex are commonly affected. Over centuries, through trial and error and deliberate experimentation, farmers have developed a wide spectrum of prevention and treatment methods. These include the use of medicinal plants, vaccination, branding, and bone-setting as well as the provision of shelters adapted to the local conditions, the exploitation of a wide range of fodder plants and many other management practices. In India ethno-veterinary medicine partly overlaps with Ayurveda, as both often use the same plants.

Allopathic, Ayurveda, homoeopathy and several others are used by dairy farmers in animal production and healthcare. Each approach is perceived as having its own strengths and drawbacks. Allopathic remedies are seen as highly potent and working fast. But they are costly and difficult to access in remote areas. Besides, they may have side effects. Farmers are also worried about 'spurious' allopathic drugs; then they pay a high price and get no results. Homoeopathy and Ayurveda, on the other hand, are seen as slow-acting drugs. For epidemic diseases and any life-threatening conditions, allopathic drugs are preferred. Worms are seen as a chronic, not very serious hazard.

The commonly used traditional remedies for worms in Maharashtra are:

a) Juice of neem leaf with water.

b) A mixture of sugar, salt and chalk in water.

c) A mixture of neem juice with turmeric & asafetida in water.

d) Juice of a kind of wild tamarind (commonly known as English tamarind) in water.

e) Sweet oil or mustard oil in water.

In Gujarat, the practice of using traditional medication is observed to be relatively low. The commonly used traditional remedies in Gujarat are:

a) Feeding of cumin seed powder in water or through feed and

b) Asafetida along-with sweet or mustard oil in water.

Doctors' Prescription Practices for De-worming

Pharmaceutical Shop Audit Report available from a market research agency is not at all useful for veterinary medicines sold in the rural area. There is no reliable information available on veterinary doctors' prescription behavior. The authors personally interviewed 22 doctors and conducted a focused group discussion to get an idea about the role they play.

Their estimates varied from 20% to 50% regarding the serious incidence of worms in cattle and buffaloes. However, they all agreed that the consequent losses are far higher in crossbred cows.

For the treatment of endo-parasites, the drug of choice amongst doctors or the most widely prescribed drug, in both the states, has been Albomar (Albendazal of Glaxo) and in a few cases Panacur (Fenbendazole of Hoechst India). For the treatment of ecto-parasites, the common practice was giving Gamma BHC or Malathion bath to the animals. Two doctors also indicated the use of Butox (Cadilla Labs) for dual treatment.

Although the doctors are aware of the efficacy of Ivermectins, they do not regularly use or prescribe it. Of the 22 doctors interviewed, only 3 practitioners from Mumbai confirmed the use of Ivermectin.

Why Ivermectin is not the largest selling drug in India for de-worming of cattle, (when it is the largest selling drug in Europe)

There are major and significant differences between dairy animal rearing practices in India and in Europe (and in the USA) which we consider to answer this puzzle. For Europe, the following aspects stand out:

- The cow is the milk animal, buffaloes are absent, and cows are more affected by worms.
- In Europe, the herd sizes are very large, in hundreds.
- Each cow has much higher milk yield, therefore losses due to worm infestation are much higher.
- Costs of manpower, particularly qualified veterinary doctors and attendants are high.
- Cost of finding out which particular cows in the herd have worms, by testing faecal samples, is very high in view of the large herd size and high cost of manpower.

It is therefore economical and convenient to do preventive de-worming for all cows at one time using a broad spectrum, de-worming drug which will simultaneously get rid of most of the endo-parasites and ecto-parasites. The visiting veterinarian, in one visit, carries out examination and treatment of all cows including vaccination, periodic deworming, etc. etc.

In India herd sizes are small. Often farmers have only one cow or buffalo in milk. The losses due to worms are low because the milk yield of the animal is low. Periodic/Preventive de-worming means that he uses de-worming drug at regular intervals say once in six months. If he de-worms his one cow/buffalo as a routine practice and the animal did not have worms, the efforts and costs are wasted. If he uses ivermectin, two times in a year, as a periodic, routine practice for a cow which did not have worms then his loss on account of the cost of drugs alone is ₹500/-. As the data collected by us shows, the probability of cow/buffalo having worm infestation which requires treatment is between 30% and

50%. In other words, the chance that the animal does not have a serious worm problem is between 50% and 70%. Therefore, if a farmer with one animal in milk adopts the practice of regular de-worming, then he will be a loser at least 50% of the times. This is a very high chance of losing on an investment decision. The losses of ₹500/- in a year are also large in comparison with his net annual income from rearing the cow / buffalo.

Does the farmer make all these calculations for the heuristic decision making? We explored this aspect during the focus group discussions with farmers. There were frequent comments and questions of the following type:

- Can I know for sure that my animal has worms before doing the de-worming?
- What are the symptoms when the de-worming drug should be used?
- Would it not be better to ensure no worm infestation takes place in the first place?
- This drug may be good for those large organized farms, I am a small man.
- I regularly feed juice of Neem leaf with water to all the cattle, worms or no worms – I do not bother; ultimately it costs almost nothing.

These comments acquire greater and new significance in light of the above discussion. The farmers do not calculate numerically and exactly the risk-return pay-off but they are generally aware of the problem. The basic psychology of 'investors risk aversion', which we studied in theory, says that investors tend to overestimate the risk when they cannot estimate it precisely. Farmers also, perhaps, under-estimate the risk and are therefore inclined not to use any costly treatment for periodic de-worming of all cattle.

The problem is further aggravated because there is no easy and symptomatic method of deciding that the animal has worm infestation which requires treatment. Symptoms like the hair on body standing up, loose motions and drastic fall in milk yield occur only when the worms reach alarmingly high levels. Significant fall (say 10%) in milk yield, irregular and delayed cycles of coming in heat happen at much lower levels of worm infestation but these symptoms can occur because of many other reasons as well. The farmer's economic losses are significant even when the level of worm infestation is not very acute. The only reliable method of detecting worms at this level is a faecal sample examination under a microscope.

Incidentally, we must anticipate and answer a question before we proceed to our recommended plan of action. The question is, "What about farmers in Europe? Do they not face the same risk of making losses?"

We have analyzed the problem from the viewpoint of a typical Indian farmer who has only one cow or buffalo in milk. The situation changes dramatically and quickly as herd size increases. The graph below shows the probability of making losses because ivermectin is used for periodic de-worming as a function of increasing herd size.

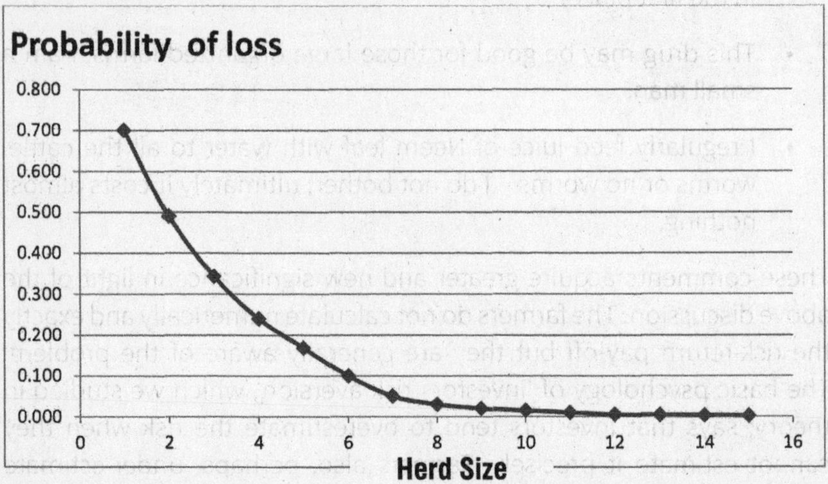

It can be seen that the chance of making a loss become 1% when a farmer has 10 cows in milk and the chance becomes less than 0.05% when herd size is larger than 15 animals in milk. In Europe, the herd size is almost always bigger than this!

Our Recommendation

We have put together most of the relevant facts. We are of the opinion that the conventional approach of promoting Ivermectin through veterinary doctors and educating farmers regarding benefits of de-worming will yield very limited results because the problem of farmer's risk aversion will not be overcome.

Government institutions are not able to efficiently deliver most of the livestock services like vaccination, de-worming etc., due to financial as well as bureaucratic constraints. This necessitates the need for providing efficient and effective decentralized services in tune with the demands emanating from the users. Such services should be delivered at the farmer's door and linked with cost recovery for economic viability.

Specific marketing strategies are required to be aggressively implemented for overcoming farmer's risk aversion. We propose a special marketing initiative, titled RAHI (RatanLab's Animal Health Initiative). The market will not be price sensitive if Ivermectin is promoted through RAHI and the company can earn good margins.

Idea of RAHI

The core activity will be a value-adding service – farmers will be offered a faecal sample examination under a microscope in their village so that they can know for sure which of their cattle need treatment for worms. This requires only a 100X microscope which is handy and cheap. The farmer can see for himself the number of worm eggs in the sample. He will be then offered immediate, on the spot treatment for the infected cattle. There will be a mobile team moving with a microscope and enough doses of Ivermectin. The team will consist of a veterinary diploma holder (equivalent to a Live Stock Supervisor in Government service) and an assistant. They will be based in the taluka town and move on motorcycle. They will visit every target area once a year. Their visit schedules will be announced through local newspapers and veterinary chemists' shops in the area and milk collection vans.

Target Areas for RAHI

The RAHI should be launched in areas where dairying is well developed. Eight districts may be selected in each state (initially 16 districts in the states of Maharashtra and Gujarat). An illustrative list of eight such districts in Maharashtra, along with the population of target cattle in these districts, is given in Annexure 1. The population of dairy cattle is not uniformly distributed amongst all the villages. Our analysis of secondary data shows that 30% of the villages have 70% of the population. These villages with high population density should be selected as the nodal villages for RAHI. The likely population of cattle in a typical nodal village, as estimated from secondary data, is given below:

Table: Target Population in a Typical Nodal Dairy Village

Type of cattle	**Average numbers**
Heifers	64
CB cows in milk	172
Buffaloes young	46
Buffaloes in milk	168
Sub Total	450
Add inflow from neighbouring villages at 20%	90
Total available target cattle	540

One RAHI team will cover 20 village clusters in a month; say 250 village clusters in a year.

Sales of Ivermectin per RAHI Team

1. A village cluster, say of three villages will have a total target population of 540 x 3 = 1620 nos.
2. Assuming at least 33% of farmers get feacal samples checked.
3. The animals checked will be 540 nos.

4. At a very conservative 20% incidence, 108 animals will test positive for worms.

5. Assuming 40% of animals which test positive are de-wormed.

6. 43 doses or say 40 doses of Ivermectin, will be sold in the village cluster.

7. Sales will be 40 doses x ₹250 per dose = ₹10,000 per day in each village cluster.

8. We estimate the sale of 10,000 doses (250 days x 40 doses per day) of Ivermectin valued at ₹25,00,000 per RAHI team per year.

Cost of One RAHI Team

Item of cost	Cost/year (Rs)
Salary of livestock supervisor	2,40,000
Salary of assistant	1,20,000
Petrol and maintenance of M/cycle	1,00,000
Local publicity	50,000
Out of pocket expenses	40,000
The total cost of one team	5,50,000

Overall Benefit-cost Analysis of RAHI

The number of villages to be covered: 6400 nos. (@ 400 villages per district for 16 districts)

Number of RAHI teams required: 27 teams (@ one team per 240 villages)

Total annual cost: ₹1,48,50,000 (@ ₹5,50,000 per team for 27 teams)

Total annual sales: ₹6,75,00,000 (@ ₹25,00,000 per team for 27 teams)

The number of doses of Ivermectin sold: 2,70,000 nos. (@10,000 doses per team for 27 teams)

Cost of promotion through RAHI per dose: ₹55 per dose; that is 22% of the sales price

An annual sale of ₹6.75 crores can be achieved in one state and the promotional cost will be less than the distributor's / retailer's margin, which will be totally saved.

Sd/-	Sd/-
Sanjay Patil	Ajay Vora
Regional Manager, Maharashtra	*Regional Manager, Gujarat*

Annexure 1

Target Cattle Population in Eight Districts of Maharashtra (Year 2010)

	Name of District	Crossbred Cows			Buffaloes			Total Target Cattle
		Heifers	in milk	Total Cross-bred	1 to 3 years	in milk	Total Buffa-loes	
1	Nashik	11408	25264	36672	25030	59584	84614	121286
2	Ahmed-nagar	46977	113101	160078	18367	46091	64458	224536
3	Pune	36793	98289	135082	26268	95882	122150	257232
4	Satara	16868	48338	65206	35669	120394	156063	286475
5	Sangli	8343	26803	35146	37893	153114	191007	226153
6	Solapur	12522	34078	46600	30513	89931	120444	167044
7	Kolha-pur	6811	28871	35682	48645	267290	315935	351617
8	Aurang-abad	9450	20895	30345	10030	31873	41903	72248
	Total	149172	395639	544811	232415	864159	1096574	1641385

Chapter 12

Jade Ring Hospital

Background

Jade Ring* Hospital was a multi-specialty hospital in Kolkata (then Calcutta). The hospital had 500 inpatient beds including 110 intensive care beds, with a staff strength of 130 consultants, 400 panel doctors and 1,100 paramedical staff. The hospital served more than 10,000 patients every year.

Dr. Vipin Ghosh had migrated to Dubai at the young age of 30. He had worked for a major hospital in Dubai for 20 years, eventually becoming the chief medical officer. However, he could not resist the urge to return to his motherland.

It had been almost six months since Dr. Ghosh, M.D., had joined the Jade Ring Hospital, as medical director. Dr. Ghosh was a worried man. In the last two months, the hospital had received two major setbacks in the district consumer court. The first case was of Urmila (age 45) who lost her eyesight due to an inappropriate amount of anaesthesia administered during a (possibly needless) surgery. The District Consumer Grievance Redressal Forum found Jade Ring Hospital negligent and asked it to pay ₹11.50 lacs to Urmila as compensation. The second case was that of Dr. Lam, M.B.B.S.

---

*The idea behind naming the hospital 'Jade Ring' originated with the founder's trip to China. Made with auspicious green jade, these rings not only look great, they are said to bring good luck. Wearing jade is said to protect a person from harm and improve the flow of Chi within your body. For followers of alternative Feng Shui healing practices in China, Jade carries a very healing, sweet, light and nourishing energy field that is accepting, loving and wise.

(age 64) who was admitted to the ICU for rapidly deteriorating health following his first round of chemotherapy administered in the hospital. Dr. Lam died of cardiac arrest caused by endotracheal suctioning. His family too had accused the hospital staff of his mistreatment on multiple occasions, and approached the District Consumer Grievance Redressal Forum. Dr. Ghosh was worried about another adverse judgement.

Both the cases had received considerable publicity in the local newspapers. Dr. Ghosh was afraid that this bad publicity would encourage other patients to file legal suits against the hospital. He also felt that these problems were the tip of the iceberg, and the cancer of poor service quality had spread far and wide within Jade Ring Hospital. This feeling was based on the expressions he saw on the faces of patients and relatives when he had casual conversations with them about the progress of a patient's health. Some of the well-wishers of the hospital had also voiced their concern, albeit very politely, regarding the deteriorating quality of health service provided by the hospital.

Dr. Ghosh discussed his concerns with other members of the board, leading consultants visiting the hospital and representatives of the staff organisation. However, the others did not share his concern.

They cited many recognitions that the hospital had received from various authorities including five accreditations from the Quality Council of India in Healthcare, certification by the National Accreditation Board for Hospitals and Healthcare Providers (NABH) and National Accreditation Board for Testing and Calibration Laboratories (NABL). They also drew his attention to the 1,500 international patients who used the hospital facilities and that the hospital was awarded 'The Best Medical Tourism Facility in India' by the Ministry of Tourism, Govt. of India. His colleagues were broadly of the opinion that the complainant patients were just a couple of exceptional nuisance elements. It was also possible that in a very exceptional case, there was a default in the service. But such a very rare exception should not cause too much worry to the management.

Planning the Patient Satisfaction Survey

Dr. Ghosh still had a gut feeling that the quality of medical service at the hospital was not up to the mark. He decided to approach the problem scientifically. While in Dubai, he had attended a course in hospital management in London. Dr. Roberts, the faculty at the course, had repeatedly emphasised the need to systematically and regularly monitor patient satisfaction.

Dr. Ghosh formed a committee of five persons to support a patient satisfaction survey. The committee comprised:

- The Managing Trustee of the Jade Ring Hospital
- The senior-most consulting physician
- The head of hospital administration
- The secretary of the Staff Association
- Himself

Dr. Ghosh decided to involve, with the approval of the committee, a very leading management institute, IIMC, in the patient satisfaction survey to increase the credibility of the survey findings. Prof. Dr. Jayant Gupta from the management institute agreed to provide the consultancy, as this was his field of specialisation.

Prof. Gupta made a detailed presentation on the methodology of the patient satisfaction survey. The professor was keen on explaining the basic concepts of measuring patient satisfaction. He said that the concerned team of Jade Ring Hospital must have an understanding of the core theoretical concepts. His experience showed that only then, any effective use of the findings to implement quality improvement programs, was likely. Prof. Gupta specially explained two theoretical foundations, namely, the Serve Qual model of Dr. Parasuraman and 'two-dimensional quality concepts,' developed by Dr Noriaki Kano. Prof. Gupta also circulated very brief reference notes. (See Annexure 1 and Annexure 2).

Prof. Gupta prepared an action plan for the patient satisfaction survey in consultation with the Jade Ring Hospital committee. The salient features of this plan were:

- The survey would also cover two other major hospitals in the town to provide a comparative picture. Dr. Ghosh would speak with the medical directors of the other two hospitals to get their cooperation. In exchange, Jade Ring Hospital would agree to share the data from the patient satisfaction survey of patients in their hospital with them.

- Patients and the attending relatives would be interviewed at their homes, face to face, by MBA students. The interviews would be conducted within seven days of the discharge from the hospital. This would ensure that patients would not feel that any negative feedback would be used by the hospital management or the staff for any penal action.
- Further, to make the respondents feel comfortable, they would be told that the survey was being conducted by the management institute and the respondents' names would not be referred to the hospital management. Only the consolidated findings for improvement in service quality would be shared with the hospital management.
- MBA students would be specially trained for this work through a two-day workshop conducted by Prof. Gupta.
- The MBA students would dig deeper, through qualitative discussions, in areas of dissatisfaction mentioned by the respondents.
- Since the survey was being conducted for hospitals run by charitable trusts, and since the findings would be used to improve the delivery of health services to the patients, Prof. Gupta would not charge any fees.
- There would not be any overhead charges by the management institute. Jade Ring Hospital would reimburse only the actual out-of-pocket expenses, mainly for local travel by the MBA students conducting the survey.
- The entire exercise would be completed within three months.
- The management of the Jade Ring Hospital would prepare an action plan for improving the health care services in consultation with Prof. Gupta.

Findings of the Patient Satisfaction Survey

Prof. Gupta and two of the student team leaders made a presentation on the survey findings. A summary of the survey findings, in tabular form, is given in Table 1 at the end of the case. As can be seen from the findings, the satisfaction of patients and relatives regarding Jade Ring Hospital is on par with two other major hospitals in the city. However, the "overall satisfaction score of less than eight is 'low' by international standards," said Prof. Gupta. Prof. Gupta also pointed out that the proportion of dissatisfied patients was a more important indicator than the average satisfaction score. Even 1% dissatisfaction meant that there were more than 100 dissatisfied patients, when the hospital was treating more than ten thousand patients every year. Dissatisfied patients would spread their views by word-of-mouth. A few would file cases in the consumer court. Prof. Gupta presented the summary table given below and requested the management of Jade Ring Hospital to quickly formulate an action plan to improve the service quality in the areas in which the patients were dissatisfied.

Percentage of Respondents Dissatisfied on an Attribute		
Priority	**Attribute**	**Percent %**
1	Directions for facilities in regional language	21
2	No noise pollution	15
3	Emergency patient received immediate help	12
4	Ambulance of the hospital arrived in good time	9
5	Disabled friendly access	7
6	I was in a clean and safe environment	4
7	Nursing staff was polite and friendly	3
8	Doctor gave adequate time to explanations	2
9	Doctor explained the reasons for medical tests	2

Prof. Gupta also shared the findings from the qualitative survey carried out through in-depth discussions by the students doing the survey.

Action Plan Report

All members of the patient satisfaction survey committee of Jade Ring Hospital took the findings of the survey very seriously. Dr. Ghosh and the team planned the actions to be taken to remove the problematic points for the patients. They are summarised item-wise in the following action plan report:

1. Directions for facilities in regional language (21% dissatisfied)

Qualitative findings: All the boards are in English and Hindi. They should also be in Bengali (and in Oriya if possible).

Action plan: All the boards will also be in Bengali, and wherever place is available the boards will also be in Oriya.

Time span: One week

Responsibility: Mr. Das, Manager (Administration)

2. No noise pollution (15% dissatisfied)

Qualitative findings: The noise that the patients complained about came from two sources. 10% of the dissatisfied patients complained about the noise coming from the building under construction in the adjoining plot. 7% complained about the loud chatting between nurses and ward boys in the general ward, particularly during the afternoon rest period and early night hours.

Action plan: The construction of the building on the adjoining plot was nearing completion and this source of noise would be eliminated within a month. Nurses and ward boys needed to be sensitized to the need to be silent so that the patients could sleep well, which was very necessary for improving the patients' health. However, it was noted that Mr. Das was doubtful whether this would be effective. Therefore, it was decided that the area at the end of the general ward, where the nurses and ward boys sat should be enclosed in a cabin with sound proof glass walls. Whether this extreme action was required should be decided by Dr. Ghosh, in his good judgement, after three months.

Time span: Four months

Responsibility: Mr. Das, Manager (Administration), Dr. Ghosh, Medical Director

3. Immediate help to emergency patients (12% dissatisfied)

Qualitative findings: The patients' dissatisfaction arose from various causes. The driveway to the 'Emergency' was blocked by vehicles without drivers. Ward boys, needed to take patients to the treatment table on stretchers, were not easily available and the relatives had to do a lot of running around to locate them. When the patient was taken inside, the hospital personnel spent time in noting down the names of the patient and the attendant, cause and history of the accident, etc., instead of attending to the patient immediately. The relatives expected a qualified doctor to attend to the patient within a few minutes, but for much of the time, only a nurse and ward boy would be with the patient. Nobody talked to the relative or to the patient explaining to them how serious their case was.

Action plan: A watchman would be appointed on a 24-hour duty to ensure that the driveway to the emergency entrance was free from obstructions. A Closed Circuit Television (CCTV) camera would be installed at the entrance of the emergency exit to record the actions taking place as soon as the patient was taken out of the vehicle on the stretcher by ward boys. The fact that the action was being recorded and was going to be reviewed by the seniors, itself would put the ward boys and the other personnel on their toes. Some of the recordings in the camera would be watched by Dr. Ghosh and Mr. Das every day. They would ask for an explanation, in case there was a delay of more than three minutes in attending to the patient. The norm would be that the nurses would attend to the patient within 90 seconds, the doctor on duty would see the patient within 120 seconds of his/her arrival. The doctor would be requested to talk to the patient and relatives regarding seriousness of the case within five minutes of the patient's arrival.

A monthly report would be prepared by a clerk in the administrative office of the number of cases in which the patient did not receive medical attention within three minutes. This report would be jointly reviewed by Dr. Ghosh and Mr. Das for the necessary corrective actions.

Time span: 10 days

Responsibility: Mr. Das, Manager (Administration), Dr. Ghosh, Medical Director

4. Ambulance of the hospital arrived in good time (9% dissatisfied)

Qualitative findings: The patients had the following things to say:

- After you call for the ambulance, you don't know when it will come. You just wait anxiously.
- After coming late, the driver said, 'There was a traffic jam.' I do not know whether it was true, or just a lie.
- The driver said, 'The address was difficult to find.' Is it so difficult to find my address?
- The driver said, 'He was finishing another duty,' but I was told that the ambulance is starting immediately.
- The driver refused to accept that there had been an inordinate delay, but the distance between my house and the hospital is only 3 kilometres. It should not take more than 10 minutes. How can it take half an hour?

Action plan: When the ambulance is booked, the attendant of the ambulance would be given the telephone number of the person calling for the ambulance. The ambulance attendant would call the patient/relative every five minutes, telling them how much longer it is likely to take. The person booking the ambulance would be given the ambulance attendant's phone number to find out the whereabouts of the ambulance. This will also help the ambulance driver in finding the address quickly as he can take directions from the patient or his relative.

A record will be kept as to when the ambulance started from the hospital and when the patient was picked up. On arrival, the patient or his relative will be specifically asked whether the ambulance arrived in time. If the patient has any complaint, it will be noted down and investigated.

Time span: Two weeks

Responsibility: Mr. Das, Manager (Administration)

5. Disabled friendly access (7% dissatisfied)

Qualitative findings: The major complaint was regarding access to the general ward. The general ward was one step higher than the level of the lobby in which the lift opened. Some patients also complained that there was no ramp to the pharmacy.

Action plan: Ramps would be constructed for the general ward and the pharmacy.
Time span: Two weeks
Responsibility: Mr. Das Manager (Administration)

6. I was in a clean and safe environment (4% dissatisfied)

Qualitative findings: All the complainants were from the special ward for tuberculosis patients. This ward, reportedly, was in an outhouse outside the main building. Patients complained of ants, cockroaches and mosquitoes.

Action plan: The pest control agency should be asked to take immediate action. All beds in the tuberculosis ward were to be provided with mosquito-nets till the nuisance of mosquitoes was eliminated by identifying the source of their breeding.
Time span: Two weeks
Responsibility: Mr. Das Manager (Administration)

7. Nursing staff was polite and friendly (3% dissatisfied)

Qualitative findings: The patients mainly complained about excessively polite nurses with very broad permanent smiles on their faces. Patients felt that the nurses were not sensitive to their painful condition. Patients also felt that the nurses were putting on a show to get maximum tips.

Action plan: This feedback would be shared with the nursing staff in a staff meeting. Peer pressure would be used to regulate the behaviour of erring nurses.
Time span: 4 weeks
Responsibility: Mr. Roy, Secretary (Staff Association)

8. Doctor gave adequate time to explain (2% dissatisfied)

and

9. Doctor explained the reason for the medical tests (2% dissatisfied)

Qualitative findings: Patients and their relatives said that they often felt the need to meet the senior consultant doctor to ask a few supplementary questions, however the consulting doctor was not immediately available to offer services, as he had left the hospital and was not likely to visit the hospital again for the next two days. They felt at a loss in such a situation. 'We, on our own enquired as to why they didn't consult the Medical Social Workers (MSWs) available in the hospital. We found that most of the patients were not aware of the medical social worker and the help available from him/her.'

Action plan: Each consulting doctor would have a MSW attached to him. One MSW might be attached to about 20 or more consultants. The MSW will also be attached to a specific ward. Their names, their mobile numbers and their job descriptions would be prominently displayed. The consulting doctors would be requested to give the name of the MSW to the patient for further advice. The MSW would maintain a register of the patients who met him/her. They would be encouraged to move around and talk to patients about their health. The MSW would not be allotted other clerical work.

Time span: Two weeks

Responsibility: Dr. Ghosh, Mr. Das

The plan was implemented with full zeal by the entire staff of Jade Ring Hospital. All the doctors and the staff were happy and proud of their contribution to the well-being of patients. The patient satisfaction survey was repeated by Prof. Gupta the following year. The average satisfaction score shot up to 9.1. The percentage of dissatisfied customers was less than 0.5% and that too only in two areas - reasonable cost of treatment and loud chatting by nurses and ward boys.

See Table 1 and Annexures 1 and 2 on the following pages.

Summary Findings of Patient Satisfaction Survey

No	Attribute	Jade Ring Hospital			Other Hospitals	
		Percentage		Avg. marks out of 10	Avg. marks out of 10	
		Delighted	Dissatis-fied		A	B
1	Proper guidance by reception clerk	27	0	9.1	9.1	9.1
2	Directions for facilities in regional language	0	21	5	8.3	9.1
3	Doctor's name plate displayed visiting hours	0	0	8	8	8
4	Disabled friendly access	0	7	5.2	7.4	7.5
5	Ambulance of the hospital arrived in good time	10	9	6.2	na	na
6	Emergency patient received immediate help	15	12	5	8	8.1
7	Registration area was comfortable	30	0	9.5	8	7.8
8	Patient area in hospital was clean	25	2	8.7	7.7	7.9
9	Toilets were clean and in usable condition	32	0	9.7	8.0	8.3
10	Canteen food was fresh and healthy	25	0	9.1	8.5	7.4
11	Waiting time less before interaction with doctor	30	1	8.9	9	8.9
12	Easy access to the medical specialists	20	0	9	8.9	9.1

Continued

No	Attribute	Jade Ring Hospital			Other Hospitals	
		Percentage		Avg. marks out of 10	Avg. marks out of 10	
		Delighted	Dissatis-fied		A	B
13	Nursing staff available quickly when required	18	0	8.0	8.2	7.9
14	Nursing staff appeared to know their job	21	0	8.8	8.9	9.0
15	No noise pollution	2	15	4.5	8.0	7.7
16	Nursing staff was polite and friendly	18	3	6.9	7.0	6.9
17	Doctor gave adequate time to explain	20	2	7.5	7.5	7.5
18	Doctor explained reason for medical tests	1	2	7.1	6.5	6.4
19	Doctor gave instructions about dosage	0	0	6.6	7.0	6.8
20	Doctor explained the side effects	0	0	6.9	6.9	7.0
23	Doctor told when to return	0	0	7.0	7.5	7.5
24	Doctor explained the chances of success	0	0	6.0	5.5	5.4
25	I was involved in the planning of my care	0	0	6.1	5.6	6.1
26	I was given enough privacy	0	0	6.7	7.0	6.5
27	I was in a clean and safe environment	5	4	6.0	8.0	8.5
28	I was treated with dignity at all times	0	0	7.0	7.1	7.0
29	Treatment that I received was effective	10	0	9.0	9.2	9.1

Continued

No	Attribute	Jade Ring Hospital			Other Hospitals	
		Percentage		Avg. marks out of 10	Avg. marks out of 10	
		Delighted	Dissatis-fied		A	B
30	Proper maintenance of records	3	0	8.8	8.5	8.4
31	Cost of treatment was reasonable	20	2	8.9	8.8	8.6
32	Time for billing and discharge was short	3	0	8.0	8.3	8.1
33	I would recommend the hospital	7	5	6.0	5.9	6.1
34	Your overall satisfaction with the Hospital	na	na	7.3	7.2	7.4

Annexure 1

SERVQUAL is a multi-dimensional research instrument, designed to capture consumer expectations and perceptions of a service along the five dimensions that are believed to represent service quality. SERVQUAL is built on the expectancy-disconfirmation paradigm. In simple terms, it means that service quality is understood as the extent to which consumers' pre-consumption expectations of quality are confirmed or disconfirmed by their actual perceptions of the service experience. The SERVQUAL questionnaire was first published in 1988 by a team of academic researchers, A. Parasuraman, Valarie Zeithaml and Leonard L. Berry to measure quality in the service sector. It represented a breakthrough in the measurement methods used for service quality research. The diagnostic value of the instrument is supported by the model of service quality which forms the conceptual framework for the development of the scale (i.e., instrument or questionnaire). The instrument has been widely applied in a variety of contexts and cultural settings, and has been found to be relatively robust. It has become the dominant measurement scale in the area of service quality.

SERVQUAL measures service quality by capturing respondents' expectations and perceptions along the five dimensions of service quality. The questionnaire consists of matched pairs of items: 22 expectation items and 22 perceptions items organized into five dimensions which are believed to align with the consumers' mental map of service quality dimensions. Both the expectations component and the perceptions component of the questionnaire consist of a total of 22 items comprising:

- 4 items to capture tangibles
- 5 items to capture reliability
- 4 items for responsiveness
- 4 items for assurance
- 5 items to capture empathy

The questionnaire is designed to be administered in a face-to-face interview, and requires a moderate to large size sample for statistical reliability.

Annexure 2

The Contribution of Dr. Noriaki Kano, Professor, Science University, Tokyo, in Terms of Two Dimensional Quality

Dr. Noriaki Kano proposed a novel and relevant classification of quality attributes as:

Must-be quality: Simply stated, these are the requirements that the customers expect and also take for granted. When done well, customers are just neutral, but when done poorly, customers are very dissatisfied. Kano originally called these 'Must-be' because they are the requirements that must be included and are the price of entry into a market. Example: Quick attention to 'emergency' arrivals.

One-dimensional quality: These attributes result in satisfaction when fulfilled and dissatisfaction when not fulfilled. These are attributes that are spoken of and the ones in which companies compete. Examples: Reasonable fees.

Attractive quality: These attributes provide satisfaction when achieved fully, but do not cause dissatisfaction when not fulfilled. These are the attributes that are not normally expected. Since these types of attributes of quality unexpectedly delight customers, they are often left unsaid. Example: The doctor addressing a patient by name.

Indifferent quality: These attributes refer to aspects that are neither good nor bad, and they do not result in either customer satisfaction or customer dissatisfaction. For example, the number of dishes in the meals served in the hospital.

Reverse quality: These attributes refer to a high degree of achievement resulting in dissatisfaction. It also points to the fact that not all customers are alike. For example, a nurse who always speaks very politely with a continuous smile on his/her face may be perceived as insensitive, and in pursuit of 'tips'.

Chapter 13

Killworm

The Customer

Rabari are one of the largest groups of livestock herders inhabiting the western districts of Rajasthan and Gujarat in India, including the great Thar Desert. Their population is estimated to be somewhere between a quarter and half a million people.

The Rabari were the traditional caretakers of the camel herds belonging to the Maharajahs. Nowadays, camels are herded by a relatively small number of Rabari families, while sheep and goat husbandry are practised by the vast majority to service a growing meat market.

The Rabari began keeping sheep about 200 to 250 years ago. During this time, they have been influencing and developing the traits of their sheep by selective breeding and recently by crossbreeding with other breeds. In this way, they have developed hardy breeds that are drought resistant, capable of walking long distances and able to produce lambs for slaughter.

Bhopa Rabari from Jamnagar and Dwarka and Vagadia Rabari from eastern Kutch migrate seasonally searching endlessly for fodder and water for their herds. They travel long distances in Rajasthan, Gujarat and Madhya Pradesh. Thankfully, barring major disasters, they return to their homelands every year.

Due to the fact that they operate under migratory conditions, Rabari pastoralists have traditionally resorted to self-treatment of their sheep. The Rabari have developed their own system of animal healthcare making use of plants, animal and mineral-based remedies, conventional drugs and traditional healers.

The Product

Killworm is a broad spectrum drench for the control of internal parasites (endo-parasites) like roundworms and lungworms in sheep. In the 1990s, the product was protected by patents and was owned by ABC Ltd., a large multinational. ABC had a very wide product mix comprising paints and speciality products including ingredients for foods, speciality polymers, electronic materials, fragrances and flavours. Killworm was a minor product in a highly diverse product mix of ABC and was, by and large, neglected by the company. The product was marketed by ABC in India for 20 years. Despite the relatively low attention paid by the company, it was the largest selling drug in its category having a 43% market share.

Many studies and field trials showed Killworm to be the most effective drug for de-worming sheep. Infestation by worms was a major problem affecting sheep and consequently the productivity of sheep and profitability of sheep rearing. At any given time, as many as 25% of the sheep in a herd suffered from internal parasites. Use of Killworm was a very attractive proposition for the sheep herders: the benefit to cost ratio was more than 6.0, at the market price and required dosage.

The Need for a New Push

Indian Veterinary Pharmaceuticals (IVP) bought the Killworm brand name from ABC in the year 2012. The new owners believed that Killworm had a much bigger market potential which remained to be exploited by ABC. The IVP management desired to expand the market rather than be satisfied with the position achieved by the earlier owner of the brand; they invited a Leading Marketing Consultancy Firm (LMCF) to design a marketing and sales strategy to quickly achieve a substantial increase in sales on a sustainable basis.

Findings by LMCF

LMCF carried out a survey. The major findings were:

- 86% of shepherds were aware of worms as a major health problem in their sheep.
- The importance of various reasons in the choice of a brand of a deworming drug was as shown in the bar chart below.

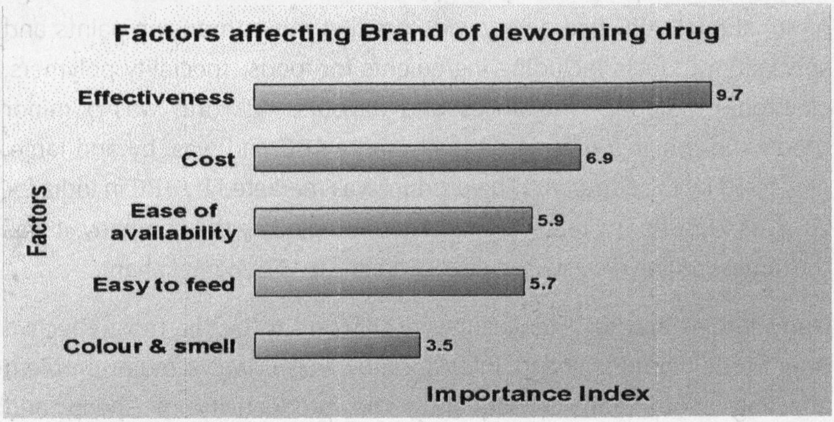

- 73% of the shepherds preferred allopathic drugs as they were more effective.
- 80% of the shepherds were aware of Killworm. Being illiterate, they recognised Killworm from a 'foreign sheep's picture.'
- The major income of sheep herders is from meat and wool. Sheep are sold for meat once or twice a year at markets in district towns. Wool is sold almost once a month. Major wool traders are based in a few commercial wool centres. However, small wool traders follow the trail of the nomads and purchase wool against cash at regular intervals.
- The shepherds use specific markets in their trail to make specific purchases. However, there are no specific/traditional places to purchase an allopathic drug.

- The shepherds move in groups from retailer to retailer to buy many necessities, bargain, and make large value cash purchases. Buying medicines for sheep is generally low on their priority list.
- Shepherds often do not buy Killworm because they do not have money. Retailers do not sell on credit to shepherds.
- Veterinary doctors, company's field sales officers and retailers have very little influence (also very little contact) with the shepherds.

LMCF's Analysis and Recommendations

The product quality was good. Brand awareness was high. The benefit-cost ratio was very favourable at the current price. The main impediment in the way of selling more Killworm was the lack of purchasing power with the shepherd when he wanted to buy Killworm. Another secondary problem was the poor availability of the drug at the retail counter.

It was necessary to make Killworm available to shepherds at a time and place when they had the money to buy it.

LMCF suggested that small wool traders should be persuaded to sell Killworm to the shepherds. Wool traders could make payment for the wool, partly in kind, in the form of Killworm doses. This would make Killworm available to shepherds at their doorstep, when they had the money to buy it. It would give an additional and significant income to small wool traders. IVP would have a monopoly on this new distribution channel.

LMCF suggested that IVP should give specially made back loaders for donkeys used by Rabari to carry their moving household. The back loaders, given as gift promotional material, should be boldly printed with Killworm and the logo of IVP.

Implementation

In the first attempt, a circular was sent to field officers to recruit wool traders to sell Killworm. Commission rates linked to volumes were also mentioned. The response was a near-total failure. The sales director was not happy. He decided to personally guide the campaign.

Wool traders and a few 'leader' shepherds were invited to meet the regional manager and managers from the head office. They were treated like VIPs. The takeover of the Killworm brand by IVP and the company's new strategy to increase sales was explained.

The development manager and regional manager moved from market to market, meeting wool traders. They made presentations on the business plan showing the wool traders the amount of money to be earned by handling Killworm.

Two-day training camps were held for small, mobile wool traders. The topics included – how to recognize a worm problem in sheep, losses because of worms, advantages of Killworm, dosage, etc. The camps were conducted in good hotels. The traders were given flip charts and gift material for sheepherders.

Results

Sales increased by 20% in six months and by 32% in 12 months.

Chapter 14

Krishi Varta

Background

Varta House Pvt. Ltd., is a leading publishing house in Marathi. (Marathi is the native language spoken by more than one hundred million people in the state of Maharashtra, which is situated on the western coast of India). The newspaper Dainik Varta is published by Varta House from four cities in Maharashtra. Dainik Varta was launched by an independent professional journalist in 1945 when most of the newspapers in Marathi were being published for a cause, mainly the Indian freedom struggle. Over the years, Dainik Varta has acquired the special position as 'undisputed leader,' for itself in the city of Nashik, where it is published. Dainik Varta is a leading newspaper in the north-south belt from Kolhapur to Nashik in western Maharashtra. This belt of western Maharashtra is an educationally, industrially and agriculturally advanced area in India.

This case, Krishi Varta, describes the launch of a new newspaper for farmers by Varta House in the year 2008.

The Newspaper Industry

Circulation of paid newspapers in the USA and Europe has been showing a declining trend over the past two decades. A survey by the World Association of Newspapers, has said the circulation fell by 3% in the U.S. and by 1.9% in Europe in the year 2007.

Asia, which is home to 74 of the world's 100 best-selling dailies, contrasted starkly with the declining newspaper readership in the west.

China and India are among the countries that have contributed to some degree of optimism in the publishing industry.

In India, the Media and Entertainment (M&E) industry grew at a Compounded Annual Growth Rate (CAGR) of 10% over three years and was expected to grow at a CAGR of 13% over the next five years.

The key growth drivers for the industry were:

- Rising digitalization
- Increasing literacy and spread of basic education
- Increase in penetration of media segments; narrow casting
- Regionalization
- Expanding international markets for Indian content
- Organized funding
- Deregulation

The potential for advertising spends remains strong. The advertising to GDP ratio in India is low (0.41%) as compared to the US (1.08%) and also to China (0.75%).

Currently, the print media has the largest share of the total advertising spend. Going forward, the growth is likely to be driven by Internet advertising while the print and television segments will continue to dominate the advertisement business.

As on 31st March 2006, there were 62,483 registered newspapers with all periodicities on the record of the Registrar of Newspapers for India (RNI), as against 60,413 at the end of March 2005.

The total circulation of newspapers increased from 15,67,19,209 copies in 2004-05 to 18,07,38,611 copies in 2005-06.

As per the annual statements received at the RNI office during 2005-06, the number of dailies being published in the country was 2130. Their claimed circulation figure was 8,88,63,048 copies.

The Situation of Marathi Daily Newspapers

- Maharashtra State had 130 Marathi daily newspapers as per the Registrar of Newspapers India Annual Report for 2005-06. Amongst Indian newspapers, Marathi holds the third position with a 130 dailies, Hindi leading with 942.

- In terms of circulation, Marathi dailies also have an edge over newspapers published in the rest of the 22 official languages of India, besides English.

- Circulation of Marathi dailies in 2005-06 was recorded at 1,05,37,174.

- Advertisement revenue earned by the Marathi press during 2005-06 was ₹5,160 million.

- Among Marathi newspapers the leading newspaper are:
- Maharashtra Times, belonging to the multi-product, multi-edition, multi-centre media house of Bennett Coleman Ltd., with The Times of India as its flagship.

- Loksatta belonging to The Indian Express Group.

- The white-collar middle class was being aggressively targeted by Sakal and Lokmat, who had recently launched a Nashik edition, the home town of Dainik Varta.

- The blue-collar working class found Pudhari and Punyanagri more attractive.

Present Situation of Dainik Varta

Dainik Varta was facing stagnation.

As can be seen from the graph below, Dainik Varta had been stagnating in terms of readership and revenues in the recent past.

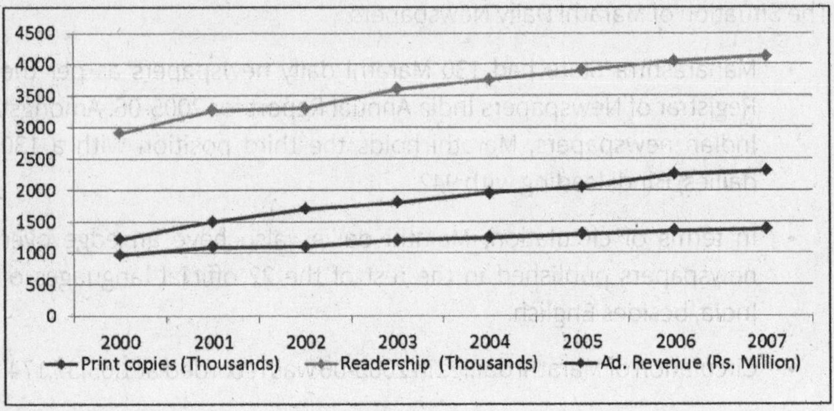

Many attempts were made in different directions to boost the sales of Dainik Varta. Some of the major efforts included:

- Starting a new edition in other towns; however, the new editions did not cross the breakeven level even after 3 years and had to be closed down.
- Starting specialized sections aimed at niche audiences; this included guidance to studies for competitive examinations, coverage of local sports events at the level of inter-school competitions, special cooking tips by housewives, review of English movies, etc. However, there was no noticeable gain in readership.
- Showing extra skin in Lifestyle pages; this resort to semi nudism came under attack from the women's lobby and, anyway, did not result in noticeably higher sales.

SWOT Analysis

In 2008, Mr. Ajay Shaha had taken the reins of Varta Papers Pvt. Ltd., as Managing Director and CEO. Mr. Ajay Shaha was a professional marketing executive. After an initial stint of two years as a journalist with the Times of India Group, he had joined IIM Ahmadabad and specialized in marketing. He had then spent 12 years as a marketing executive in various publishing houses. Under the leadership of Mr. Ajay Shaha, Varta Papers Pvt. Ltd., took various initiatives to modernize the management style.

The management of Varta House Pvt. Ltd., carried out an intensive Strength–Weakness–Opportunities–Threats (SWOT) analysis in collaboration with an expert consultant. The outcome of this exercise is summarized in the pictograph below:

Strengths	**Weaknesses**
• High brand equity • Dynamic leadership • Financial reserves • Many editions • Large readership	• Tradition bound editors • Core group of conservative readers • Price sensitive demand • Old technology

Opportunities	**Threats**
• Digital revolution • Growing market • Link with infotainment • Virgin market segments	• Aggressive competition • Entry of multinationals • New media competing for advertising revenue

Research

The management of Varta Papers Pvt. Ltd., carried out a market research exercise to understand the readers' profile and reader satisfaction through an independent professional market research agency. The major findings of the market research are summarized below.

Market

Summary findings of qualitative research through Focused Group Discussions (FGDs): There were ten FGDs, with 15 participants per group,

- There should be an international news affair supplement – in Marathi or English.
- Dainik Varta should start a helpline service for the general public and act as a solution provider.
- In book reviews, award-winning books must be covered.

- Industry-wise upcoming trends should be given.
- Dainik Varta should provide more national news.
- In the television schedule, details of English channels like HBO; Star Movies should also be given in Dainik Varta.
- More local sports coverage.
- Positive news on the front page.
- Restart cartoons.
- Information about travel and tourism.
- Area wise supplements should be given.
- Readers' poll of newly released movies.
- Agriculture news and development should be given.
- 100 days ago - News follow up.
- Business biographies of successful companies.
- Articles on environmental awareness.
- Open forum.
- Encourage better 'Letters to the Editor.' (Give an award to the five best letters).

The satisfaction of readers with 'Dainik Varta' across various dimensions is depicted in a Radar Chart below:

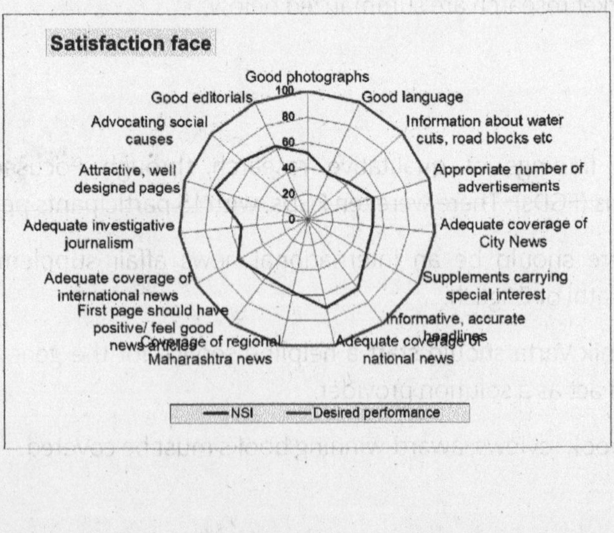

Occupational Composition of Readers of Marathi Daily Newspapers

Occupation of readers	Marathi daily newspapers						
	Maha-rashtra Times	Lok-satta	Loka-mat	Sakal	Pudhari	Dain-ik Varta	Punya nagari
White collar	30.2	32.1	31.2	28.2	21.4	26.3	23.8
Blue collar	16	16.7	16.4	20.3	26.2	21.3	23.7
Traders	8.8	10	9.4	9.7	9.7	9.6	9.6
Profession-als	6.7	6.5	6.6	6	4.5	5.6	5
Students	12.1	10.1	11.1	9.1	10.6	10.9	10.7
Homemak-ers	10.5	9.5	10	9	9.8	9.9	9.8
Farmers	2.3	2.1	2.2	3.2	4.2	3.2	3.7
Retired	11.2	11	11.1	11.3	11.1	11.1	11.1
Unemployed	2.2	2	2.1	3.2	2.6	2.4	2.5
	100	100	100	100	100	100	100

The occupational pattern in the above table revealed that farmers constituted a very small percentage of readerships of all the Marathi newspapers, despite being the single largest occupational group. The traditional reasons for farmers not reading newspapers were low literacy and insufficient disposable income. However, these reasons might not be valid at the beginning of the 21st century, after a lot of development in independent India in general and the impact of the 'green revolution' in particular. Therefore, as desired by Ajay Shaha, the market research agency carried out a supplementary survey of farmers in western Maharashtra. The major findings of the supplementary survey of farmers were:

- 30% of male farmers and 17% of women farmers were literate. 10% of the farmers had completed secondary schooling.
- 20% of the farmers had net assets (including land, house, agricultural equipment, consumer durables and bank balance) of more than a million Rupees.

- The farmers stated two main reasons for not buying newspapers:
    - The first reason cited by more than 90% of the prospective farmers was that the newspaper reached their village after 10 a.m., and by that time they had to leave for their farms. Therefore, it was only possible to read the newspaper in the evening –and by that time the news had become stale.
    - The second reason was, the news was very city-centric; there was very poor to no coverage of news which was of critical interest to farmers like prices of agricultural produce, level of water in irrigation dams, etc.

A New Initiative

Mr. Ajay Shaha recommended to the Varta editorial team that a daily newspaper should be launched for rural farmers since:

- This was the single largest occupational group in India.
- The needs of this group were distinct and easy to satisfy.
- Currently, there was no such newspaper, and therefore no competition.

There was a lot of opposition from the editorial and circulation teams. The major points of discussion between the editorial team members and Ajay Shaha are summarized in the following paragraphs.

Editorial team member 1: News is news. It comes through PTI, UNI and our correspondents. Everybody wants to read about 9/11 and Sachin's century. What do farmers want that is different?

Ajay Shaha: Yes, like anybody else, farmers are interested in such major developments. But they are also interested in attacks of pests, the current water level in irrigation dams and prices of flowers in Amsterdam markets. When you cover the union budget, you report in detail about changes in income tax rates; farmers are not interested.

Editorial team member 2: Why can't we have a supplement for farmers? We have supplements for every group of readers – women, children, youth. We will have a supplement for farmers.

Ajay Shah: Yes, I am aware of the practice of supplements. As a marketing professional, I fail to grasp it; it is like selling a cake of soap in which one corner is for the dry skin of grandma, another corner is for the tender skin of the baby, and so on. A supplement cannot carry screaming headlines of interest on the first page. A supplement does not give the feel of a newspaper specially published for farmers.

Editorial team member 3: How about a weekly? 'A Farmer's Guide to Modern Agriculture'?

Ajay Shaha: Farmers want news, news about topics of their interest, presented through their perspective. I am not talking about educational booklets.

Editorial team member 4: What is this about news through farmers' perspective? Is my perspective not good enough?

Ajay Shaha: Perhaps not good enough. When onion prices go up, you cry foul; farmers want you to be happy. When it rains you write about clogged water drains and traffic jams; farmers want you to be celebrating. Yes, we will require reporters and an editorial team which identifies with farmers.

Editorial team member 5: Rural farmers are illiterate, how will they read a newspaper?

Ajay Shaha: Literacy rates in rural India are lower than those in urban areas, but we estimate that there are more than 20 million literate persons in rural Maharashtra. That is a very large and very attractive number.

Editorial team member 6: Rural people are poor. Will they pay ₹2/- every day for a newspaper?

Ajay Shaha: There is not much difference in the average income of rural and urban households when income in kind is accounted for. Urban poor are poorer than rural poor, urban rich are richer than rural rich. We estimate that at least 25% of rural households have disposable incomes, which are sufficient to easily afford a daily newspaper.

Editorial team member 7: Rural area is highly dispersed. Road network is poor. Currently, our paper reaches most of the villages after 10 a.m. if it reaches at all. What is the point in distributing a newspaper if it is going to reach the farmer after he has gone to the farm?

Ajay Shaha: Well, at least for now, it is not necessary to reach every village before 7 a.m.; it is sufficient if we reach villages with a population of more than 1500. Even then we will reach more than half the market. Moreover, the news in which farmers are interested gets generated mostly during the day time. You can start printing by say 10 p.m. and stop at say 11.30 p.m. That gives you two to three hours extra for covering the extra distance. We have worked out the detailed logistics with costs. Distribution is physically possible and economically viable.

Editorial team member 8: Will it be economically viable? Will advertisers look at it?

Ajay Shaha: As I already said, you can finish the printing of Krishi Varta before you take up printing of your main paper, therefore you don't require investment in press at all. More importantly, the rural market is attracting the attention of everybody. Agri-input products like seeds, fertilizers and cattle feed are sold only in rural areas, their sales are huge. Now traditional urban marketers like Levers and Titan are keen on expanding in rural areas. There is no specialized media today to reach rural consumers. Krishi Varta will be the first such medium. We have a list of 200 companies who are big advertisers and are keen to expand in rural markets.

Editorial team member 9: Will we get competent staff?

Ajay Shaha: I have searched for agricultural graduates who have done post-graduation in journalism and are currently working as journalists. We have 23 names. Not a very long list, but not bad to start with.

Editorial team member 10: We have no previous experience. How should we plan the page-wise content? How many pages? What size?

Ajay Shaha: We need to do some more research, that will suggest some answers. And there is always scope for learning by experience.

Krishi Varta was launched on 1st May (Maharashtra Day, International Labour Day) 2008. It sold 1,10,000 copies on the first day. It broke even during the second month of publication and became economically viable in the third month. It made it to the Guinness Book of World Records as the first ever newspaper for farmers published anywhere in the world. It is the only newspaper for farmers anywhere in the world. The glass ceiling was broken.

Chapter 15

Leaf Miner

It was the second meeting, on 10th January 2016, of the 'Group of Seven' after passing out from Panjabrao Deshmukh Krishi Vidyapeeth, Amaravati. They were meeting in the university campus, at the residence of Professor Dr. Vijay Patil, who was a 28-year-old bachelor and the mentor of the group. The seven members were Anil More, Milind Chavan, Vasudha Deshmukh, Vilas Nimbalkar, Shankar Kendre, Subhash Joshi and Arun Kone.

The story of the 'Group of Seven' starts with a notice prominently displayed on the notice board of the university. The notice said:

Agri Clinics and Agri Business Centres Scheme

The Ministry of Agriculture, Government of India, in association with NABARD* and MANAGE*, has launched this unique scheme to take better methods of farming to each and every farmer across the country.

This program aims to tap the expertise available in the large pool of agriculture graduates. Irrespective of whether you are a fresh graduate or not or whether you are currently employed or not, you can set up your own agriclinic or agribusiness centre and offer professional extension services to farmers.

Agriclinics: These are envisaged to provide expert services and advice to farmers on cropping practices, technology dissemination, crop protection from pests and diseases, market trends and prices of various crops in the markets, and also clinical services for animal health which would enhance productivity of crops/animals.

Agribusiness centres: Agribusiness centres are envisaged to provide input supply, farm equipment on hire and other services.

In order to enhance viability of the ventures, the scheme covers full financial support for training and handholding, provision of loan and credit linked back ended composite subsidy.

A total of 10 MSc final year students were interested in starting agriclinics/ agribusiness centres in their villages. They consulted Prof. Vijay Patil. Prof. Patil enthusiastically supported the students and said that the scheme by the central government for starting agriclinics and agribusiness centres was very good. Loans were available from banks at a concessional rate. There were subsidies from the central and state governments. He also said that as 'in charge of the extension activities' at the university, he would extend support from the university in this good endeavor.

Seven out of the ten finally decided to start agriclinics, and formed the 'Group of Seven'. The group decided to meet at least once a year to exchange notes on their experiences and explore how they could support each other.

The first meeting of the 'Group of Seven' after the first year, ended on a very positive note. All of them had started agriclinics, and their business plans had been approved by the district authorities. They had also attended a special training program in Nagpur. The necessary credit was approved by the banks. All had opened small offices at the talukas. Their families were happy and they had complete family support. They were all set to 'Go'.

The second annual meeting of the 'Group of Seven' commenced after a good lunch (courtesy Mrs. Vijay Patil). Prof. Vijay Patil requested each of them to narrate, very briefly, the developments that had taken place in the past 12 months.

Vasudha: I was getting a good response to the pest control advisory service which I had started. So, I expanded my activities and started an agribusiness centre as well. I have bought two tractors, two roto-vectors and all the necessary attachments. Now, I hire out this equipment with drivers and skilled operators. This is earning me a decent income.

Shankar: I have started an artificial insemination centre. I am also offering services for the detection of worms in cattle and treating the infected cattle with vermicide. I am doing more business through the artificial insemination centre and worms control program than through agriculture advisory services. Soon, I will be starting my own small centre for collecting goats' milk and converting it into cheese. I am going to Baramati to attend a training program for making cheese from goat milk. If any of you have any inputs, I would welcome them.

Vilas: I had a very bad experience on my own farm. I planted BT cotton along with many others in my village. My cotton attracted all kinds of pests. I lost almost 70% of the crop. Other farmers in my village did equally badly. I had no energy left to run the agriclinic. How can I advise other farmers when I cannot protect my own farm? I think that my cotton was attacked by pests because the seeds I got for BT cotton were outright spurious. I want to hang all those cheats who manufacture spurious seeds. I am really sad and angry.

Anil: My village is drought-prone. No programs in agricultural development can be very successful in my village unless the availability of water is increased. My village is between hill slopes and a river. When it rains, a lot of water flows from the hills into the river, but afterwards, the hills, the land and even the river are dry. I therefore, decided that my agriclinic should diversify its activities into watershed development. I motivated the villagers to work with Paani Foundation. This foundation, established by actor Aamir Khan, aims to harness the power of communication to mobilise, motivate and train people in this mission to eradicate drought. It offers training in scientific watershed management, leadership and community-building. The work has begun, and at present, it is emotionally very rewarding. I am sure that drought in my village will be a thing of the past in two more years. After that, my agriclinic will be very helpful to farmers in taking up more profitable and sustainable agriculture based on the available water.

Subhash: All of you are aware of the huge misfortune that befell me. My father and mother both died in a car accident. All of you gave me a lot of emotional support during that traumatic period. My sister's marriage was scheduled to happen within the next 15 days. We postponed the marriage.

She got married after six months. I was really burdened with a lot of family responsibilities. I am coming out of it now, and hope to look after my farm as well as my agriclinic this year. I once again thank you for your support during my traumatic days. Thank you.

Arun: Just yesterday I received the good news! I have been selected for the fellowship of the Indian Agricultural Research Institute (IARI) for doctoral research in plant genetics. I will be going to Delhi in a few weeks. I would like to hand over my agriclinic, which is not doing badly, to anybody who wants to take it over, any takers?

Milind: I am the last one in this round and we have time. So, I hope you don't mind if I take a little longer. My experience is very similar to that of Vilas. The difference is that I suffered in the case of groundnut crop instead of cotton. A number of groundnut farmers along with me suffered because of Leaf Miner that vigorously attacked our crop. I used chemical pesticides and saved 80% of the crop.

The other farmers in my village were not so fortunate. When I noticed Leaf Miner in my farm - those typical white designs on the leaf - I enquired with other farmers whether my farm was an exception. I understood that they also had Leaf Miner in their groundnut crop, and some leaves were already becoming yellow and getting crumpled. I suggested to them that they should spray chemical pesticides quickly to save the groundnut crop.

They looked at the sky, spread their hands and said, “Well, we hope that the rain God helps us”. As you know, if it rains very heavily, which happens in our area around two to three times in the Kharif season, the Leaf Miner larvae get washed away. The infected crop is saved without spending any money on pesticides, and without the effort of spraying the pesticide. The sky did get cloudy three to four times during this period igniting hopes of the farmers.

But the rains were very light, and it showered only twice. The farmers kept on waiting for the rains. Then they said, ‘Now it is too late. The surviving crop will yield almost no groundnuts. Now, it is not worthwhile to spend money on pesticides to save this crop.’ Almost all the farmers in my village lost around 80 to 90% of the crop. My agriclinic lost very good business of supplying and spraying pesticides. I am wondering where I went wrong. I feel that we should have an aggressive program of educating farmers in timely use of pesticides and the futility of depending on help from uncontrollable, unpredictable sources like rains. I am working on a scheme on how to do it. I would like this to be a cooperative effort amongst all of us.

Vasudha: No, No and No. I am totally against promoting the use of chemical fertilizers and pesticides. We are poisoning mother earth. We must learn to do agriculture without using poisons. We must find pest-resistant varieties and biological enemies of these harmful pests. But we must not use these poisons. They not only poison the soil, but they also poison our bodies and kill us. I very strongly request all of you to let agriclinics be centres for organic farming, farming without the use of poisons.

Milind: Vasudha, I appreciate your sentiments. Even I would like to avoid using chemical pesticides whenever possible. But when a pest like Leaf Miner has attacked the standing crop of groundnuts, what do you do? Do you let this pest feast on the groundnut leaves while farmers are denied the rightful returns of their efforts?

Arun: Let us understand clearly this poisoning of food affair. Yes, when we use poisonous chemical pesticides on green vegetables like spinach or lady fingers, it is quite likely that the residual pesticides will go into our stomach. Of course, even in the case of vegetables, I understand, if the customer washes the vegetables thoroughly, then most of the pesticides get washed away. But green vegetables are not the issue right now. The story is different in the case of groundnuts. Vasudha, even you will agree that the groundnut grows below the ground. It is protected with the shell of the tough kernel. The pesticide against Leaf Miner is being sprayed on the leaves which are above the ground. The Leaf Miner generally stays on the upper side of the leaf. Therefore, the pesticide is also spread from above. Isn't it rather far-fetched to imagine that this pesticide on top of the leaves travels below the ground to get inside the kernel and into the groundnut?

Vasudha: The rain washes it into the ground, Arun, you are being pseudoscientific. You don't love nature. You don't want to live with nature. What kind of human beings are you?

Prof. Patil: Hold it, hold it. We are all students of agriculture as a science. Let us not become emotional and personal. Integrated pest control is a serious issue to which a large number of agricultural scientists have devoted their careers. I suggest we study the subject in greater detail. We cannot do that in a group discussion.

My suggestion is that we hold this topic for the time being. Let us all go home and study the topic, from books, the Internet and in the fields. Let us meet again in three months after we have exchanged notes. Yes, saving farmers' groundnut crop must be our priority. Minimizing the use of chemical pesticides must also be our priority. We should try to find a way forward which would satisfy both the sides. Ok? Please start sharing facts and views on our group through emails and WhatsApp. Let us tentatively decide to meet in the first week of April 2016 to discuss this topic in greater detail and formulate an action plan.

All members of the 'Group of Seven' agreed to the suggestion made by Prof. Patil.

Group of Seven: Messages by Emails and WhatsApp: Sub – Leaf Miner

10.1.2016 Vasudha

Here is a link to a small film on 'The Life Cycle of the Leaf Miner'.
https://www.youtube.com/watch?v=lmu1G30Nltg&t=57s

- The adult lays shiny white, beautifully sculptured 0.5-0.8 mm long eggs singly on groundnut leaflets and shoots. The eggs hatch in 2-3 days.
- The young caterpillar is creamy-yellow with a dark-brown head. The caterpillars mine the leaflets near the midribs and proceed towards the margins by feeding on the green tissues in between the epidermal layers.
- After a week, the caterpillars emerge from the mines, fold a leaflet, or web together two or more leaflets, and continue to feed on the green tissues.

- The caterpillars molt thrice. The larval period lasts for 9-17 days. The caterpillars grow to about 6-8 mm long and are moderately stout, pale-greenish or brownish with a black head and prothoracic shield. The cuticle is smooth except for a few scattered, short, bristly-hairs which arise from minute blackish chitinous warts.
- The pupal period varies from 3-7 days. Moths are small, 8-10 mm in length and greyish. The adults live for 5-20 days. The total life cycle from egg to adult is completed in 15-28 days.

18.1.2016 Arun Kone

I came across the following. Should we throw it in the dustbin as propaganda of the pesticide lobby, or is there a possibility of finding some truth there?

Minimizing and Monitoring Residues

The crop protection industry helps to minimize residues in crops by training farmers on the proper use and lowest possible application levels of pesticides.

Regulators set very strict limits on pesticide residues. Consumers are protected by existing government legislation pertaining to maximum allowable residue levels on foods. Independent experts have concluded that regulated residue levels do not pose a threat to human health.

Any pesticide residues that may be on supermarket foods are well within safety limits and therefore, do not pose a health risk.

Systems are in place to monitor that residues are within safety limits. Hundreds of thousands of samples worldwide are analyzed for residues year after year. Testing shows that virtually all foods meet safety standards in terms of pesticide residues. Both organic and conventional foods are inspected by government authorities to avoid health risks.

Any pesticide residues that may be on supermarket foods are well within the safety limits and therefore, do not pose a health risk. Due to huge safety margins, these residues are not a risk to human health, even if the legal limit for residues is exceeded. Nor are consumers at risk with potential exposure to multiple residues in food.

Pesticides are only approved for use if their potential residue levels are deemed safe for all consumers. Safety limits are set by authorities for each pesticide based on the amount of potential residue that can be consumed in a lifetime without posing any risk to health. https://pesticidefacts.org/topics/human-health-and-pesticides/ "

20.1.2016 Prof. Patil

Leaf miner (Aproaerema modicella Deventer) was endemic to South India, but now it appears to be a pest of economic importance in many states.

The major groundnut growing states are Gujarat, Andhra Pradesh, Tamil Nadu, Karnataka, Rajasthan and Maharashtra. These constitute around 80% of the area and production. The total area under groundnut cultivation is about 8 million hectares, and the annual production is over 9 million tonnes of pods. Groundnut plays a significant role in the livelihoods of small farmers in the rain-fed area. In India, groundnut is cultivated during kharif, rabi and summer seasons under various cropping systems. The national average production of rabi groundnut is higher (1600 kg/ha) than kharif (1000 kg/ha). Rain-fed groundnut cultivation coupled with an attack by a variety of insect pests and diseases is the major reason for lower productivity.

I have located a research paper (https://niphm.gov.in/IPMPackages/Groundnut.pdf) which compares the incidence of pests on various crops before and after the Green Revolution. The paper states that, in 1960, the incidence of pests in groundnut was 5%. By the year 2000, it has gone up to 15%.

In short, the 'Pests in Groundnut' is a problem of increasing magnitude, and we are on the right track in trying to find a method to combat this problem on a priority basis.

25.1.2016 Vilas

This supports what Milind told us about farmers hoping for the rains: "The thrips feed on the upper surface of groundnut leaves. Under dry conditions and heavy infestations, the leaves become dry and plants become stunted. The thrips are easily washed away by rains because they inhabit the upper leaf surface. There is rarely a pest during the higher rainfall periods.

5.2.2016 Subhash

Milind, this may be useful while planning control of Leaf Miner: "The chemical control measures may be taken when the pest crosses an economic threshold level of 1 larva per 1 meter row. (www.ikisan.com/tn-groundnut-insect-management.html)"

15.2.2016 Vasudha

The following is a comprehensive program for controlling Leaf Miner without chemical pesticides:

- Early sowing (before 15th of July) of rain-fed groundnut reduces the incidence.
- Use light traps for monitoring pest incidence.
- Setting up of pheromone traps.
- Weed-free crop reduces Leaf Miner incidence.
- Leaf Miner prefers soybean for its early occurrence. This can be monitored on soybean, and first-generation larvae can be collected and destroyed.
- Grow pearl millet or lablab as an intercrop in groundnut (1:4 ratio).
- Mulching with a straw of pearl millet or other crops in drylands helps to reduce the incidence of Leaf Miner.
- Regulate irrigation in the growth period so as to avoid drought stress, which increases pest incidence (or) spray water one or two times, which in turn minimizes the pest population.

- Spray Neem seed kernel extract (15 kg/ha) or Neem oil (15 lit/ha) or Neem leaf extract (25 kg/ha).

16.2.20 Arun

Is there a reference for Neem seed oil or...?

16.2.20 Vasudha

My Dear Arun Kone

Please read the following carefully. Please check the authenticity of the reference. Sleep peacefully!

"Neem oil disrupts the lifecycle of the Leaf Miner and prevents the larvae from becoming adults. AzaMax and Azatrol contain the active ingredient azadirachtin, which is extracted from the Neem seed using patented technology. Both products are OMRI listed for use in organic production and are safe to use on vegetable crops.

Apply to any food or non-food crop up to and including the day of harvest. For Leaf Miner and other difficult to control pests, apply at a maximum rate of 1.0 to 1.6 oz. per gallon of water (28 to 45 gms. per 4.5 litres of water). Two to three (2-3) applications should be scheduled at 10-14 day intervals until the pest pressure has ended."

(https://www.planetnatural.com/forums/topic/leafminer-neem/)

27.2.2016 Anil

The following underlines the need to use chemical pesticides:

The present study was undertaken to assess the relative abundance and extent of damage caused by the various pests attacking groundnut in the Marathwada region of Maharashtra during the 2012 and 2014 kharif seasons. Selective applications of insecticides were deployed in field experiments to assess the damage caused by the key members of the groundnut pest complex, namely the Aphids, Jassid, thrips, defoliators, Leaf Miner and Gram Pod Borer. The experiment was laid out in paired plot design with two treatments, replicated sixteen times. Pooled results showed that groundnut crop left unprotected is highly infested by pests and recorded significant yield reduction to the extent of 26.74% as compared to crops protected through chemicals (Agriculture Update Volume 12 | TECHSEAR-1 | 2017 | 58-6).

4.3.2016 Vasudha

Friends, I am also aware of the limitations of biological control; for instance, "Though about 25 species of hymenopterous parasites were found to attack the Leaf Miner eggs, larvae and pupae on groundnut, no large scale release and augmentation has been tried."

10.3 2016 Shankar

This is another finding, in continuation of the contents of Anil's mail: "https://www.arccjournals.com Abstract: Studies on the estimation of yield losses of groundnut due to major insect pests revealed that the highest pod (1367 kg/ha) and fodder (2947 kg/ha) yield, as well as CBR of 1: 6.51 was obtained in the plot sprayed with dimethoate 0.03%, chlorpyriphos 0.05 %, profenophos 0.05 % and profenophos 40% + cypermethrin 4 % 0.044% at 15 day intervals starting from 20 days after sowing till harvest of the crop. The avoidable yield loss due to major insect pests of groundnut was recorded to the tune of 48.57% in the pod and 42.11% in fodder in the untreated control plot. The data on yield in protected plots revealed that 94.45% additional yield in pod and 72.74% additional yield in fodder could be realized over unprotected plots." /journal/legume-research-an-international-journal/ARCC557

25.3.2016 Milind

Friends, I stand educated through your emails. Thank you. Now it is time to act.

I have also discussed the issue with some pro-change farmers in my village. I have come to the conclusion that the main bottleneck in controlling Leaf Miner from the ground is the farmer's tendency to postpone actions which involve incurring additional cost. In the case of the Leaf Miner, the possibility that the rain will wash away the pest gives a boost to this tendency.

I have formulated a scheme to overcome this tendency of farmers and protect the groundnut crop from the Leaf Miner. The scheme has the following salient features:

The Group of Seven will announce The 'Bhuimoog Bachao' scheme (Bhuimoog = Groundnut/Peanut, Bachao = Save; both are Marathi words)

The group, with support from Prof. Patil and the University, will produce an audiovisual film, of about 15 minutes duration, showing the life cycle of the Leaf Miner, the damage caused by Leaf Miner and the preventive measures that can be taken.

The film will have data on how many times it has rained heavily, that is more than 25 cms., within 24 hours, which is the minimum intensity of rain required to wash away Leaf Miner, in the last 100 Kharif seasons. This will clearly show that the chances of rains coming when required to wash away the Leaf Miner are less than 1 in 50.

Preventive measures advised to the farmers will be:

- Early sowing, by July 15th, to reduce the chances of Leaf Miner.
- Intercropping with pearl millet or lablab and avoiding intercropping by soybean.
- Intensive weed control and mulching with a straw of pearl millet.

A novel incentive scheme will be announced. The farmer who is the first from his village to report the occurrence of Leaf Miner in his farm will get three sprays of appropriate pesticides free of cost under the Bhuimoog Bachao scheme. This will demonstrate to the remaining farmers that action is possible, action is available and action is being taken. This will create 'action urgency'.

The next five farmers who report Leaf Miner will get the first spray free for one acre of land.

Ten petromax traps will be placed in strategic locations to catch and count the Leaf Miner. This will make the remaining farmers aware that they are susceptible to attack by Leaf Miner in the near future

The Group of Seven will maintain an adequate stock of Neem seed oil, organic pesticides extracted from Neem seeds and also stocks of chemical pesticides. When the seven of us act together, we will be able to reduce the minimum required total stock to be kept as a ready stock of pesticides. We will try to resource 25 species of hymenopterous parasites which are natural enemies of Leaf Miner; although we may not be able to do so immediately. But we will be on the lookout for these insects becoming available in large enough numbers.

We will monitor very closely, through the recording of systematic qualitative and quantitative observations, the effect of each of the actions. Farmers who do not participate in the scheme would be our control group. We will be able to continuously discuss data generated to plan more effective actions.

When all seven of us act together, we will be able to provide pest control to more than 2,000 farmers. Such a massive action will create massive propaganda.

I am sure; within the first two years, we will be able to demonstrate very effectively, the benefits of integrated pest control practice under the Bhuimoog Bachao scheme.

(End of e-mail correspondence).

The group met on the 10th of April and discussed the Bhuimoog Bachao scheme. Almost everybody had some minor suggestions and some reservations; however, they decided to go ahead.

In the kharif season in the year 2016, 247 farmers from 25 villages took advantage of Bhuimoog Bachao scheme. The maximum losses recorded because of Leaf Miner by a participating farmer were 15%. The average losses, because of Leaf Miner in farms of farmers participating in Bhuimoog Bachao scheme were 3.5%. The losses in farms which were not protected by the Bhuimoog Bachao scheme averaged 37%, with a maximum of 97%.

In the year 2017, 730 farmers from 35 villages participated and benefited from the Bhuimoog Bachao scheme. In the year 2018, 1730 farmers from 65 villages participated. The Group of Seven found it difficult to cope with the workload. Each of them earned more than ₹1.5 lakhs from the Bhuimoog Bachao scheme.

The Group of Seven has now become known as the Bhuimoog Bandhus (Brothers of Groundnuts) in the 100 villages where they operate.

Chapter 16

Mascerhanas Motors

Mr. Daniel Mascerhanas established Mascerhanas Motors in the year 1965 when he was 31 years old. He had obtained two dealerships, one for Light Commercial Vehicles (LCVs) from ABC Motors Ltd., and another for two-wheelers from XYZ Motorcycles Ltd., based on his financial strength and political connections.

Mascerhanas Motors had two showrooms in Panjim, Goa, on the outskirts of the city towards Madgaon, on the National Highway from Mumbai to Karwar. The showroom for LCVs was named 'Durga' and the showroom for two wheelers was named 'Shanta'; obviously the names were derived from the Hindu goddess of Goa, 'Shanta Durga'.

Mascerhanas Motors was the first automobile dealership in independent Goa and did good business until the end of the century. Mr. Daniel Mascerhanas was interested in sports and politics. He had financially supported Churchill Brothers Sports Club during the club's early formative stages. He was also an ardent fan of football and Churchill Brothers Football Club. Mr. Daniel Mascerhanas was elected to the Goa assembly in 1995 on the ticket of the United Goans Democratic Party (UGDP), the party founded by Mr. Churchill Alemao, the Chief Minister, who was his personal friend.

Daniel Mascerhanas had two sons: Peter and Paul. Paul looked after the Shanta showroom for two-wheelers while Peter managed the Durga showroom for LCVs. Peter and Paul had joined their father's business in their late twenties and were designated as general managers. Both of them held an MBA degree from a reputed management school in Goa. Neither of them was interested in football or politics. They were interested in picnics, parties, wining and dining. Their father thought that they needed to be watched carefully. As it is, Daniel was a hard taskmaster.

Daniel had seen a job description of a general manager of an automobile showroom in a handbook given to him by the sales director of the manufacturing firm. He had made his sons responsible for all the tasks of a general manager mentioned in the handbook which were: paying close attention to daily operations; ensuring that all employees understood and followed policies and procedures, submitting daily reports on the cash flow; preparing monthly financial statements; ensuring that records are correctly maintained; taking necessary steps to resolve customer complaints. All these responsibilities were on paper. Paul and Peter did not have any authority to incur any expenses not approved by their father in advance. Neither Paul nor Peter appreciated the strict financial control of their father. They carried out all the above duties without really applying their minds.

This, in a way, suited the management style of Mr. Daniel Mascerhanas, as he was very conservative in his approach. He believed in the minimum of everything. Minimum stocks, minimum staff, minimum training to the staff, minimum wages, minimum maintenance, minimum service, minimum attention to customer complaints!

In addition, there was a major task which both Paul and Peter handled with enthusiasm. This duty was entertaining the executives from the head office, who came for pleasure trips to Goa. Sometimes, the Japanese representing the company collaborating with the principal manufacturer also arrived in Goa. Paul and Peter arranged fishing cruises for these visiting dignitaries and kept them happy with a generous supply of wine and seafood.

Mascerhanas Motors had done quite well during the first 35 years. Sales had grown at an average rate of 7% to 10% every year. The costs had increased almost at the same pace; the profits remained steady. However, the situation had started deteriorating in the 21st century.

All the competing brands had their showrooms in Goa. Two new competing brands had entered the Goa market after the year 2000. The sales were almost stagnant after 2010 for LCVs as well as two-wheelers.

Mr. Daniel Mascerhanas however, did not change his 'minimum of everything' approach. He felt, bad times would come and bad times would go. Money saved is money earned. If his sons were allowed to spend money, then they would squander it away and soon the situation would become worse. He did not listen to his son's requests for the renovation of the showroom, increase in stocks, improvements in service to the customer. And only Mr. Daniel Mascerhanas had the authority to sign cheques!

Mr. Daniel Mascerhanas died on 24th January 2014 at the age of 80.

Paul and Peter reviewed the financial situation with their chartered accountant. They estimated that for the year ending March 2014, Mascerhanas Motors would have a cash surplus of only ₹2 lacs and a book loss of ₹20 lacs after accounting for a depreciation of ₹22 lacs. They also made a quick estimate of the likely income and expenses in the financial year 2014-15 and discovered, as they had expected, that if nothing changed, there would be a cash loss of ₹12 lacs and a book loss of ₹32 lacs. It was obvious to them that they could not continue with the 'minimum of everything' policy.

Paul and Peter knew that they had a major challenge on hand. As a first step they decided not to split the parent company of the two showrooms; they decided to stick together.

It was a coincidence that Paul and Peter were invited to a Next-Gen program, meant for family members who would inherit a family business, organized by their alma mater management institute, at the end of February 2014. The residential program was for seven days, the fee was only ₹50,000 per participant and the admission for spouses was free. Paul and Peter decided to join the Next-Gen program with their wives, Mary and Jyotsna. They thought, it would be a good break and a place to do some fresh thinking, even if nothing else was gained.

Incidentally, both Mary and Jyotsna were management graduates. Paul and Peter had fallen in love with them when they were studying for an MBA. Each couple had two children, one son and one daughter, who were studying in high school and junior college. Mary and Jyotsna had been housewives so far and had no direct experience of business. However, their husbands had shared the developments in their respective showrooms with them, almost on a daily basis, over the last 15 years.

The brothers were really influenced by the visiting American professor, Martin Rand, who was the course director at the residential program at their institute. Prof. Rand handled the topic of 'customer satisfaction and service delivery' as a means of improving business growth and business profitability. Professor Rand had visited about 20 dealerships and retail outlets in western India and had held in-depth discussions with consumer organizations as his preparation for conducting the course. Prof. Rand impressed Paul and Peter with the following key themes:

- Dealers in India were passive stockists. They only stocked the product and delivered it to the customer on demand.
- The principal manufacturer did everything else, viz., determining the customers' needs, designing the product, manufacturing, advertising the product, driving the customer to the showroom, deciding the stocks to be maintained at the point of sales, deciding dealers' staff-strength, training dealers' staff.
- Showrooms were nothing but passive display rooms.
- Dealers, particularly automobile dealers, thought that servicing a product was lowly. It was blue-collar work which did not suit their white-collar 'businessman' status. They neglected service as far as possible and provided it only because the principal manufacturer insisted on it.
- Dealers generally recruited unemployable distant relatives as salespersons.

Professor Rand recommended that every participant should read 'You Shall Be Satisfied' by Bob Tasca. The professor read out the following review of the book, "Bob Tasca is, quite simply, the world's most effective practitioner of customer satisfaction. His accomplishments are astounding. His small Ford dealership is consistently among the world's best in sales volume, and industry executives from all over often visit it, in order to learn from his operation. Though he sells a generic product, Tasca has at times achieved the unheard of feat of capturing 24% of his metro market, and he regularly sees 65% of his customers return - triple the loyalty rate of his competitors. In 'You Will Be Satisfied,' he reveals how anyone, whether shoe salesman, software company middle manager or bookstore owner, can drive customer loyalty to dizzying heights. In the book's short, punchy chapters, real-life anecdotes and bulleted lessons, readers will find the knowledge and tools they need to send their sales soaring."

At the time of summing up the workshop, Prof. Rand once again strongly recommended the book saying, "I love that Bob Tasca is very practical about how to get, and keep customers. Most people think that it is more difficult than it is. Although it is impossible to please "everyone" this book tells how and why it is important to try to do it anyway. Bob Tasca not only applies this philosophy to his business, but also in everyday life. It is a very good book and I have passed it around to many associates."

The book, 'You Shall Be Satisfied' by Bob Tasca, was circulated as a complimentary copy at the end of the course. All four Mascerhanas read the book. They found it not only educative, but also entertaining. They discussed it in detail and were charged with the idea of making service the principal business activity of Mascerhanas Motors.

Peter, Paul, Mary and Jyotsna decided to work as one team and take one showroom at a time for planning a detailed action program. They started with Durga, the showroom for commercial vehicles.

The first task was to understand the customers and to describe them and their needs in a detailed profile note.

Peter knew the profile of his customers. He prepared the following note:

- Customers are self-employed men.
- Customers bought a new light commercial vehicle – 4 to 6 Tonner for any one of the following reasons:
    - The old LCV has run its life and has to be replaced.
    - He wanted to expand his business; there were enquiries he had to often refuse because his vehicle was already booked. A close

relative, most usually a younger brother, was now available to join him in business.

- He was driving a smaller vehicle, mostly a three-wheeler, within the city. He now wants to handle larger cargo over longer distances.
- He has worked as a driver of an LCV. He has now accumulated enough money to pay for the margin money of a new LCV and wants to be his own master.
- He is a wholesaler who uses the LCV to make deliveries.

Peter described some special features of the LCV transport business of his customers as:

- His customers drove the LCV in a radius of about 150 kilometres around Panjim.
- They generally carried agricultural produce from farmers to the taluka places, to district centres and even as far as Belgawi and Kolhapur.
- They carried fish from the coast to inland markets.
- They also carried construction material on behalf of contractors to building sites. The construction material consisted generally of cement bags, steel reinforcement bars and bricks.
- They also carried material within the city for various purposes like shifting of a house, or delivery from a wholesaler to a network of retailers.
- Occasionally, they carried cattle.
- Occasionally, they carried human passengers.
- An overwhelming majority of the vehicles ran on rural roads which were not in good condition.
- The owners could not avoid the temptation of an extra buck earned through overloading.
- They were also given to driving fast in the hope of reaching the destination early and making an additional trip during the day.

- The overloaded vehicle, driven rashly on bad roads with potholes, meant that the vehicle's life was less.
- As it is, given the nature of mechanical parts in friction with each other, the spare part requirements were bound to be regular. With the special conditions of use; breakdown of the vehicle, while in service, was a common phenomenon.
- Repair of a vehicle required parts which were not easily available in rural areas.
- Consequently, the downtime of breakdown vehicles was high.
- This resulted in significant losses to the transporter because of the wasted time. Sometimes, the fresh vegetables/fish being transported became stale and there was a loss of value to the farmer/fisherman who demanded compensation from the vehicle owner.

Paul, Peter, Mary and Jyotsna then sat together to do a Strength, Weakness, Opportunity and Threats (SWOT) analysis for 'Durga' and the LCV business.

Strengths

- Product: the LCV brand was the best in its class; it delivered value for money.
- High, 30%, margin on spare parts.
- Good relations with the principal manufacturer.
- Good personal relations with senior managers from the principal company.
- The dealership had made a profit continuously for the last 45 years.
- A good relationship with bankers.
- Good public image, particularly because of the sponsorship of football matches.
- Dependable relationship with political leaders and senior government officials.

- Happy customers, who did not expect much once they got their vehicle.
- A good relationship with LCV-finance agencies that approved finance at the table in the dealership itself.

Weaknesses

- Very poor sale of spare parts. The sale of spare parts could be up to 50% of the vehicle value. Actual sales of parts were less than 10% of the value of vehicles sold.
- The market was flooded with spurious parts which had a very poor life and which caused consequential damage to the good parts in the vehicle.
- Very poor income from servicing the vehicles. Customers did not come to the dealership for service once the vehicle was out of the warranty period. They believed that the service at the dealership was very costly and of poor quality. Some customers even suspected that when the vehicle was given at the dealership for servicing, good parts were taken out and poor spurious parts were fitted.
- Old and untrained staff, both at the sales counter and in the workshop.
- Poor relationship with local roadside mechanics who generally contributed foul word-of-mouth talk regarding the quality of service at the dealership.
- The poor look of the dealership since no major renovation had been carried out in the last 15 years.

Opportunities

- The market was growing with the growing economy at a rate of 8 to 10% per annum.

- Customers did not knowingly buy spurious parts as they were aware that the losses due to the failure of these parts in terms of vehicle downtime were much more than the cost-saving if any. Spurious parts were not sold cheaply as that would indicate to the customer that the part was spurious.

Threats

- The principal company was thinking of appointing one more dealer in Panjim and one more in Madgaon. This would result in direct competition and a significant loss of sales.
- The likely losses next year would mean that banks would then be reluctant to extend finance.
- The cash loss would really reduce the scope for making upfront investments to improve service; it might even be difficult to finance the renovation of the showroom, which was long overdue.

The scheme designed by Peter, Paul, Mary and Jyotsna had two major components:

One: Promote the use of original spare parts bought from Durga.

Two: Develop a partnership with roadside mechanics.

Promote the use of original spare parts bought from Durga

The scheme to promote original spare parts was described by a tag line in Marathi, the local language of Goa, as **'शांता तुमच्या दारी । शांती तुमच्या मनी.** It said that, 'Goddess Durga is out to destroy the spurious parts.' The line rhymed with the popular prayer of goddess Durga.

The scheme had the following rationale and features:

- The cost of parts required for repairing a vehicle damaged in an accident was covered by the insurance company. However, the cost of parts required to be replaced because of normal wear and tear was not covered by insurance. Generally, no loan was available from banks for buying spare parts. The owner had to pay in cash for the parts.

- Though the amounts required to buy parts were not very large at one time, the owners often found it difficult to raise this money at short notice. The notice was short as the requirement of the parts became clear only when the mechanic noticed the need at the time of service. For a vehicle, the lifetime value of parts, over a span of 12 years of life, on an average was 50% to 60% of the purchase cost of the vehicle.
- The scheme offered the buyer an option to book lifetime purchase of parts, at the time of purchasing the vehicle. The buyer would pay 40% extra of the vehicle price at the time of purchasing the vehicle; in exchange, he will be assured of a free supply of genuine spare parts as and when they were needed over the next 12 years.
- Since the servicing was to be done at the Durga workshop or by a mechanic trained and authorized by Durga (see Chalenge Saath Saath scheme below) there was very little chance that parts would be fitted unnecessarily.
- The risk of rising prices of parts over the next 12 years was taken care of for the vehicle owner as well as Durga. The value of all the parts was received today at today's prices and the money would remain with Mascerhanas Motors earning an interest at around 12% which was more than the escalation in spare part prices. (Escalation in the spare parts prices during the last decade was only 7 to 8% per annum).
- The finance companies agreed to finance this extra 40% amount when the vehicle was purchased.
- Consequently, an LCV owner could avail of an amount of 90% as a loan for spare parts and did not have to worry about raising money at short notice for parts required to service the vehicle.
- If the vehicle met with an accident, then the value of parts replaced would be billed by Durga to the insurance company along with service charges as was done usually.

- Existing owners of vehicles could also join the scheme by a one-time purchase of lifetime spare parts. The amount to be paid was dependent on the remaining life of the vehicle. A detailed table of the value of the spare parts for the remaining life of the vehicle was worked out carefully by Peter in consultation with the service engineer of ABC Motors and his own senior mechanics.

Two: Develop a partnership with roadside mechanics

'चलेंगे साथ साथ' 'Chalenge Saath Saath', that is, 'We Shall Walk Together' was the short title for the scheme developed for building a fruitful relationship with roadside mechanics. The features of this scheme and the rationale behind it are explained below.

- Seven to ten roadside mechanics, having locations at critical road junctions and who had high potential to develop into good mechanics and partners of Mascerhanas Motors will be selected. They will be told that they had been selected after a careful search and offered membership of 'Chalenge Saath Saath' mechanics club.
  - Mechanics already working in the Durga workshop will be asked whether they were interested in starting their own workshop if 90% of the initial investment was available as bank finance. If more mechanics volunteered, then only three of them will be taken in as part of the initial team; the remaining, at least seven, will be the roadside mechanics.
  - Roadside mechanics or their sons will be recruited to join the scheme. Initially, they will join as an apprentice under training in the 'Skill Development Program' of the central government run by ABC Motors, so that their stipend could be paid through government funds.
  - These mechanics will be invited for four one-day orientation programs in the Durga workshop.
  - After the mechanics have attended four orientation training sessions at the Durga workshop they will go to the ABC factory for a one-

week training program. All their lodging and boarding expenses will be paid by ABC Motors.

- At the ABC Motors factory, they will be shown the factory, so that they understand the assembly of the vehicle in detail.
- At ABC, the apprentice mechanics will also see an exhibition of spurious parts and photographs of the damage caused by the use of spurious spare parts.
- On return from training at ABC, they will be given a stock of all the parts required regularly, on credit, by Durga.
- If the vehicle serviced by the local mechanic was covered under the lifetime spare parts plan then the local mechanic will use parts from his stock and demand replacement from Durga.
- If the vehicle serviced by the local mechanic was covered under the warranty period, then the mechanic will be paid his service charges by Durga. These service charges will generally be 5% more than what the mechanics otherwise charged. This will give more business to local mechanics and local mechanics will not look upon themselves as competitors of Durga.
- There will be a tea stall adjoining the Durga showroom and Durga workshop. All LCV owners, LCV drivers and all local mechanics would be welcome to spend as much time as they want at this tea stall. They will be served tea, free of cost. This will mean that the tea stall will become a gossip centre and word-of-mouth information exchange for LCV owners and mechanics. Tips on the operation of LCVs, as well as opportunities for business, will be exchanged.
- All mechanics joining the 'Chalenge Saath Saath' scheme will get a board declaring 'Associate of Durga Motors and ABC Motors'. The board will say that the mechanic has been trained at ABC Motors and uses genuine spare parts bought through Durga from ABC Motors.
- All vehicles sold by Durga and/or serviced by partner-mechanics will carry an attractive sticker "**बनावटांची विनाशकारी । दुर्गाही भारी ॥** with a photo of Shanta-Durga goddess.

- Mascerhanas owned a marriage hall in Panjim. This hall would be made available at a concessional rent to owners buying lifetime spare parts under the **बनावटांची विनाशकारी । दुर्गाही भारी ॥** and the mechanic members of 'Chalenge Saath Saath' club for marriages of their near relatives. Each marriage would be attended by the entire Mascerhanas family and a major memento gift will be given by the Mascerhanas family to the newlyweds.

Right from the beginning, both the schemes were designed keeping the service engineer and area sales manager of ABC Motors in the picture.

- ABC Motors agreed to give a stipend to the mechanics under the Chalenge Saath Saath scheme for one year.
- ABC also agreed to host the factory visit.
- ABC offered an additional discount of 5% on parts purchased in bulk by Mascerhanas Motors and credit term of six months for these parts.

The financial working showed that the scheme would be very profitable if 20% of the new vehicles were part of life-time sale of spare parts under **बनावटांची विनाशकारी । दुर्गाही भारी ॥** and 40% of the vehicles on the road were serviced by mechanics of the Chalenge Saath Saath club.

Renovation of the Durga showroom, including a good tea stall adjoining Durga, was an integral part of the two schemes and the scheme was presented in an integrated fashion to the bank. The approval of the bank was received in 15 days.

Implementation

The lifetime spare parts scheme did not require much preparation. **बनावटांची विनाशकारी । दुर्गाही भारी ॥** was launched on 1st of May 2015. By March 2016, 22% of the buyers of new vehicles had opted for the scheme. Additionally, 10% of the vehicles which were less than three years old had been covered under the scheme.

Recruiting mechanics for Chalenge Saath Saath was a bit difficult. Mechanics were sceptical about joining an orientation program at the Durga workshop. However, they readily agreed to visit the ABC Motors factory. Two mechanics from the Durga workshop expressed a desire to start their own workshop in partnership. The visit to ABC Motors motivated the mechanics. Expecting dropouts, Peter had selected 15 mechanics for the visit to ABC Motors. Twelve of them showed eagerness to join Chalenge Saath Saath. Peter and Paul did not waver from the decision to have only 10 mechanics in the club. They selected 9 out of 12 who were interested, along with one of their own mechanics who had expressed a desire to start their their own workshop in partnership with the Durga workshop.

Chalenge Saath Saath scheme was launched in full earnest in December 2015. By March 2016 about 30% of all vehicles on the road were already being serviced by members of the Chalenge Saath Saath club.

The tea stall at the dealership was a great success. On any one day, at least 50 vehicle owners, drivers and mechanics sipped tea at the stall and exchanged news and gossip.

The marriage hall was also in good demand. By 31st December of 2017, a hundred days of the marriage hall had been booked by mechanics and vehicle owners.

Looking at the success of the scheme, ABC Motors decided to promote the scheme with select dealers all over India. ABC requested any two of the four-member team from the Mascerhanas family to act as "resource persons" to guide the selected dealers. Mascerhanas asked ABC Motors to wait for a year, as all four of them needed to concentrate on their own dealership operations for some more time before they could venture into being "resource persons" for other dealerships.

'Shanta' Showroom for Two-wheelers

Meanwhile, in June 2015 itself, all four Mascerhanas had started working on the 'Shanta' showroom for two-wheelers of XYZ Motorcycles.

Paul and Jyotsna wrote the customer profile:

- 80% of the customers are men. However, a woman customer is generally accompanied by a man who has a significant role in making the decision.
- Most of the customers are in the age group 20 to 35 years.
- Customers in the age group of 25 to 30 are more concerned about pick-up and top speed; younger and older customers are more concerned about mileage.
- Almost all customers avail of the finance scheme. They prefer a finance scheme of longer duration and smaller monthly instalments. They are less sensitive to the interest rate in comparison to the size of monthly instalment.
- Customers are not sensitive about the service; 50% of them miss the first warranty service during the recommended period.
- Customers are not bothered about the quality of parts; they rarely discuss the quality of parts with the mechanic.
- Young men are now totally into buying motorcycles. Women mainly buy auto-gear, button-start scooters. However, some women are now showing interest in buying motorcycles.
- Mopeds and geared scooters are totally out of fashion.
- Customers listen to the sound of the engine while buying a new motorcycle, for them, this indicates the quality of the engine which they believe differs from piece to piece even when the brand, the model and the period of manufacture is the same.
- Customers give importance to having a test ride on the vehicle they are going to buy. 30% of the customers reject the first motorcycle offered to them, although the same motorcycle may be purchased by another customer on the same day!
- Customers are not very price-sensitive, perhaps because their down-payment is only 10% of the purchase price. They go in for

the latest fashionable model which will be noticed by people on the road.

- Most of the customers have a personal relationship with a roadside mechanic and value his opinion about reliability and trouble-free working of the vehicle.
- Pilots, that is, motorcycle taxi drivers, are a special group. Generally, they buy a second-hand motorcycle at a highly discounted price as they do not get loans from a finance company for buying a new vehicle.

As they had done for Durga, all four of them sat together, to brainstorm the SWOT analysis for the Shanta showroom selling two-wheelers of XYZ motorcycles. They discovered that most of the SWOT points for Shanta were very similar to those already jotted down for Durga. These points covered: a strong brand of motorcycles, good relationships with XYZ Motors, a good relationship with finance agencies for two-wheelers, a good relationship with bankers, goodwill among the customers, financial problems and the likelihood of losses in the coming years, poor relationship with roadside mechanics, poor sales of spare parts and low income from service operations. The special additional features in the SWOT analysis, different from those in Durga, were the following:

Strengths

- Most of the two-wheeler customers belonged to the age group of the four Mascerhanas and therefore they understood and related with these customers much better than with the LCV owners.
- The goodwill amongst young men due to sponsorship of football matches was more significant in the case of Shanta customers.

Weaknesses

- The salesmen at the counter were old and untrained.

- The conversion ratio at the counter was at two in ten. This was rather low.
- Many customers did not avail of the service at Shanta workshop.

Opportunities

- Service was an untapped market which could grow manifold.
- Conversion at the counter could improve from the current 2 in 10 to 3 in 10, thereby giving a 50% increase in sales.
- Motorcycle taxis were a unique phenomenon in Goa. This represented a unique opportunity specific to Goa for Mascerhanas Motors.

Threats

- The financial constraint for taking new initiatives.
- A stock of 30 unsold mopeds lying in the company store-house for more than a year,
- Possibility of XYZ Motorcycles opening a new showroom in Madgaon.

The scheme designed by the four for Shanta showroom was ready by December 2015. This scheme had three components:

One: Pick-up for the vehicle to be serviced.

Two: Promotion of a motorcycle taxi.

Three: Improving salesmanship at the counter.

Pick-up for the vehicle to be serviced

This component was titled '**शांता तुमच्या दारी । शांती तुमच्या मनी ॥** (Shanta at your door-step, for your peace of mind)

Rationale

The current practice at the Shanta showroom was that customers were expected to bring the motorcycles for servicing in the morning. The motorcycles were accepted for servicing on a 'first-come, first-served' basis. If the customer came late, he was not sure whether his motorcycle would be taken in for servicing; it depended on how many motorcycles had been accepted on that day. The workshop had the capacity to service 30 motorcycles every day. If the workshop had a full load, the customer was told that the motorcycle could not be serviced on the same day; he was welcome to leave the motorcycle and collect it the next day evening. If the customer could not spare his motorcycle for two days, then the disappointed customer took back his motorcycle. He might or might not bring it back the next day. There were no records kept to find out how many times customers did not bring the motorcycle for servicing. Often, customers did not bring the motorcycles for servicing to the Shanta workshop, if they realized that they could not reach the workshop before 10 a.m.

For a motorcycle outside the warranty period, the charges for servicing at the Shanta workshop were reportedly 10 to 30% more than the charges of the local mechanics.

The customer could stand in front of the local mechanic and observe his vehicle being serviced, which generally took less than one hour. The customer then felt sure that the servicing was done properly and no good parts were replaced by cheap spurious parts.

The Shanta workshop received, on an average, 20 vehicles every day for servicing against a capacity to service 30 vehicles per day. Currently, the Shanta workshop operated around break-even level.

Jyotsna made a quick calculation based on 'rule of thumb' norms available with the service engineer of XYZ Motorcycles and the senior mechanic at the Shanta workshop. Given the number of motorcycles which Shanta had sold during the last 15 years, (this was the reasonably expected life of the motorcycle), there were 12,000 motorcycles sold by Shanta on Goa roads. Assuming they required at least two services during a year, the total service requirement was 24,000 services during the year. Even if the

Shanta workshop operated at its full capacity of 30 vehicles per day and 300 working days in a year, the total number of vehicles that could be serviced was 9,000. This showed that only 40% of the total service market could be served by the Shanta workshop; the remaining motorcycles had to be serviced by roadside mechanics. Shanta was losing ₹200 per motorcycle not serviced. This worked out to ₹(15,000 x 200), or ₹30,00,000 of the service market. There was a 15% margin on service fees. The Shanta workshop was losing ₹4,50,000 in net income. Additionally, almost an equal amount was being lost due to loss of sale of spare parts.

Jyostna and Mary asked, "Why is the workshop running only one shift from 9:30 a.m. to 5 p.m.? Why can't the workshop run in two shifts, or for that matter in three shifts? All women run their kitchens in two shifts! In that case, the capacity of the workshop can go up to 27,000 vehicles per year which is clearly sufficient to carry out 24,000 services in a year. The additional shifts require only additional manpower. Interestingly, the additional manpower could be recruited under the Skilling Program launched by the central government and aggressively pushed by the state government. In such a case, salaries of the junior mechanics will come mainly come from the government. Consequently, the profit margins could increase further." Paul and Peter were initially taken aback by this suggestion by their spouses, but they quickly saw the logic in it and agreed.

The question was how to get all these vehicles to the Shanta workshop for service?

All four of them had brainstorming sessions with their own service manager, service engineer and regional sales manager of XYZ Motors. They also discussed the problem with a number of friendly customers. Finally, the idea of picking up the vehicle from the customers' residence came apparently from nowhere; and subsequently, everybody took credit for it.

Features of pick-up for the vehicle, **'शांता तुमच्या दारी'**

A Shanta mechanic or a pilot (see the scheme below for promoting motorcycle taxis) would go to a customer in the morning, after taking a prior appointment, on a moped owned by Shanta. He would give the moped to the customer for his use during the day and bring the customer's vehicle back to be serviced at the workshop. After the vehicle was serviced, he would take the vehicle back to the customer and collect the moped given to the customer for his use during the day.

The two main attractions of the scheme for the customer were: (a) He was being provided with a vehicle for his use while his own motorcycle was being serviced. (b) His time of travel for two trips to the workshop was also saved.

Mary and Paul had done an advanced course in computing, just out of interest. They saw a great challenge in this idea. The dealership had addresses of all the customers to whom the vehicles had been sold during the last 20 years. Of course, some addresses would have changed, vehicles would have changed hands, but the data would be valid for almost 80% of the customers. Using these addresses, Paul designed a computer program so that the mechanic or the pilots staying closest to the customer could be assigned to a specific customer for picking up his vehicle.

The workshop started working in three shifts. However, even then, the number of mechanics working in the Shanta workshop did not prove sufficient for collecting the customer's vehicles on the way from their home to the workshop. This is when the second component of the scheme, 'promoting motorcycle taxis,' came in handy. Twenty pilots were required to be assigned the job of bringing the vehicles from the customers' houses to the service workshop and taking them back to the customers.

The 30 mopeds lying in stock in the Shanta stockyard for more than a year became a major asset for the scheme.

The mechanic or the pilot would fill one litre of petrol in the motorcycle, and 1 litre of petrol in the moped, while exchanging the vehicles when picking up the customer's vehicle for service. The petrol would be filled from safety bottles in the two-wheelers, in the presence of the customer.

If parts were required to be replaced during the servicing, customers' prior approval would be taken over the phone.

A five-person call centre was set up to contact customers on the telephone, take the appointments and do service follow up. Later, the call centre activity was expanded to also provide booking services for motorcycle taxis that were parked outside the Shanta Workshop, ensuring a regular income to the pilots in the scheme.

The logistics involved complex planning. Paul and Mary did very good programming to take care of it. There was a provision to send an automatic SMS to the customer alerting him that the service was due and offering him home pickup and home delivery.

Service charges for **'शांता तुमच्या दारी । शांती तुमच्या मनी ॥'** were only ₹400 including the cost of two litres of petrol. If any parts were required to be replaced then the price of the parts was extra.

There was no compulsion for the customer to join the scheme. This was an additional option. The customer could still bring the vehicle to the workshop on his own and collect it in the evening by paying a fee of ₹200, as he had been doing earlier; and of course, he was still free to get his motorcycle serviced from the local mechanics.

Implementation

The scheme was launched on 15th August 2016.

Initially it was only launched in one area on the Panaji-Madgaon highway where the concentration of customers was the highest and the number of customers bringing their vehicles to the Shanta workshop was low.

For the first month, the customers could not believe that such a pick-up service was available. They suspected some catch. There used to be a lot of questions to the telephone operators and to the mechanics who went to pick up the customer's motorcycle. However, that this was an extremely convenient and reliable service, spread very quickly by word-of-mouth.

In three months, the workshop was running in two shifts. It was clear by mid-2017 that the third shift of the workshop would have to be started by January 2018

Promotion of the MotorcycleTaxi

Rationale

Goa is the only state in India where motorcycle taxis have been legalized since 1981. There are about 300 motorcycle taxi stands spread all over the state. Motorcycles with yellow mudguards are to be seen at these motorcycle taxi stands. The motorcycle drivers, called pilots, carry one pillion rider. There is no metering of these motorcycles. The fares are decided by convention and through bargaining. A typical pilot earns up to ₹500 per day. This is a good employment opportunity for unemployed youth.

The Mascerhanas team decided to promote motorcycle taxis with support from the Shanta showroom. The scheme was titled, 'My pilot - your pilot'. The major features of the scheme were:

- A youngster would join Shanta Motors as a trainee apprentice.
- Their salary/stipend will come from the central government under the 'Skill India' program, through XYZ motors, for one year.
- The apprentice will receive comprehensive training in driving and maintenance of motorcycles.
- The apprentice will do the work of bringing customers' motorcycles to the workshop for servicing and delivering them back to the customer. They would drive the moped to their homes and go to the new customer on the moped, the next day morning. The fact that they could travel to the house on a two-wheeler at the cost of the company was a major fringe benefit.
- An apprentice, who was sincere and hardworking, in the first six months, would have an option to become a pilot. He would be given a motorcycle to drive on a rent of ₹100 per day by Mascerhanas Motors.
- If his performance was good in the first year, he would be given a loan to buy the motorcycle by a finance agency. Mascerhanas Motors would stand guarantee for this loan.

- A motorcycle taxi stand would become operational outside the Shanta Motors showroom. Customers could phone the call centre and the Shanta Motors showroom to call for a motorcycle taxi.

Implementation

- The scheme started with 20 apprentices in May 2016. By the end of 2017, 16 of them had become pilots.
- Shanta Motors had a waiting list of 210 youngsters wanting to join the 'My pilot- Your Pilot' scheme.
- Mascerhanas Motors approached a very reputed software design firm, through XYZ Motors to design a satellite-based program using which motorcycle taxis could be ordered by customers from their home and they could monitor the arrival of the pilots, just as in case of Ola or Uber cars. The software company accepted the contract and the call system promoted by Mascerhanas Motors was likely to be operational in Goa by December 2018.

Improving Salesmanship at the Counter

The purpose of this scheme was to increase conversion at the counter. The scheme was named 'Sell, Sell and Sell, (3S)'. The major features of 3S were:

- All existing salesmen above the age of 45 will be offered voluntary retirement or positions as backroom clerks.
- New, smart looking boys and girls in the age group of 25 to 30 will be recruited to man the sales counters.
- Prof. Saxena, a popular professor of salesmanship in a management institute, will be retained to conduct a seven-day workshop in benefits-selling for the new team. The new team would be made very proficient in understanding product features, converting them into benefits, focusing on correct benefits as per customer's specific needs, using objections as an opportunity and closing the sales.

- Every prospect will be explained the service pickup scheme with its advantages.
- All customers will be offered drinking water through small sealed bottles of mineral water.
- Customers will be offered paper napkins with a freshener in the summer months.
- The showroom would have a good tea/coffee vending machine from which tea or coffee will be served to each customer.
- The customer will be asked to choose any of the new motorcycles for taking a test drive.
- A salesperson-wise record will be maintained of the conversion ratio.
- Anonymous customers will be sent to the Shanta counter regularly by Prof. Saxena. Prof. Saxena will share the feedback of these anonymous customers and conduct a three-hour revision workshop for the salespersons, every month.
- Every year, all the sales team members will go for a one day picnic with Paul, Peter, Mary and Jyotsna. Prof. Saxena will conduct team-building games during this picnic.

- Every month the salespersons with the highest conversion ratio will be rewarded with a one-month bonus salary.

Implementation

- The scheme was implemented by the end of the year 2016. There were no problems in implementing the scheme.
- The conversion ratio which was 2 in 10 at the beginning of 2015 had risen to 2.5 in 10 by the end of 2016 and to 2.8 in 10 by the end of 2017.

Postscript: The sales of Mascerhanas Motors showed a very positive improvement, as can be seen from the table below:

Percentage (%) Growth Over the Previous Year

Year ending March	Durga showroom		Shanta Showroom		Average total growth
	Vehicle Sales	Service and Parts	Motorcycle Sales	Service and Parts	
2015	6	15	15	10	14
2016	7	15	22	25	17
2017	5	30	20	15	20
2018	6	20	10	10	15

- ABC Motors, XYZ Motorcycles and Mascerhanas Motors received special letters of appreciation from the Government of Goa for having trained 55 apprentices under the Skill India Program and having provided permanent employment to 50 of them by December 2018.
- As resource persons for ABC Motors, Paul and Peter individually visited eight LCV showrooms all over the country to promote the service and sale of genuine spare parts.
- Prof. Saxena invited Ms. Mary Mascerhanas and Ms. Jyostna Mascerhanas as visiting professors to the management institute. They proved to be very popular lecturers.
- Ms. Mary Mascerhanas is now working on a scheme to promote women pilots for motorcycle taxis.
- Mrs. Jyotsna Mascerhanas is now working on a scheme to promote fisherwomen as owner-operators of LCVs for delivering fresh fish.

Chapter 17

Pinto Products

Background

Paul Pinto was a second-generation Goan in Pune. He was a commerce graduate and had completed his MBA from a reputed institute in Pune. Paul's father was a senior officer in the Indian Army. Paul's mother, Margaret, was a small scale entrepreneur. She made speciality Goan sweets like guava cheese and Bebinca and sold them as 'Pinto Products' to Goan people staying in Pune. Incidentally, some Goans staying in Mumbai also bought Pinto Products when they came to Pune. Margaret treated this business as a hobby rather than as a commercial enterprise. The total sales turnover of Pinto Products, in a month, rarely crossed ₹1,000.

Paul had a streak of entrepreneurship in him. He was in charge of running the college cooperative store when he was doing his bachelor's degree in the commerce college. He doubled the sales in two years. While doing his MBA, he tried his hand at selling the Pinto Products, namely Bebinca and guava cheese, on the World Wide Web. However, he could not manage the logistics problems of delivering the products, in good condition, to widely dispersed customers who ordered on the net. He stopped this effort as his father told him to concentrate on studies.

The Beginning

Now that he had graduated, Paul was keen to develop his mother's hobby into a proper business, manufacturing Goan sweets. As a first step, without revealing his identity, he collected feedback from the customers of Pinto Products. He found that the customers were very happy about the quality of the product and felt they got great value for money. Some of them said, 'these are the best products available, not only in Pune and Mumbai but also they are better than most of the products available in Goa'.

Paul's father had bought a small piece of farmland on the outskirts of Pune where he had plans to construct a farmhouse once he retired from the Army. Paul found that the plot could easily be converted into a non-agricultural one, on which a small cottage industry could be set up. The professor who taught Paul finance management as a visiting faculty during his MBA course was on the board of a cooperative bank. He knew Paul as an intelligent and disciplined student. He said that he would recommend Paul's case to the bank. Paul was therefore assured of getting finances on attractive terms.

Paul personally studied the production process used by Margaret with four women helpers. He visited the Institute of Catering Technology in Pune and invited the professor there to see the manufacturing process used by Margaret. He said that the processes could be mechanized to a significant extent and with 10 workers it should be possible to produce Goan sweets like guava cheese and Bebinca to the tune of ₹2.5 million per month. He also checked the documents with Margaret and assured Paul that Pinto Products had all the necessary permissions and compliances for making and selling packed food products through retail stores, anywhere in India.

The costing and calculations of economics showed that even if the production was only worth ₹1.5 million per month, it would generate a contribution of ₹0.5 million per month towards fixed costs and surplus. (Incidentally, the cost of the raw material was about ₹8,00,000, cost of labour about ₹2,00,000 and expenses on energy and other things ₹1,00,000) The total investment, excluding the investment in land, was likely to be about ₹40,00,000. The payback period, therefore, was less than a year! This was quite an attractive proposition. Paul showed his calculations to his classmate, who was the topper in the discipline of finance. He verified Paul's calculations independently. The director of the bank, who taught him finance during his MBA, was also impressed.

After all this initial work, Paul turned his attention to selling, which he considered to be his forte, as he had specialised in marketing, and passed with flying colours during his management studies.

Paul discovered that starting his own retail outlet at a convenient location in Pune, say on Main Street, was much more expensive than setting up the entire manufacturing unit. It was also not clear whether there would be adequate footfalls at this retail outlet, as Goan sweets was a speciality item known to Goans but not popular amongst the Maharashtrian consumers.

Paul, therefore, came to the conclusion that the product must be sold through at least 50 select outlets in Pune, the majority of them in the camp area and Khadki Cantonment, as most of the Goans in Pune stayed in these areas. Paul went around these areas requesting leading shopkeepers to stock Pinto Products, but the response of the shopkeepers was lukewarm.

They were willing to stock a small quantity, only 'on a sale basis,' of payment; that is, Paul should visit after 15 days and collect money if the product was sold or take back the unsold products. Paul decided to try his luck and placed the product, on a sale basis. Paul had prepared nice danglers, by hand, to display in the shop windows. He placed products worth ₹10,00,000 in 50 shops.

After 15 days, Paul took a round of these shops with fresh product stock. He was hoping that he would be able to collect at least ₹7,00,000 to ₹8,00,000 and restock the retailers with additional products worth ₹15,00,000. However, Paul was sadly disappointed when he found that most of the shops had removed the danglers and together, they had sold products worth only ₹3,00,000. They had unsold stock worth ₹7,00,000 which shopkeepers insisted on returning saying that the product had become stale. Very few of them were willing to accept fresh stocks. Paul could not place products worth more than ₹3,00,000 with the shopkeepers. This was obviously not good.

Paul knew that he had to find some novel method of selling the products, but nothing came to his mind. He called three of his classmates for a cup of coffee. Sitting in Cafe Coffee Day they explored many wild ideas. Eventually, it was Erica who came up with the first most brilliant one. Then others came up with supportive ideas. They called it the P P (Pinto Products) Brain Wave.

The P P Brain Wave

Major upper-middle-class and middle-class residential societies, with more than 100 flats in the society, were identified in the Pune Camp and Khadki area. 40 housing societies in the camp area and 22 housing societies in the Khadki area were selected on the basis of size, presence of Goans and accessibility.

Paul and his friends took a gift basket of Pinto products to the president and secretary of each society, presented the gift basket and asked for permission to promote these products in the society through a novel promotional scheme. Forty-eight housing societies granted permission for the promotional scheme to be launched in the evening hours from 4 p.m. to 8 p.m., without using any loudspeakers and on the condition that no litter would be left behind.

Two vendors selling gas balloons to children were identified. Two hand-carts were prepared with a lot of signage and space to display and keep stocks.

At 4 p.m., the gas balloon vendor entered the residential society with his flying gas balloons. Alongside, a young sales girl/boy pushed the Pinto Products hand-cart. The balloons were in multiple colours and carried the 'Pinto Products' logo.

The children in the society automatically gathered around the carts. Each child was given a balloon and a sample product of Bebinca or guava cheese. They were told, "The balloon is yours to keep, take this product to your house, and ask your mother whether she would like to buy it. You come back either with the product or with the money printed on the label. In either case, the balloon is yours." The children enthusiastically carried the product back to their homes. In 70% of the cases, the product did not come back. When, at the end of the day, stock-taking was done, it was found that all the stocks could be accounted for. No customer had kept the product at home without paying for it. At the rate of two housing societies per day, 30 housing societies were covered in 15 days. The same exercise was repeated after 15 days.

Paul put up two billboards, one in the camp area on the main street and one in Khadki Bazar, both carrying a simple tagline, "The best of Goa now in Pune - Pinto Products".

Two housewives were recruited for a special job. Each housewife was given a route map. On that route, she would go to every possible retailer for Pinto Products and ask for Pinto Bebinca. She would express vociferous disappointment on discovering that the Pinto product was not in stock. Next time, she would aggressively ask the shopkeeper, "Why don't you keep it?" Every day, each would cover about 10 shops. They continued to do so for a month. Some shops were visited thrice, or even four times.

After a month, Paul went to the shops again, asking them whether they would like to stock Pinto Products. This time he dictated the terms, saying stocks are available only if bought on a cash basis. Almost 90% of the shops agreed to stock the product. They allowed Paul and the salespeople to display the product prominently in the shop windows.

Within 3 months, Pinto Products were well established in the retail network of the camp and Khadki Cantonment and were moving fast enough to ensure a sale of ₹15,00,000 per month. Paul was now wondering whether he should cover other areas of Pune or move on to prime areas of Mumbai like Colaba and Bandra West or whether he should quickly add additional products or go slow and consolidate his position in the existing market.

Chapter 18

Quality Circle of Farmers

ABC Sugars Ltd., is a large private sector sugar producer in South India. ABC Sugars has five factories dispersed in the southern states. The major activity of ABC Sugars is to crush the sugarcane produced by farmers in areas neighbouring the factory and convert it into crystalline sugar.

ABC Sugars also produces the Merry brand of candy, which is popular amongst children all over the country. ABC Sugars was continuously facing the problem of unscrupulous small scale producers producing candies and selling them as Merry candies. ABC Sugars retained Global Consultancy Limited to plan strategies and action programs to meet this menace of spurious manufacturers. Global Consultancy experts did work on this problem but success was proving to be difficult.

While this assignment was on, the Managing Director of ABC Sugars, Mr. Krishnan, invited Global Consultants to participate in another meeting. The agenda of this meeting was not at all connected with the assignment on hand. The problem being discussed was how to get more sugarcane for crushing.

It was likely that the factories would operate at only 60% capacity during the present season because enough sugarcane was not available. A major reason for less sugarcane being available to the factories was a fall in the per acre yield of sugarcane because of a poor monsoon and inadequate availability of water in the dams for sufficient irrigation.

Another reason was the intense competition between sugar mills to attract supplies from farmers producing sugarcane, who were not necessarily in the close neighbourhood, given the shortage of sugarcane.

Low capacity utilization was a serious problem because at the ruling prices of sugar, the factories could run in profits only if the capacity utilization was more than 80%.

Attracting distant farmers for supplying the sugarcane to the factory was not a very attractive proposition because the prices required to be paid to these farmers as compensation for cost increased due to long distance transport, and incentives for undertaking such transport were high.

This problem of shortage of sugarcane for crushing was a frequent one, occurring once in every three to four years. The Managing Director of ABC Sugars, Mr. Krishnan, wanted to explore ways and means to find a long term solution to this problem.

One possible solution being discussed was to encourage additional farmers to take up planting of sugarcane. This was not a very viable solution in the long term because the additional area under sugarcane would fight for the scarce resources of water from canal irrigation and might not therefore contribute, on the whole, much additional sugarcane.

Another possible solution was to educate and guide farmers in the use of improved technology like drip irrigation which uses water more efficiently and also to encourage the use of correct seed stock, fertilizers and pesticides, so that the production of sugarcane per acre improved significantly. Mr. Krishnan had invited Global Consultants to participate in this meeting, called to discuss how to increase the yield of sugarcane per acre, to get some fresh out of the box ideas from them.

Global Consultants had, in the past, participated in implementing 'quality circles' in the automobile industry, where they had achieved excellent results. (The term 'quality circle' is defined by Professor Kaoru Ishikawa in his 1985 handbook, "What is Total Quality Control? The Japanese Way" - A quality circle is a group of workers who do similar work, who meet regularly to identify, analyse and solve work-related problems.) Global Consultants knew that the Japanese movement of 'quality circles' had been adopted mainly by mechanical and chemical engineering factories in India. The movement had not spread to sugar factories, leave aside to farmers growing sugarcane.

Global Consultants made a bold suggestion to Mr. Krishnan that the quality circle movement should be enthusiastically accepted by ABC Sugars. The movement would begin within sugar factories, for which the procedure was well established and standardized. They suggested that the movement should also be taken to the sugarcane farmers. Farmers growing sugarcane in a village should be organized in quality circles. These quality circles should be the group activity centres to promote improved sugarcane cultivation technology among the farmers in the village.

There was immediate and spontaneous opposition to this suggestion from senior managers of ABC Sugars. Even some board members joined the chorus of opposition. Their general opposition was, "This is an urban fad, and will not work in interior rural areas. Farmers are illiterate, ignorant and reluctant to change. This Japanese technique might have worked in modern factories, where workers are well paid, well-educated and afraid to lose their jobs. Farmers have nothing to lose if they don't participate. We want to woo them to get their sugarcane in our factory. If we tell them to do fancy things, they will go away!"

Mr. Krishnan was himself a farmer having a five-hectare farm. He had graduated in agricultural engineering before taking his first job with a tractor manufacturing company. He had first-hand experience of the quality circle movement and the results it had achieved in the tractor factory. He knew that adopting quality circles amongst sugarcane farmers would require evolving special procedures and processes; manuals would have to be prepared and they would have to be made available in local languages. Mr. Krishnan did not agree with the negative views held by officers of ABC who had an urban upbringing and orientation. He was happy that Global Consultants were showing faith in farmers. He requested Global Consultants to go ahead and prepare manuals and an action plan for launching quality circles amongst farmers.

Global Consultants found this to be a challenging task. They also saw a good business opportunity in spreading quality circles amongst farmers of various states, once their efforts succeeded for farmers supplying sugarcane to ABC Sugar Limited. They decided to go ahead.

A quality circle manual for sugar cane farmers was prepared by Global Consultants based on:

- 'An E-Learning Manual for Total Quality Management,' by the United Nations Industrial Development Organization & Japanese Standards Association.
- In-depth discussions with field officers of ABC Sugars.
- In-depth discussions with progressive farmers.
- Guidance from professors in agricultural universities.

The summary of the eleven major topics in the manual is given Annexure 1.

Implementation

- The quality control manual was translated into Tamil and Kannada.
- Global Consultants realised that the attitude of field officers of ABC Sugars would be a major problem. They had a “we know it all” attitude and were used to dictating instructions to farmers. Quality Circle aimed at enabling farmers to make good decisions. The attitude of the field officers had to change. Field officers were trained in a seven-day, full time, workshop at the beginning of the ‘off’ season to re-orient them.
- 140 quality circles were set up in 110 key villages over the span of four months.
- Mr. Krishnan attended 92 quality circle meetings without prior notice.
- It was found that, when left to themselves, the quality circles often excluded scheduled caste farmers and women farmers. In seven villages special quality circles of women farmers were formed.
- Generally, young, rich farmers showed initial enthusiasm but then absenteeism soon became the rule. On enquiries, it was found that these young rich farmers preferred to spend their time in nearby towns, often spending the money at dance bars!

- Middle aged, educated farmers with medium sized farms were the main strength of the quality circles.
- Farmers took keen interest in general human relations skills topics, like benefit communication, art of active listening and transactional analysis.
- Interference of local political leaders was a major nuisance.
- The schemes to make more economical and productive use of irrigation water, were the most discussed topics at the quality circles.
- The participating farmers demanded priority in harvesting their sugarcane according to their preference. Mr. Krishnan instructed the field officers to accommodate, to the extent possible, requests from QC member farmers in this respect.

Results

Quality circles were implemented in the sugarcane catchment area of ABC Sugars Ltd., under the leadership of Mr. Krishnan. The next year the monsoon was good and cane production was good. But more importantly, the total receipt of sugarcane at the gate of ABC factories was 5% more than the earlier best year of ABC Sugars since its inception.

Postscript 1: ABC consultants had meanwhile identified a few retailers who sold spurious Merry candies. Some of them shared the source of their spurious supplies after ABC field officers used 'sam, dam, dand' (negotiation, payment, force). Of the three tactics dand – the threat of police action - worked most often. ABC consultants continued tracing backwards the source of spurious supplies of Merry candies. Surprisingly, the trail went back to three official distributors of Merry candies appointed by ABC Sugars. This information was shared with Mr. Krishnan who did not act aggressively on the information, like discontinuing the distributorship, filing a police complaint etc., because he knew that these distributors were close relatives of the directors of ABC Sugars Ltd.

Postscript 2: Global Consultants were invited to set up quality circles of farmers by three co-operative sugar factories in Maharashtra and one private sugar factory in UP.

Annexure 1

Summary of the eleven topics in the Quality Circle Manual for Sugar Cane Farmers:

1. **The human dimension to a quality circle:** Participating farmers get a lot of satisfaction from improving skills, and from using new skills together with other farmer colleagues to achieve meaningful targets.
2. **Quality circle activities:** Farmers identify problems in their agriculture, usually related to product quality and quantity; together they set about finding solutions. Farmers use quality control concepts and techniques, and try to be creative in seeking solutions.
3. **Introducing quality circle activities in your farms:** The aim is to encourage the development of farmers. Participating farmers must make sure that they take an approach that suits the working environment, and the character and climate of their fields.
4. **Quality circle leaders: Lead farmers and members:** The quality circle 'lead farmers' will be the driving force behind the activities. Select leader farmers who can create an atmosphere where everyone will feel free to express their opinion.
5. **Quality circle training:** Quality circle training is aimed at achieving a team of farmers who are motivated, creative, and good at solving problems by using quality methods.
6. **Quality circle meetings:** Quality circle meetings help farmers to work together towards the same goals. Team members exchange ideas and information, get to know each other, and develop a spirit of cooperation and a sense of solidarity.

7. **The quality story:** Quality circles address the five priorities, viz., quality (Q), costs (C), deadlines and productivity (D), safety (S), morale (M).

8. **The basic procedures for quality circle activities:** Once quality circles are set up, there are a wide range of procedures to follow.

9. **Evaluation of quality circle activities:** Regular and appropriate evaluation of quality circle activities will help to motivate farmers and to revitalize activities. There are two forms of evaluation: self-evaluation by farmers, and evaluation by lead farmers.

10. **The RADAR questions:** The RADAR questions will help you to focus on this discussion:

    R - Are these ideas relevant to my crop?

    A - How would I apply each of them in my sugar cane fields?

    D - What difficulties might I meet and how would I overcome them?

    A - Are there any additional actions that I might take, not mentioned in the text?

    R - What resources would be needed? At what cost? How could they be acquired?

11. **The 6-point structure:** The 6-point structure will help farmers to write their action plan:

    1. Problems: Problems you have in your fields, in the area you have just discussed.
    2. Proposals: Your proposals for improvement.
    3. Obstacles: Obstacles to implementation and how these could be overcome.
    4. The resources required, those available and how to meet the short fall.
    5. Assessment: Ways of assessing the results of implementing these proposals.
    6. Benefits: The benefits your proposals would bring.

Chapter 19

Quality Machine Tools (QMT)

Part 1

Quality Machine Tools (QMT) is a famous machine tool manufacturing company. Their specialty is general-purpose, semi-automatic machine tools. A1 Boilers (A1B) had been their customer for the last 10 years. They are also their next-door neighbour in Kurla, Mumbai. Almost all the machines on the shop floor of A1 Boilers are supplied by Quality Machine Tools.

Vijay Patil, a young sales officer working with QMT, was a graduate mechanical engineer from Walchandnagar and had done his MBA from IndSearch Pune. QMT was his first job.

Vijay received an enquiry for a semi-automatic lathe machine from A1B. The machine was required for the training division of A1B. Vijay knew that there had been changes in the purchasing department of A1B. The purchase manager of A1B, who had a longstanding relationship with QMT, had retired. The new purchase manager David Awale had come from outside the company, and had a reputation for being a hard negotiator. Vijay did not want to begin his relationship with the new purchase manager of A1B on the wrong foot. He, therefore, decided to quote the lowest possible price so that the purchase manager did not feel that Vijay quoted a very high price initially and then gave a large discount at the time of bargaining. Vijay quoted a price of ₹5,50,000 with the possibility of a discount of only ₹10,000, in case Mr. Awale insisted on a discount.

Within two days Vijay received a phone call from Mr. Awale, who sounded agitated. He said, "Vijay, I know our companies have a long relationship.

But the quotation you have given is way above my expectations and the going market price. I have quotations from two other reputed companies. The maximum price is ₹5,00,000. The other competitor has quoted ₹4,50,000. I am here to save money for my company. Please drop your prices. I will give the order at ₹4,75,000. I am giving you an extra ₹25,000 in view of our relationship. Take it or leave it. Let me know your acceptance by tomorrow."

Vijay was taken aback by this frontal attack. He did not know what to do. He rushed to his boss, Mr. Bhatia. "Sir, can I reduce the price by ₹75,000 as a special case? They are our old customers," he asked. "Have you padded up the quotation by that much?" asked Mr. Bhatia. "No sir," said Vijay. He continued, "I have quoted the lowest possible price, I have a margin of only ₹10,000." Mr. Bhatia grew stern, he said, "Then why are you asking me? Being our old customer is a good reason why A1B should give us a good price. Go and get the order. Vijay, it is your call. I don't want to lose this order. Do not open doors for the competitors." Mr. Bhatia then changed his tone to that of a friendly advisor and continued, "Vijay, now that you have asked me, I can make a few suggestions. See if you can reduce some safety gadgets and reduce the cost and take Mr. Awale for dinner, I will sanction the expense but get the order. Good luck."

Vijay was at a loss. He had a feeling that David Awale would not budge and if it came to the crux, he would give the order to the competitor. That would be a disaster, and the fact that Vijay's confirmation in the company was due, made him more nervous.

Dear Reader, take a pause here and think of a solution for Vijay within the framework of the concept of marketing. "The marketing concept is the philosophy that firms should analyse the needs of their customers and then make decisions to satisfy those needs, better than the competition."

Part 2

Vijay was worried. When he reached home, Vijaya, his wife realized that something was troubling Vijay. "What is it?" she asked him. Vijay said, "Yes, I was about to consult you anyway."

Vijay and Vijaya had fallen in love when they were studying engineering in the same class. While Vijay went on to do his MBA, Vijaya proceeded to complete her M.Tech in mechanical engineering and was now working as a teaching assistant in workshop practice in an engineering college in Mumbai.

Vijay briefly described the situation regarding the enquiry from A1 Boilers. Vijaya thought about the problem. After dinner, she said to Vijay, "I have been thinking about the enquiry you have from A1 Boilers. I have not done an MBA like you but I have some experience of training young men in using lathes in my own workshop practice sessions. You said your company has a long standing relationship with A1 Boilers; the enquiry is for a lathe in the training division; right? In that case, the production lathes they have on their shop floor have to be similar to the ones you are going to supply to their training division. Now, as a trainer, I can tell you that I would definitely go in for a lathe which is very similar to a lathe on my shop floor for training my apprentices. Your lathe is the best lathe for A1 Boilers. And yes, do not worry about losing your job, you are good, there are ten jobs waiting for you if you lose this one!"

Vijay was listening very attentively to Vijaya. Suddenly the correct sales strategy started unfolding, step by step, in front of Vijay's eyes.

The next day, Vijay met Mr. Varma, the training manager of QMT, and described the situation with A1 Boilers. He then outlined a possible solution he had in mind and asked him for his advice. Mr. Varma said that he knew Mr. Datar, the training manger of A1 Boilers, quite well and that it would be good idea to involve Mr. Datar at this stage as anyway, he would be involved in the decision making at the final stage. They both went to Mr. Datar and discussed Vijay's ideas. Datar enthusiastically supported Vijay's idea. Vijay then prepared a revised offer for Mr. David Awale. The salient features of this revised offer are summarised below:

Salient features of the revised offer

- The lathe will have extra safety gadgets as it would be used by apprentices. However, in view of the relationship between QMT and A1 Boilers, there would be no extra cost for the additional safety gadgets.

- QMT will supply large training display flexes on how to use the lathe safely for accurate and high speed machining.
- QMT will sponsor visits of apprentices from A1 Boilers to the QMT factory, so that the apprentices can see how the lathes are made and assembled. This will improve the understanding of the trainees regarding operations of a lathe. This will be a goodwill and relationship gesture on the part of QMT.
- QMT service engineers are often on the shop floor of A1 Boilers to service machines which had been supplied by QMT. The service engineers will help in training apprentices on routine maintenance and servicing of lathe machines. This will help both the companies in the long run because maintenance calls for QMT service engineers will go down and also the downtime of machines on the shop floor of A1 Boilers will decrease. This will result in savings for both the companies in the long run.

Vijay discussed this proposal with Mr. Bhatia, who was very appreciative. He pointed out that the competitors, who had quoted a lower price, must be from Ludhiana and they could not match factory visits or help by service engineers in training. Vijay knew that Mr. Bhatia was also happy because the cost of these add-ons was not going to be debited to the sales account!

Vijay personally met Mr. David Awale and explained to him the salient features of the revised offer and the benefits to A1 Boilers. Mr. Awale was highly impressed by the customer centricity of the young Mr. Vijay Patil. Vijay received the order from QMT for the lathe machine from A1 Boilers in two days at the price he had originally quoted.

Vijay received his permanent job confirmation appointment letter, before the end of his probation period, on the first of the next month with three additional increments in appreciation of the quality of his work. At the dinner to celebrate Vijay's confirmation Vijaya was pleasantly surprised to receive diamond ear rings from Vijay!

Chapter 20

Shakti Motors: Fight Them, Kill Them

Background

Shakti Motors manufactured commercial vehicles, namely trucks and buses, in a very wide and deep range of product mix. Mr. Dinesh Pant had joined Shakti Motors as vice president, commercial, a couple of years back. He had been recruited from outside the automobile industry because the chairman of Shakti Motors felt that there had been too much in-breeding of managers in Shakti Motors and they confined themselves to inbox thinking and actions.

Dinesh Pant, a graduate automobile engineer and a post-graduate in management had made his career in marketing household consumer durables, starting with kitchen appliances. His last job, before joining Shakti Motors, was Vice President, Marketing, of a leading television brand. On joining Shakti Motors, Mr. Pant had taken new initiatives in improving the service at the dealership and promoting the exchange of vehicles. Consequently, the retained value and the resale value of the old vehicles had gone up, and the new vehicles had become more appealing to the buyers. In appreciation, the board of directors of Shakti Motors had recently promoted Mr. Dinesh Pant as joint managing director

The market for commercial vehicles had grown consistently at a rate of 5% to 10% per year over the last decade. However, the company was currently in trouble because the market had suddenly stopped growing, primarily as a consequence of the stagnation in the Indian economy. Additionally, a large number of well-known foreign brands had entered the Indian market during the last 15 years and were fighting to gain a share in the market.

Mr. Pant was looking into ways of coming out of the market stagnation. Of course, he couldn't do much about the state of the Indian economy or the entry of new competitors, but one segment of the market to which he had not given enough attention during the first two years was the after-sales market for spare parts. This was partially due to the fact that the contribution of the sales of spare parts to the total sales was very small. In a total sale of approximately ₹2,50,000 million, the sale of spare parts in the after-sales market, by Shakti Motors, accounted for less than ₹2,000 million.

It is often said that the lifetime value of the after-sales market in trucks or buses is equal to the initial sales price of the vehicles. This after-sales market in commercial vehicles comprised tyres, batteries, bodies of buses, mechanical spare parts and servicing. Mr Pant knew that when the market for new vehicles was not only stagnant but declining, it was imperative that addition to sales from every source was fully exploited. During the last two years, he had seen many presentations from the spare parts team explaining why the market share of Shakti Motors in spare parts of its own vehicles was this small. He asked his executive assistant Jacob, a young MBA from an IIM, to summarise the major points from these presentations.

Jacob's Note: The Market for Spare Parts and Our Current Situation

- A major component of the after-sales market is tyres, batteries, body parts of buses and service. These are not within the scope of supply of Shakti Motors. The after-sales market of interest to Shakti Motors is spare parts, particularly engine and transmission parts. The total size of this spare-part after-sales market is only about ₹20,000 million.
- There are three groups of suppliers of spare parts: (1) Shakti Motors. (2) Manufacturers who supply to Shakti Motors but also supply the after-sales market under their own brand name.(3) Manufacturers who make imitation and me-too products often claiming that they are supplied by Shakti Motors.The market share of the three major groups is:
    - Shakti Motors 10 to 15%

  - Suppliers to Shakti Motors selling under their own brand names 30 to 40%
  - Me too, spurious, illegal manufacturers 45 to 60%

- The engine and transmission parts are mainly made of special quality steel and require accurate machining and advanced heat treatment processes.
- Shakti Motors supplies spare parts through authorised dealers of vehicles.
- There are a large number of multi-brand spare parts shops selling parts to mechanics and vehicle operators. These shops are normally grouped together in select localities within the town.
- Spurious, fake, substandard parts are often sold in packaging very similar to the original packing used by Shakti Motors. (Read the story told by Mr. Navlakha, former General Manager, Spare Parts, Shakti Motors in Annexure 1).
- The prices charged by fake and spurious manufactures are the same as the prices charged for original parts by Shakti Motors. Manufacturers of spurious parts do not charge a lower price because that would announce that the part is of lower quality.
- A customer does not knowingly buy the spurious parts. The reason being that if a vehicle fails on the road because of spurious parts the consequential damages are very large and fatal.
- Shakti Motors fixes the selling price with 100% to 150% mark-up on the manufacturing cost or procurement price. The logic is: since the turnover is low it should be compensated by higher margins per unit.
- The cost of making the spurious parts is very low because high-quality steel can easily be substituted by low-quality steel and the costly heat treatment could be avoided altogether, while making the spurious parts. Consequently, the margins available to the spurious manufacturers are very high.

- It is commonly believed that some unscrupulous authorised dealers and authorised service stations also trade in spurious parts. They also use spurious parts in servicing the vehicles which come to them during the warranty service period.

- It is also suspected that some of the managers of Shakti Motors are working hand in glove with spurious part manufacturers and help them to push their products through trade channels.

- Large transport operators have their own workshops. They purchase parts directly from the vehicle manufacturer if the manufacturer offers good discounts. Otherwise, they purchase their requirements from market wholesalers. Market wholesalers offer significant discounts of up to 40% on the list price.

- These large wholesalers also generally operate their own retail shop and carry a ready stock of most of the fast-moving items of all the brands. There is a countrywide network of the large wholesalers of spare parts. In case of need, they can purchase a part from any wholesaler in India and make it available to the end-user within 7 to 10 days. The vehicle manufacturers take much longer to supply a part if it is to be supplied from the company warehouse.

- The small operators and roadside mechanics buy the vehicle parts from multi-brand retail shops in the city. The multi-brand retail shops offer credit for a period of up to 45 days and/or discounts up to 20% on the list price.

- The main channel of Shakti Motors for the supply of vehicle parts to vehicle owners and mechanics is through authorised dealers appointed for the purpose of sale of vehicles. Whole-sellers, retailers, mechanics, authorised service stations and vehicle owners are expected to purchase parts from vehicle dealers.

- Authorised Shakti Motors dealers offer discounts (up to 15%) and credit facility (upto 30 days) for parts only to a very few customers, and that too at their discretion.

- Company dealers are mainly interested in selling new vehicles. They generally neglect the service and spare parts business. They perceive the service and spare parts business as a headache which involves stocking a large number of parts and employing a large number of people doing blue-collar work. The return on spare parts and on servicing is much lower than the return on the sale of vehicles.
- Being an automobile dealer having a large showroom for commercial vehicles is seen as a prestigious business in the hierarchy of retailing. Servicing the vehicles and selling spare parts is ranked at a much lower level on the retailer status hierarchy scale. This is also a reason for neglecting the business of servicing and selling parts by automobile dealers.
- The company insists that every authorised dealer buys an allotted quota of spare parts every year from the company. Since this business is neglected, the stocks of spare parts keep on piling up. Generally, auto dealers auction these parts. Wholesalers enthusiastically participate in these auctions. Wholesalers form cartels for participating in these auctions. They buy the parts at a much lower price than the company list price. This is one reason why they can afford to give large discounts to regular customers. 'Go to the auction in a three-tier sleeper, return from the auction in first-class AC,' is a common jocular jest amongst the spare part wholesalers.
- It is very difficult for an ordinary truck/bus operator or commercial vehicle owner or a mechanic to judge the quality of a spare part like a gear. All steels with grease look more or less similar. The quality of steel, the kind of heat treatment the part has undergone and the dimensional accuracy to the level of a few microns is very difficult to judge without using very sophisticated and costly instruments. Therefore, users and mechanics have to rely on source credibility to judge the quality of the parts.

- The spare parts department is currently headed by a vice president who has risen from the ranks within the spare part organisation, starting as a field sales officer. Almost all managers in the spare parts department have been in the department since they joined Shakti Motors. Most of the field officers are in their area for more than 10 years. Field officers have extremely good personal relationships with dealers, spare part wholesalers, authorised service stations and large institutional buyers.
- The spare parts department has no long-term strategy to gain a significant market share. Their annual plan generally involved tactics like:
    - Push large stock on the dealers at the year-end. This takes care of performance in the balance sheet. Then increase the prices in May- June to compensate the dealers. (This also made the whole-sale dealers and the spurious manufacturers happy).
    - Pressurise the materials department to sign contracts for supply of parts only with those parties who agreed not to sell the products under their brand name in the open market. (The materials department did not always oblige because many suppliers of parts had a monopoly on the technology for making parts through specialised processes like investment casting, powder metallurgy, case hardening, etc.)
    - Occasionally, file a police complaint regarding a totally fake product sold in packaging very similar to that of Shakti Motors.
    - Generally, practice 'a live and let live' policy. The attitude of personnel in the spare parts department is: The fake parts mafia is hand in glove with the local police, politicians, spare part wholesalers, some large dealers and a few managers in Shakti Motors (who knows?). Fighting with the mafia can endanger not only your career but also your life. Do not take on the spare parts mafia. At the most, you can fight the branded products supplied by your own large suppliers.'

New Initiative

Mr. Pant read Mr. Jacob's note very carefully. Although Mr. Pant was, on the whole, aware of the situation, reading the comprehensive summary prepared by Mr. Jacob made him realise that a whole new strategy and its bold implementation was an urgent necessity.

As was felt by the chairman two years back while recruiting Mr. Pant, Mr. Pant now felt a need to infuse fresh outside blood to do out of box thinking. He invited Mr. Suresh Joshi, who had worked with him earlier in TV marketing as general manager, to join Shakti Motors as senior vice president, sales. He also invited Global Consultants, a leading consultancy firm, to provide support in the area of market research. Sometime later, he also invited ABC trainers to take on the responsibility of training the mechanics. Mr. Pant, Mr. Joshi, Mr. Jacob, and consultants from Global Consulting and ABC trainers burned the midnight oil for the next six weeks and came up with a comprehensive strategy summarised below.

Strategy for Spare Parts: Kill the Spurious

Preamble: The spurious and fake parts being fitted in buses and trucks of Shakti Motors are not only eating into our market for spare parts but are also causing great damage to the reputation of our company, which is based on the performance of our vehicles. A number of reports show that the major cause of serious accidents is low-quality fake parts. These spurious parts also reduce the life of our vehicles. Allowing them to flourish and dominate the market is outright criminal. The marketing and sales strategy will be 'Kill the Spurious and Fake Supplies.'

Target: Our simple target is to reduce the share of fake, low-quality parts to less than 10% from the current 50% to 55% in the next three years. Each and every action of Shakti Motors must be designed and executed towards this goal.

Strategic Actions

- A new brand will be created for spare parts called 'Shakti Original.' The tag line will be 'Shakti original parts are strong so as to prevent accidents and increase vehicle life. The quality of Shakti original parts is guaranteed by Shakti Motors, the makers of Shakti Vehicles.

- A new distribution channel will be created for 'Shakti Original' parts. Exclusive distributors will be appointed for 'Shakti Original' parts. There will be at least one distributor of 'Shakti Original' parts in each state and union territory. There may be more than one distributor for 'Shakti Original' parts in some large states like Maharashtra, Madhya Pradesh and UP. The distributor will be responsible for supplying the parts to retailers, mechanics and fleet owners in his territory, and will do business only in 'Shakti Original' parts.

- The mark-up deciding the sales price of 'Shakti Original' parts will be a flat 80% on the manufacturing cost or the purchase price of the part, instead of the current practice of 100% to 150% mark-up. 55% of this margin will be passed on to the parts distributor who will then be able to pass on a discount of up to 45% to the wholesaler, retailer, fleet owners and mechanic. This will lead to a lowering of prices, making them less attractive to manufacturers of fake products. Eventually, Shakti Motors should get the same profit from the spares business - what is lost in margins would be more than recovered through increased turnover.

- 'Shakti Original' parts will be supplied in well-matched and balanced sets. This reduces the mechanics' labour of ordering parts separately and matching them.

- Retailers will be offered specially designed display boards saying, 'Shakti Original' parts are available here. The board will be available to those retailers who give an undertaking that whatever they buy in the boxes which look like genuine boxes of 'Shakti Original' parts will be bought only from authorised distributors of 'Shakti Original' parts. This will improve the source credibility. A directory of authorised retailers will be compiled and published. This will guide buyers to retailers who sell 'Shakti Original' parts.

- A new scheme will be started in which a buyer can buy a lifetime supply of spare parts at the time of purchasing the vehicle itself.

For instance, he will pay about ₹1,00,000 extra when buying a vehicle worth ₹9,00,000. He will then get a free supply of all the spares required for the vehicle throughout its life. The only additional condition will be that the vehicle will be serviced at an authorised service station. (Workshops of large fleet owners will also be authorised for this purpose). This scheme has three advantages for a customer: (a) The buyer of the vehicle will get bank finance for spare parts, which is currently not available. (b) The buyer will be assured of getting high-quality original Shakti parts. (c) The buyer will be protected from any future increase in the prices of parts.

A special scent will be added in all the boxes of 'Shakti Original' parts. We will ensure that the scent is available exclusively to Shakti Motors from the aromatic manufacturer and that it will not be easy to copy. Consequently, when a mechanic opens the box of 'Shakti Original' parts, the scent will confirm that the parts are original and of high quality.

- Our service engineers will conduct training camps all over the country for roadside mechanics as well as retailers' salespersons. There will be a special session in this program to explain why making good quality parts is not easy and why advanced technology is required to make 'Shakti Original' parts.
- A field sales officer for spare parts and a field service engineer will remain posted in a particular geographic area for not more than two years. They will then be transferred to either a state which has no common boundary with their current state of posting or they will be transferred to the factory.
- A detective agency having all India presence will be appointed to make mystery customer visits at various counters selling spare parts for Shakti Motors, to check whether fake parts are being sold at the counter. In case the parts are found to be fake, the detectives will immediately file a police complaint of cheating against the retailer.

- Whenever a bus or a truck of Shakti Motors meets with an accident in which a person is killed, the accident will be investigated by a team of specially trained engineers. The team will investigate whether the accident was caused by a low-quality, fake part. If such a cause is found, the engineers will provide all the evidence to the police and ask them to investigate and book the culprit for causing the death of a human being.
- A legal agency will be appointed to pursue all the police complaints vigorously and ensure that culprits are charged with crimes and are punished.
- The public relations department of Shakti Motors will be responsible for giving publicity to the cases filed against fake part manufacturers so that others get the message.
- Shakti Motors will explain these initiatives against fake parts at various forums of the automobile industry and try to get similar action plans implemented by other automobile manufacturers and also by reputed manufacturers of quality spare parts. Shakti Motors would lead a broad front of the automobile industry against the fake part manufacturers.

Results: Sales of 'Shakti Original' parts crossed ₹1,000 crores within the next two years.

(This case study is based on real-life happenings in three different automobile companies in three different and overlapping time periods. The quantitative figures about market size, market share, mark-ups etc., should be treated as indicative.)

Annexure 1

Story told by Mr. Navlakha, former General Manager, Spare Parts, Shakti Motors.

"About a couple of years before my retirement, in the year 2015, I had gone to Japan to explore the possibility of buying some of the spare parts from Japanese manufacturers. While inspecting the parts made by the Japanese, I noticed the special kind of cardboard packing boxes which had been marked with engraved watermarks. The process appeared unique. On enquiries, I found that in Japan there are special purpose machines engraving watermark logos on cardboard boxes. I thought that if we could pack spare parts in such specially watermark cardboard boxes then the spurious parts manufacturers would not be able to copy our packing and the distributors and retailers and even the final buyers will know that the parts are genuine, coming from Shakti Motors. I ordered four machines, got a few sample boxes made and came back to India.

Immediately, there was a conference of dealers in Delhi. I proudly displayed the new boxes with the engraved watermarked logo of Shakti Motors at the conference and confidently said, "My dealer friends, now you do not have to worry about spurious parts looking very similar to the genuine parts. Within two months, our parts will come in these special boxes. Please ensure you are buying parts in boxes engraved with watermarked logo. Half of your worries regarding spare parts will be over." I came back to the head office and got busy with my normal work.

The machines arrived from Japan but it took a bit longer than anticipated to get them cleared by customs. The machines were being installed when I received a phone call from a leading dealer in Delhi. He said, "Boss, what is my crime? What have I done to deserve this kind of treatment?" I said, "What happened?" He said, "The market is flooded which Shakti spare parts in the new boxes you showed during our conference, but the supplies I have got today are in the old boxes. Who will now buy them from me? Why have I not been given supplies in new boxes?"

I was shocked. We had not supplied any spare parts in new boxes. The machines for printing the boxes were still to be installed and become operational. But, 'hats off' to the entrepreneurial spirit of the manufacturers of the fake and spurious products! They imported the machines and started using them even before us. I realized that it is not easy to fight the fake and the spurious."

Chapter 21

Simco

Part 1

South India Matchbox Company (SIMCO) is a large company manufacturing match boxes. The company was in serious trouble. Their sales had been declining for the last two years.

The Chairman of SIMCO knew that something was basically not right. He hunted for an expert marketing manager from fast-moving consumer goods companies. He found Mr. David, a young, dynamic and upwardly moving manager in a major FMCG company. Mr. David was appointed director of marketing and also made a board member. The Chairman told him, "You have only one task, get me a market share of 60% from the current share of 40% within two years."

Mr. David called a meeting of his senior managers to understand the situation and the reasons for the declining sales. The following is a summary of what the senior managers said.

VP Sales: The problem is the competition from small-scale and backyard manufacturers. Their costs are very low. Almost all processes are manual without any consideration for workers' safety and health. They also do not pay any tax. They can afford to sell the matchbox for 40 Paisa against our price of 50 Paisa. On top of it, they offer a margin of 10 Paisa per matchbox to the retailer as against the margin of 5 Paisa per matchbox by us. Most of the people who buy matchboxes are poor. They don't care about quality. The retailer offers them a cheaper brand and they are happy. The retailer makes more money by selling these brands. In the last two years, Khadi and Village Industries Commission (KVIC) have made special efforts to promote this backyard manufacturer; that has really aggravated the problem.

Head, Product Development: We have put in a lot of effort to make our product better. We have substituted cheaper wood. We have promoted plantation of this new variety of trees to reduce the cost of raw materials. However, competitors have also started using the cheaper wood; we don't have a monopoly on the source. We have developed special damp proof, high friction surfaces. We have developed a technology so that the head of the matchsticks does not fall off and burn a hole in the customer's shirt. But customers don't seem to care.

Advertising Manager: We have never really spent on advertising. We spent less than one-fourth of 1% of our sales on advertising. This is really low for an FMCG product. Sir, you are from the FMCG industry, please give me ten times larger budget for advertising. Then we can make customers aware of the advantages of SIMCO matchboxes.

General Manager (Sales): Sir, we must adopt an aggressive sales strategy. We will identify those areas in which the small, local manufacturers are most vulnerable. We will drop the price selectively only in that area to 35 Paisa per matchbox and give a margin of 15 Paisa to the dealer. Yes, we will incur losses in that small market. But the competition will be wiped out in three months. We will then raise our prices. We will call it a clearance sale. We will keep this rolling from one market to another. Within two years we would have more than our earlier market share. The backyard manufacturers would have learned their lesson, they will think ten times before entering the market again.

Mr David closed the meeting saying that he will think about their suggestions and convey his decisions soon.

Part 2

Mr. David checked as to when the last market survey was carried out to determine the customers' needs and buying behaviour. He found that no such study had been carried out for many years and that the company did not have a market research department. Mr. David realised that he did not have time to commission a formal market research assignment with a professional agency. Further, he also knew that if the agency came up with some new findings, then it would be difficult to sell them to SIMCO's marketing and sales staff that had been with the company for 20 to 40 years. He decided on an aggressive tactic.

Mr. David called a meeting of all marketing and sales people up to the level of area managers at the head office and told them, "I know that in this room we have more than 1,000 years of experience in selling matchboxes, but I am new. I'm going to the market and will stand at a paan shop and observe what buyers do. All of you will do the same for two days in the next week. This will be our dipstick research. Send me a summary of your observations within 10 days from today."

The following phenomenon was observed repeatedly by Mr. David at paan shops in the Dharavi slum in central Mumbai. A similar observation was reported by almost all managers who went to poor localities.

The Observation: A customer comes and asks for a matchbox. If he was a smoker, he named the brand of the cigarette or bidi but he did not name the brand of the matchbox. The retailer offered a matchbox to the customer - sometimes a SIMCO matchbox, more often another brand. The customer took the matchbox and shook it near his ear. If it was a SIMCO matchbox, he returned it; if it was another brand, he bought it.

Mr. David did what the customers did and found that a SIMCO matchbox made a lot of noise while competing matchboxes did not make any noise. Many other executives also reported this observation.

Obviously, the customer was checking as to whether the matchbox was full. If the matchbox made a noise, it meant it was somewhat empty. He wanted the promised 50 sticks for his money.

Mr. David then asked his production department as to why SIMCO matchboxes made a noise? The answer was simple. SIMCO matchboxes were filled by automated machines in the factory. This required the stick to be shorter than the box so that the sticks could easily slide into the tray of the box. The tray could not be filled up to the brim because then the tray might not slide into the cover easily. For easy and speedy manufacturing SIMCO engineers had provided a large clearance between the stick and the tray and the extent to which the tray was to be filled. The engineers did not know that the customers listened to the sound of the matchbox!

Under Mr. David's instructions, the clearances were reduced to the minimum. The 'sound' of SIMCO matchboxes almost vanished.

Within six months SIMCO market share rose from 40% to 45%.

Everybody was happy but Mr. David knew that he had to get 15% more market share within another 12 months.

Chapter 22

Soya Sathi

The Bhartiya Krushi Sewa Sangh (BKSS) is a Non-Government Organization (NGO) established in 1932 by Acharya Devidas, a Gandhian who devoted his life in the service of Indian farmers. Today, BKSS, a charitable public trust, is involved in the activities of watershed development, animal husbandry including improving breeds, biodiversity conservation and women's self-help groups. Although they have an all India presence, BKSS activities are mainly focused in the states of Karnataka, Andhra Pradesh, Maharashtra, Madhya Pradesh and Gujarat. The total staff strength is 740 full time volunteers.

BKSS was headed by Shri. Mohan Devidas, grandson of Acharya Devidas, for over fifteen years. Mohan Devidas was a post-graduate from the Institute of Rural Management (IRMA) at Anand in Gujarat and a graduate in agricultural sciences.

The BKSS trust is funded mainly by donations that come as a part of the Corporate Social Responsibility (CSR) funding by large private sector organisations and funding by central and state governments for implementing government schemes. BKSS has an annual gross turnover of around ₹500 million.

A special meeting of the Board of Trustees and some key volunteers had been convened in the year… by Mr. Mohan, to consider a proposal received from International Biotech Limited. Persons present in the meeting were:

Representing the BKSS

Mr. Mohan Devidas: Managing Trustee (MD)

Ms. Sheetal Deshmukh: Trustee, Director Finance (SD)

Mr. Ramakrishna Desai: Trustee, Director Diversification (RD)

Mr. Suresh Bhandari: Manager, Information Technology (SB)

Mr. Satish Verma: Expert, Farm Economics (SV)

Ms. Surekha Pandit, Volunteer, Services Delivery (SP)

Mr. Anil Verma, Volunteer, Services Delivery (AV)

Representing International Biotech Limited

Mr Partha Chakraborty: Marketing Director (PC)

Mr. John D'souza: Head, Crop Sciences (JD)

Transcript of the proceedings of the meeting:

Mohan Devidas: Welcome to all. All seniors, including our guests, know each other. Let me specially introduce our two young colleagues, Surekha Pandit and Anil Verma, who have joined our organisation recently. They are graduates from IRMA with brilliant academic careers and have been recruited in our new division called Services Delivery, which is currently under my direct supervision.

As you are aware, we have done considerable work to improve the lives of Indian farmers. So far, we have worked mainly in the peripheral areas to farming, like animal husbandry, watershed management, agro-based industries, and so on. We have not looked into the core issue of agricultural productivity. We realise that this is a deficiency which we must correct. We have to work directly to improve the productivity in terms of the per acre yield of the farms. I believe that this is a core issue and it is becoming more and more urgent. Every day we receive reports of farmers committing suicide. Usually, the main reason for the suicides is the loss of crop because of bad monsoon or related reasons. The farmer is unable to repay loans taken at a very high interest rate from the local money-lenders. A more basic reason is that a farmer is unable to create reserves in a good year, which will help him to tide over bad times, because the productivity is low. We have, therefore, decided to deliver services to farmers to enable them to increase the productivity of the land.

My two young colleagues are the first volunteers in this new division.

It is an interesting coincidence that we decided to form this new Service Delivery division and one of our major donors, International Biotech Limited, have approached us for collaboration in this area of improving farm productivity. I will now request our guests from International Biotech Limited, to share with us their ideas on the collaboration so that we help the farmers to improve productivity.

John D'Souza: Thank you sir for giving us this opportunity. Let me come directly to the point. At International Biotech we do considerable work to improve farm technology. We strive to enable farmers to raise farm productivity. As you rightly mentioned, low productivity of Indian farms is a serious issue. I present to you the summary finding of productivity in Indian farms in global comparison. The data have been compiled by The Economic Research Unit of OECD, a reputed organisation.

Summary Finding of Productivity in Indian Farms in Global Comparison.

Crop production, Tonnes/hectare				
Country	**Wheat**	**Rice**	**Maize**	**Soybean**
Argentina	3.2	4.5	7.1	2.9
Australia	1.7	7.3	6.5	1.9
Brazil	2.5	4.2	5.8	3.1
Canada	3.3		10	2.6
China	5.4	4.7	6.1	2.1
European Union	5.8	4	NA	NA
India	3.1	2.6	2.7	0.8
Israel	2.8	1	3	1
Japan	4.1	5.1	1	1.7
Pakistan	2.8	2.6	4.8	0.5
Russia	3.1	5.3	4.4	1.5
Thailand	1	2	4.2	0.3
United States	3.1	5.9	11.1	3.3
World	**3.4**	**3.1**	**5.8**	**2.7**
India/World	**0.91**	**0.84**	**0.47**	**0.3**

As you can see from these data, the productivity of Indian farms is much lower than the highest achieved in the world. More worrisome is the fact that Indian productivity is low for all major crops even in comparison with the global average. This difference is much less for wheat and maximum in case of Soybean. In case of Soybean the productivity in India is less than one-third of the global average. We should start work where the problem is most serious and the gains would be very significant.

Soybean plays an important role in boosting the oilseed production in the country. It stands second, among the nine oilseed crops, next only to groundnut in production in the country. It has an outstanding nutritive value with 43 percent biological protein, 20 percent oil and is also very rich in vitamins, iron, minerals, salts and essential amino acids. Soybean flour is extensively used in manufacture of insecticides, disinfectants, and also is a rich medium for culturing antibiotics. The Soybean protein is rich in lysine and the oil extracted is edible with fairly high unsaturated fatty acids. Consumption of Soybean may also reduce the risk of colon cancer, possibly due to the presence of Sphingolipids. Which is why, Soybean is considered a miracle crop of the present century.

Soybean is grown mainly in the states of Madhya Pradesh, Maharashtra and Rajasthan and in areas which depend mainly on rain-fed agriculture. The table on the screen shows how soybean is a major crop in these three states.

Soybean in India			
State	Sowing Area	Yield	Production
	Lakh Hectares	Kg/hectare	Lakh Tonnes
Andhra Pradesh	1.8	877	1.6
Chhattisgarh	1.3	865	8.0
Gujarat	1.3	925	1.2
Karnataka	3.2	911	2.9
Madhya Pradesh	54.1	1094	59.2
Maharashtra	36.4	1054	38.4
Rajasthan	9.2	1025	9.4
Others	1.1	955	1.0

What are the reasons for this low productivity in Soybean? There are many reasons: Soybean is a 'kharif' crop which depends on monsoon rains; poor rains, poor yield. Also, Soybean is a hungry crop; it uses a large number of nutrients from the soil. When farmers cultivate Soybean in the same land year after year, the productivity goes down unless the farmer is able to replenish the nutrients in the soil by using organic and inorganic fertilizers including micronutrients. After a bad year because of a poor monsoon, the farmer does not have the money to invest in correct application of fertilizers. Soybean is also prone to attack by pests.

There is one more important reason. The reason is competition by weeds. Weeds are a common problem in all crops. Studies made some years ago showed that globally, weeds are responsible for decreasing production of the eight most important food and cash crops by 13.6 per cent, leading to an economic loss of $100 billion. However, weeds are a far more serious problem in Soybean. I show you on the screen a recent report from a research funded by a premier Agricultural Research funding institute in our country:

"Weeds are misfits and are one of the major limiting factors of Soybean production throughout the world. The losses caused by weeds and the cost of weed-control are among the most expensive items in Soybean production. The losses caused by weeds exceed the losses from any other category of agricultural pests like insects, nematodes, diseases, rodents, etc., as the weeds compete with crop plants for their nutrients, soil-moisture, space and sunlight and sometimes also serve as hosts for various pests and diseases. Generally, an increase in one kilogram of weed growth corresponds to a reduction in one kilogram of crop growth as weeds remove plant nutrients more efficiently than crop plants. When yields from un-weeded plots from different studies are compared, the reduction in yield of Soybean is approximately 50-60 percent, although more reductions are encountered when certain highly competitive weed species predominate."

So how are weeds to be controlled? There are three main traditional methods. (a) The crop residue, in the form of straw and leaf, is burned in the farm so that the stock of weed seeds left in the soil will get destroyed. (b) The upper layer of the soil is exposed to the sun by hoeing, so that the sun-rays kill weed seeds. (c) After the Soybean crop is planted, weeds start growing; remove the weeds by loosening the soil with a sickle and uprooting the weed with hands. This work is generally done by women. Weeding with hands needs to be done 20 to 40 days after sowing; more frequently, if necessary. All these methods may prove adequate if they all are practiced in tandem and correctly. However, that is very difficult nowadays. Agricultural labour is scarce and costly. Labour for de-weeding by hand is required during the narrow time-slot by Soybean farmers. Farmers do not get women workforce in adequate numbers at a reasonable cost. Also, if manual de-weeding is done without care, then it will damage the crop itself.

International Biotech has a solution, a pre-emergent weedicide, brand name for which is 'Weedabort'. Weedabort has been created especially for the Soybean crop. Weedabort attacks all the weeds which grow in the Soybean crop and does not damage the crop at all. Weedabort is to be sprayed in the Soybean farm about three days before or after sowing. This can be done mechanically by a single man using a spray-gun. He can spray two hectares of land in one day. Our field-trials show that Weedabort is able to control weeds in Soybean crop to the extent of 95%. This is a very high efficacy. The crop productivity almost doubles. The gains of increased productivity compare well with the cost of spraying Weedabort. The benefit-cost ratio is more than 2:1. I must mention in this context that Weedabort is already the largest selling weedicide for Soybean in USA and Europe.

We think that Bhartiya Krushi Sewa Sangh should take a lead in educating farmers. Adopting this new technology would improve productivity and enable farmers to save money to overcome a bad season, as rightly said by the chairman.

Partha Chakraborty: So, how do we collaborate? Our proposal is very simple. Your organisation has high credibility with the farmers. BKSS will design a program to educate farmers and to popularize Weedabort amongst them. BKSS will implement the program and also monitor the results in terms of the gains in productivity, so that we are all convinced about the efficacy of your inputs. You recruit the necessary manpower, train them, you design the educational material.

International Biotech Limited will reimburse all the costs at actual, no questions asked and give a 10% fee for your supervisory efforts. We will manage the physical distribution of Weedabort. Give us your budget, we will submit it to our board and I am sure they will approve it. Let us start this joint activity in three districts of Madhya Pradesh and Maharashtra to begin with. After a review at the end of this kharif season, you can decide to extend it to all Soybean areas in India. Our target should be to double the productivity of Soybean farms within a span of next five years.

Mohan Devidas: Thank you John and Partha. Very informative and educative presentation made in a very short time; thank you once again. As I said earlier, we have also been focusing on increasing agricultural productivity and Soybean is one major crop receiving our attention. My colleagues have done some work in the area, I am sure they can make important contributions. Satish, would you like to begin?

Satish Verma: Sir, I had heard about Weedabort and had started collecting some relevant information. I wrote to some agricultural universities in Maharashtra and MP about weeds in Soybean. I compiled a list of major weeds that occur in Soybean crop.

Major Weeds in Soybean Crops		
S. No.	**Common Name**	**Botanical Name**
1	Nut grass /Moutha	Cyperus rotundus
2	Bermuda grass/Dubgrass	Cynodon dactylon
3	Sawa	Echinochloa crusgalli
4	Gazzer grass	Parthenium histrophorus
5	Field bind weed	Digera arvensis
6	Field bind weed	Convolvulus arvensis
7	Choti dhudhi	Euphorbia geniculata
8	Badi dhudhi	Euphorbia hirata
9	Gokhru	Xanthium stromarium
10	Hazardana	Phylenthus niri
11	Kass	Saccharum spontaneum
12	Amerenthus	Amerenthus viridi
13	Pili sengi	Melilotus indica
14	Jangali choulai	Ameranthus viridi

Does Weedabort act effectively against all these weeds that are encountered in India? As we know, weeds in a tropical country like India are bound to be more diverse and different than those that grow in the fields of Europe and USA.

John D'souza: I do not have a ready list of the weeds which are controlled by Weedabort. I will definitely get that list from our R&D and share it with Mr. Satish. However, let me re-state that we have tested Weedabort in fields in MP and Maharashtra with 95% control of the weeds and significant gain in productivity.

Satish Verma: I do not doubt your findings at all; but it is good to be twice sure in these matters concerning investment by farmers who have very low risk buffers.

I have also another fear nagging me. If these current weeds are controlled then is there a likelihood that new weeds will come up which are resistant to Weedabort? I am not talking about existing weeds undergoing genetic mutations to develop resistance. I know that will take a very long time. I am talking about biological competition. There is a biological competition between weeds. The weeds which now grow predominantly suppress the growth of other weeds in Soybean farms. Once these dominating weeds are eliminated, the weeds which were suppressed in the biological competition will have a field day. We will then require another pre-emergent weedicide to control these new weeds! Please do not misunderstand me. I am not against using a chemical weedicide, but I foresee problems. We must plan strategies to counter possible emergent dangers.

One simple strategy that comes to my mind is not giving up manual weeding completely. We should advise farmers to do at least one manual weeding to remove the weeds which survive and grow despite the spray of Weedabort. This will prevent the danger of new weeds growing freely. Of course, we will have to work out the cost implications of using pre-emergent weedicide and one round of manual weeding, say 40 days after sowing.

Sheetal Deshmukh: Yes. I think we can do that quickly. We have been tracking the cost of various farming operations for some time. We have even computerised the data. International Biotech can give us the cost of Weedabort spray per hectare and we can quickly estimate the cost of one spray of Weedabort along with one manual weeding. If Mr. Chakraborty can tell the cost now, I think Suresh will be able to tell us the cost of these two operations immediately. We can look at the benefit-cost ratio of combining spray of Weedabort with one manual weeding. Suresh can you do this?

Suresh Bhandari: Yes ma'am, we can do it, but not that fast. Give me a day. Meanwhile, I have been referring to online sources for the role that IT can play in this endeavour. I came across a very interesting possibility. Allow me to project it for your consideration:

Weed Seed Wizard

The Weed Seed Wizard is a computer simulation tool for use in cropping situations across Australia. It can be used to explore different weed management scenarios side by side and help users decide where a new practice (or tactic) or rotation may fit into their specific system and location.

The 'Wizard' uses farm-specific management inputs and modelled competition to predict grain yield and weed seed production. Changing management practices can alter crop or weed numbers. This will affect the grain yield as well as the number of weed seeds produced and their subsequent return to the seed-bank.

The input of management practices into the model is very flexible. It is based on a timeline using specific management records and can be used to look at past or future years:

The 'Wizard' fine-tunes to specific locations:

- Users can input the crop they have sown in the past or what they may sow in the future, the specific sowing times and rates as well as the viability of the seed.
- Specific herbicides or mixtures can be added and their control percentages quickly adjusted to portray herbicide resistance or poor herbicide application, for example:
    - Particular harvest management strategies can be inputted and subsequently changed to suit the location, for example where a wet harvest affects the amount of weed seed dropped or where rain after haymaking may allow weeds to re-grow and set seed.
    - Multiple weed species can be considered simultaneously for the same paddock.
    - Users choose their own weather file. The specific weather predicts the loss of dormancy for each weed species and matches this with the rainfall to determine the timing of their emergence from the weed seed-bank.

- Users also choose their soil type. The different soil types combine with the weather file to determine how much water is in the soil profile and when germination will occur.

- Different tillage practices can be added. The 'Wizard' matches where the weed seed is within the soil profile from the chosen tillage practice with the soil moisture of the chosen soil type to further predict the germination of each weed species.

(A free download is available from: https://dafwa.agric.wa.gov.au/weed-seed-wizard-0.)

Suresh Bhandari: Weed Seed Wizard is in public domain. The Australians are available for consultation. I joined BKSS hoping to use IT for the benefit of the Indian farmers. Many of my colleagues, I know, have a similar motive. I am enthused. Let us adopt the Weed Seed Wizard.

Sheetal Deshmukh: Very Good. Weeding has been traditionally a 'women's specific' work in agriculture. With weedicide sprays sprayed by men riding tractors, with use of Wizards, are we planning to evict women from their traditional wage-earning work? What will they do? We run more than 200 self help groups of women. We are struggling to find work. How many papads can we roll? There are not enough stomachs to feed on these papads!

I insist that the task of using weedicides and using computer based programs should be handed over to the women's self-help groups. If necessary, we will form special purpose cooperatives of women in villages. The cooperatives will handle contracts for weed removal. The women's group will decide when to use chemical weed killer, when to use mechanical implements and when to use women's labour. There is no point in making a working woman idle and then trying to find her alternative employment. I assure you that we have educated women in our women's self-help groups who can operate computers. Of course, they will need training, which I am sure our IT people will be happy to provide.

Mohan Devidas: Well said, Sheetal. You know we are with the women; we have a 'Woman First' policy, which we implement in every sphere. Yes, sometimes we men overlook the difficulties of women. Thank you Sheetal for reminding us of our commitment to equal opportunity for women. Now, Ramakrishna, you have not spoken so far. Incidentally, I like to call you by your first name so that I accumulate some 'punya' every time I call you. So, the floor is yours.

Ramakrishna Desai: Thank you, sir. I am not very familiar with this business of weeds and killing them. But there was a talk of weed seed bank just now when we had a presentation on Weed Seed Wizard and I remembered my father. Our ancestral house had a small lawn. My father, after his retirement from the Army, was fastidious about his lawn. He wanted the lawn lush green without any weeds. He did not want to use chemicals if he could avoid them. But at his age of 80, it was not possible for him to pluck out the weeds by hand – he had no gardener. I remember my father used to collect a sample of the soil for which he had a special cylindrical tool. Exact small measured quantity of soil used to come out in this tool. He would then collect the soil sample in a pan and count the seeds using a lens. If the weed seed bank was large, he would use a chemical, can we use some similar technique for our farmers? It is unlikely, I believe, that all farms have equally large weed seed banks. The extent of weed growth can be anticipated by the density of weed seeds in the soil which can be easily measured in advance. I think this may be feasible and will avoid unnecessary use of chemicals. These are my memories; the technology may be much more advanced now.

Mohan Devidas: Very interesting. We must explore. My young colleagues, Surekha and Anil, will you like to say something?

Surekha Pandit: No Sir.

Anil Verma: No Sir.

Mohan Devidas: How do we go ahead? We are fortunate to have a collaboration with International Biotech. We must help farmers to control weeds in Soybean farms and produce more Soybean per acre. We are Gandhians. We must adopt technology so that weakest of the weak gain the most. I request Surekha and Anil to work under the guidance of Ramakrishna to produce a blueprint for action. The plan must include all farmers of Soybean in a village; but the plan must help not only the smallest farmer but also that 35-year-old widow who works in a Soybean farm to remove weeds. Burn midnight oil, if you have to, but make the blueprint ready in two weeks. Good working. God bless you.

....

A plan was prepared by Ms. Surekha Pandit and Mr. Anil Verma under the guidance of Mr. Ramakrishna Desai.

The plan was called **Soya Sathi.**

Objective

To increase farm productivity of the Soybean crop, by controlling the weeds growing amongst the crop.

Conditions

- All farmers in the village growing Soybean would be eligible to benefit from the scheme.
- The smallest farmer will benefit from the scheme.
- The women who do the work of de-weeding will not lose their employment.
- The possibility of new weeds growing (because the currently dominant weeds get eliminated) should be minimised.

Geographic Spread

In the first phase, that is, in the coming kharif season, 20 villages in Madhya Pradesh and 20 villages in Maharashtra will be covered.

These villages will be selected in such a way that there are actively functioning women's Self-Help Groups (SHGs) in these villages and the total land under Soybean is more than 100 hectares.

In the second phase, that is the next kharif season, the program will be extended to 200 villages in Maharashtra and 200 villages in Madhya Pradesh.

Subsequent spread will be decided in a review after two seasons.

Collaborators

- International Biotech Limited
- Australian International Cooperation Service
- Involvement of ITC Ltd., a major player in Soybean procurement through their e-Choupal, should be explored.

Project Design

In every village the women's Self-Help Group (SHG) will be the agency for implementing the Soya Sathi programme.

The project will start by testing the soil in each Soybean farm for a weed seed count.

A least 20 women from each SHG will be trained. The training will consist of:

- Scientifically collecting the soil samples and measuring weed seed count.
- Using hand tools for removing weeds. They will be provided with specially designed sickles to easily uproot weeds.
- SHG workers will be trained in using a back mounted spray gun for spraying Weedabort. The women will be specially trained to take correct precautions so that the weed spray does not affect their health. Women will be provided with specially designed, easy to handle, masks for this purpose.
- Women will be trained in using the promotional material to educate and motivate farmers to participate in Soya Sathi.

A three-day training program for 25 women from each SHG will be held in the village for this purpose.

Each SHG will be provided with a computer which has a built-in program to store, classify and retrieve the relevant information. The computer will have the 'Weed Seed Wizard' program. Three women from each SHG will be trained in using this program through a ten-day residential course conducted on the BKSS campus.

A team of two women from the SHGs, will contact farmers and explain to them the service offered under Soya Sathi. At least 10 teams will be operational in each village. These women, who do the promotional work, will be remunerated at a rate which is at least 15% higher than the going wage rate for removing weeds.

International Biotech will reimburse the expenses on account of:

- Providing computers to self help groups
- Preparing software
- Training women in using the 'Wizard' software
- Audio visual material made for training the women from self-help groups
- Visual material to be used to promote the 'Soya Sathi' scheme to the farmers
- Promotional visits to farmers by two member teams of self-help groups

The estimated cost for this project, is ₹1,90,000 per village having 100 hectares under Soybean cultivation. The actual cost may vary according to local conditions. The final budget would be prepared, in consultation with the SHGs, once the villages have been selected, International Biotech will supply Weedabort to each SHG, at the office of the SHG in the village, in quantities requested by the SHG, at a price which will be 20% less than the MRP.

Integrated Weed Management

The de-weeding program of Soya Sathi, will be dove-tailed to the farm size and the density of weeds as measured by weed seed count. A strategic combination of manual weed removal and use of pre-emergent weedicide, namely Weedabort, is summarised in the table below;

Farm Size of Soybean Farm	Weed Seed Count		
	Low	Medium	High
Small (Less than one Hectare)	Hand weeding – once 20 days after sowing	Hand weeding – once 20 days after sowing	Hand weeding –twice 20 days after sowing 40 days after sowing
Medium (1 to 2 Hectares)	Hand weeding – once 20 days after sowing	Hand weeding– twice 20 days after sowing 40 days after sowing	Weedabort – Pre sowing Hand weeding –once 20 days after sowing
Large (More than 2 Hectares)	Hand weeding – once 20 days after sowing	Weedabort – Pre sowing Hand weeding –once 20 days after sowing	Weedabort – Pre sowing Hand weeding –once 20 days after sowing

As the Soya Sathi program becomes popular it will also take up the task of educating the farmers on crop rotation and inter-cropping, particularly with corn and maize.

Submitted for the approval of the Trustee Committee

Surekha Pandit Anil Verma Ramakrishna Desai

Postscript: Mr. Mohan Devidas: Managing Trustee (MD) forwarded the note prepared by Mr. Ramakrishna Desai and his young colleagues to Mr. Partha Chakraborty: Marketing Director, International Biotech Limited, for his consideration.

After two weeks Mr. Chakraborty informed Mr. Mohan Devidas that International Biotech Limited was unable to proceed with the scheme for the time being. No reasons were stated.

Chapter 23

ABC Motors: Right Diversification?

10th December 2018

From: Navin Banerjee,

Head, Policy Planning Cell, ABC Motors.

To: Managing Director, ABC Motors.

Subject: Diversification

Background

Our diversification into very light commercial vehicles in the year 2010 was the right decision, as the market in this segment has grown at an average growth rate of 9.5% per year during the last five years.

Overall, in the last five years, the sales of all automobiles have grown at 7.1% per year and sales of commercial vehicles have grown at 3.1% per year as shown in Table 1.

Table 1: Sales of Automobiles 2013 to 2018

Category		2013-14	2014-15	2015-16	2016-17	2017-18	Average Growth Rate Per Year (%)
Passenger Vehicles	Nos.	25,03,509	26,01,236	27,89,208	30,47,582	32,87,965	
Growth over Previous Year	%	-6.1	3.9	7.2	9.3	7.9	4.4
Commercial Vehicles	Nos.	6,32,851	6,54,948	6,85,704	7,14,082	7,56,453	

Continued

Category		2013-14	2014-15	2015-16	2016-17	2017-18	Average Growth Rate Per Year (%)
Growth	%	-2.7	3.5	4.7	4.1	5.9	3.1
Tractors	Nos.	6,96,828	6,26,839	5,71,249	5,81,500	7,11,400	
Growth over Previous Year	%	18.0	-10.0	-8.9	1.8	22.3	4.6
Three Wheelers	Nos.	4,80,085	5,32,626	5,38,208	5,11,879	6,35,698	
Growth over Previous Year	%	-10.8	10.9	1.0	-4.9	24.2	4.1
Two Wheelers	Nos.	1,48,06,778	1,59,75,561	1,64,55,851	1,75,89,738	2,01,92,672	
Growth over Previous Year	%	7.3	7.9	3.0	6.9	14.8	8.0
Grand Total	Nos.	1,84,23,223	1,97,24,371	2,04,68,971	2,18,62,128	2,49,72,780	
Growth over Previous Year	%	3.5	7.1	3.8	6.8	14.2	7.1

Heavy commercial vehicles continue to be the major component of our product mix, constituting 70% of our sales; and the sales of heavy commercial vehicles have grown at a slower rate of 1.9% per year.

This market for heavy commercial vehicles has been showing a strong recessionary tendency in the last few months. The sharp decline in the sales of medium and heavy commercial vehicles in November 2018 is most glaring. The volumes of Ashok Leyland Ltd., fell by 18% year-on-year, while those of Tata Motors Ltd., contracted 24% year-on-year.

In view of the cyclical variations and very slow growth rates in the market for commercial vehicles, it is necessary that ABC Motors diversifies.

I suggest that ABC Motors should enter the field of tractors.

Why Tractors?

Sales of tractors have grown at a rate of 4.1% per year in the last five years. Tractor sales have been very buoyant in the recent past. The sales grew by 22.3% over the previous year in the year 2017-18 and the growth has been more spectacular in recent months.

For 2017-18, Mahindra & Mahindra, the country's top tractor manufacturer, reported a 21% increase in domestic sales. The domestic sales of TAFE, India's second-largest tractor maker, rose by 16%, to about 1,36,000 units. Sonalika Tractors also recorded a 26% growth rate at 86,700 units.

The data in Table 1 suggest that the sales of commercial vehicles and tractors are cyclical, but the cycles are out of phase; when commercial vehicle sales grow significantly then the tractor sales show a negative growth, and when the commercial vehicles sales show a negative growth or stagnation then tractor sales show a large growth. Diversification into tractors will not only increase the growth rate but will also stabilize the sales of ABC motors.

John Deere Tractors, which are in the sixth place in terms of market share, have shown the largest growth in sales of 41%. This indicates that despite the established leadership position of Mahindra and Mahindra, the market is open for smaller players and new entrants to grab a significant share.

Although nearly 4.3 million tractors are in operation, the demand for tractors is far from reaching saturation in India. Only 19% of Indian rural farming households that can afford a tractor have purchased one yet.

A reason for the sustained demand for tractors is the relatively easy availability of loans from banks. Loans for agricultural tractors are classified as loans for the priority sector. Some state governments offer subsidies on tractors, sometimes as much as 50% for woman farmers. The loans given to farmers against mortgage of land are difficult to recover. In case of default in repayment of the loan for tractor, the financing institution can take possession of the tractor; and there is a good market for second-hand tractors.

Independent, market-watch agencies, Kotak and ICRA, project that the tractor market will grow at a rate of 7% to 8% per year.

Our engineering knowledge, manufacturing technology and plants for producing heavy commercial vehicles are more than adequate for producing good quality tractors. Additional investment required by ABC Motors for setting up a manufacturing unit of tractors will be marginal, while addition to sales will be substantial.

Our network of dealers for commercial vehicles is spread wide and deep all over India. The dealerships of ABC Motors at district and tehsil towns can take up the sale of tractors immediately. We will not have to make any special efforts to set up a new dealership network.

What Kind of Tractor?

Although Indian tractor manufacturers have tried to develop a tractor design to suit Indian conditions, the results have been rather marginal. This is very clear from the fact that all tractor manufacturers offer one and the same tractor everywhere in India although the crops, the soil conditions and the use of tractors varies greatly from the fertile planes of the Punjab to the rocky soils on the Deccan plateau and the muddy paddy fields in almost the entire coastal region.

I came across a very interesting write-up on the web-site of a Japanese manufacturer of agricultural equipment; some highlights are:

- Agricultural practices are dependent on soil and climate and traditions, they greatly vary geographically.
- The cropping pattern, cultivation practices depend on types of soil and sizes of farms.
- Features of agricultural machinery are heavily governed by these factors.
- We must design products according to the needs of each area.
- We should understand the needs of the farmers.

I recommend the above approach for designing a new tractor so that it is pre-sold in various market segments.

I had a discussion with five tractor dealers, ten tractor salespersons and 25 knowledgeable farmers who use tractors. My very preliminary and tentative recommendations deal with three aspects, namely, (a) safety of the tractor operator, (b) different models for different regions and usage, (c) value engineering to maximize the benefit-cost ratio of various features in the ABC tractor. I describe each of these aspects in the following paragraphs.

Safety of the tractor operator: Reliable data on the extent of tractor accidents in farms and roads are not available. The Indian Council of Agricultural Research (ICAR) did carry out a survey of accidents in agriculture and the limited data collected from a few sample villages indicated that the fatalities due to agricultural accidents were 21.2 per 1,00,000 workers per year. The major source of accidents were farm machines namely tractors, threshers, chaff-cutters, cane crushers, sprayers and electric motors, and other sources namely snake-bites, drowning in wells/ponds and lightning. Tractors alone accounted for 43% of the total fatal accidents. However, accidents in remote villages are likely to be under-reported; by lowest estimates, there are at least 5,000 fatal accidents, every year, because of the overturning of tractors.

In developed countries, tractors overturn sideways if the load in the trailer is not properly balanced. This is a reason in India too. However, my discussions with farmers indicate that tractors overturn upside down, and crushing the driver under the tractor is the most common cause of fatal accidents because of the tractor design in India. The overturning of the tractor occurs under two extremely opposite conditions: On the Deccan plateau, when ploughing is in full swing, the plough may engage with hard rock in the soil. This is as if there is sudden braking and pulling from behind and the tractor may overturn backwards. In the Gangetic plains and paddy fields, the front wheels may suddenly dip into a pond which is unexpectedly deep or soil which is unexpectedly soft. In that case, the tractor may overturn on the front wheels.

Currently, farmers use makeshift technology to overcome this life-threatening danger. They attach heavy cement bags in the front or rear, depending on whether the danger would be overturning on the back wheels or front wheels; sometimes they fill water in the rear tires to make them really heavy so that the tractor does not overturn on front wheels.

These are not very effective solutions. Moreover, they also increase the load which the tractor carries and extra fuel is burned to carry this extra load.

Non-fatal accidents because of tractors would perhaps run into hundreds of thousands. In addition to the overturning of tractors, accidents are also mainly because of:

- **Power Take-Off (PTO):** Loose clothing like dhotis, lungis, kurtas get caught in the power take-off shaft. Additionally, many work practices such as clearing a plugged machine, lead to an operator's exposure to operating PTO shafts. Other unsafe practices include mounting and dismounting a moving tractor, reaching for control levers from the rear of the tractor, and stepping across the shaft instead of walking around the machinery. An extra rider on the tractor while PTO power machinery is operating is another exposure situation.
- **Collision on the roads:** Relatively faster-moving vehicles on the road ram into tractor-trailers from behind because trailers have no lights in the rear, not even reflective indicators.

Tractors from ABC motors should have safety mechanisms which are better than the indigenous solutions as given below.

- While ploughing rocky soil when the plough engages with hard rock and pulls back the tractor, the plough should automatically disengage from the tractor.
- The ABC tractor can also have a sensor in the front for judging the depth of the ponds and softness of the soil while working in plain muddy fields.
- The ABC tractor should keep all components of PTO systems shielded and guarded.
- The ABC tractor should have a facility to put rear indicator lights on trailers.

The above solutions are those suggested by farmers. I am sure our engineers will improve on these solutions. One thing is sure, if the ABC tractor is seen as much safer and less life-threatening, then it would be the first choice of the farmers.

Different tractors for different terrains and uses: I understand that the Indian terrain can be divided into three main groups: flat lands like planes in the Punjab, rocky soils on the Deccan plateau and muddy paddy fields in the entire coastal region. The pulling power, the accessories the farmer is likely to use with the tractor, the turning radius of the tractor and track width, all these differ according to the terrain. ABC tractors should have at least three different models: one for India north of Vindhya, second for India south of Vindhya, third for the coastal belt.

The tractor as a transporter is imagined to be used for last-mile connectivity from the village to the farm. However, in India, a tractor is used for transporting farm produce over longer distances and tractors ply on tar roads and highways. When the tractor is likely to be used more often for this purpose then the tractor may have synchromesh gears and also a special gear for driving at a speed between, say, 30 km/h to 50 km/h.

Need for value engineering: The ABC tractor is likely to have additional safety gadgets. This is bound to increase the cost of the tractor. Can a farmer pay this additional cost? When the ABC tractors are designed specifically for a type of terrain, then the sales of that model will be restricted to a particular geography. This would mean higher costs because the total sales potential of the tractor model would be low. ABC motors must therefore carefully explore areas of possible cost reduction.

My preliminary qualitative research with farmers and tractor sellers indicates that a large number of farmers never use some of the special tractor features, for instance, track width variation and power take off.

Track width variation means the width of the wheel track can be adjusted by re-positioning the inner "hub" of the wheels in relation to the outer "rim." Most of our tractors are equipped with adjustable-track-width wheels. But very few farmers use this facility.

Power Take-Off (PTO) in tractors is to be used to operate rotary implements, attachments like a rotovator, power harrow, compressor etc. PTO is also not used by a significant section of tractor users.

If these and such other features, which are not used by a majority of farmers, are eliminated or are made optional then the additional cost due to safety gadgets and terrain-specific designs can be fully or partially compensated.

Once the decision to get into tractors is taken 'in principle,' we should:

- Commission detailed comprehensive market research to understand the needs of Indian farmers and tractor users, to design appropriate features for the ABC tractor.
- Carry out a systematic value engineering and value analysis to maximize the benefit-cost ratio of the ABC tractor.

Summary

Diversification into tractors is recommended because the tractor market is growing and ABC Motors already have the necessary production and distribution facilities.

The tractor to be introduced by ABC motors should be designed to be safer and in line with farmers' needs.

Submitted for consideration of the Top Management
Sd (Navin Banerjee)

Mr. Ravi Shukla, Managing Director of ABC Motors, found the note sent by Mr. Navin Banerjee really relevant and worthwhile. He circulated the note to all the six vice-chairmen of ABC motors for their comments.

Postscript 1: When the agenda of diversification was taken up at the board meeting of ABC Motors, there was a 10 minute discussion on the note. The Chairman, Mr. Chandrasekhar Chitale, issued the final instructions, "Let us get into tractors. The initial capacity will be 5,000 in a year. The tractors will be produced in our plant line for mid-sized commercial vehicles. Initially, only one all-terrain model of 35 HP should be produced. We should not invest in any costly safety gadgets or systems, as farmers will not pay for them."

Postscript 2: The 35 HP tractor under the brand name 'Bull' was launched by ABC Motors in September 2019. It was very similar to the large selling model of Mahindra Tractors and had no special safety features. The initial response of farmers and dealers to 'Bull' was rather poor; with 980 tractors being sold in the first 6 months.

Chapter 24

Joy Consumer Durables

Mr. Suresh Chopra was the sales director of Joy Consumer Durables, popularly known as JCD. JCD was the largest manufacturer of high-value consumer durables in India. They held a market share of 23% in colour TVs. The other products of JCD included washing machines, air-conditioners and microwave ovens. Mr. Suresh Chopra, sales director (and as he liked to insist, a member of the board), called Mr. Dinesh Oberoi, VP marketing and Mr. Vivek Doshi, general manager, market research, for an important meeting to discuss the dealer development strategy.

Suresh Chopra opened the meeting. He said, "I have called you to discuss a very important issue. As you can see, I have not involved many people because what we discuss and plan in this meeting must remain confidential for some time.

I'll start with the personal experience I had in Kolkata, which has shocked me. I had flown to Kolkata for a private family function and did not involve any of our sales teams in Kolkata. After the function was over, there was some time for me to spend in Kolkata before I boarded the return flight. I decided to walk into a major television showroom. I had hoped that nobody would recognize me and I was relieved when that was the case. I could then act as a mystery customer.

A look at the TV sets on display showed that Sony and Haier were prominently displayed with their 48" screens. Both were showing the National Geographic channel with colourful animals and flowers coming alive on the screen. After searching a bit, I could see a 28" Joy colour TV in a corner. It was playing some local Bangla channel with poor picture quality. On the first impression, a customer would think that the picture quality of Joy was far inferior to that of Haier and Sony.

I then enquired with the salesperson whether they had a bigger, colour Joy TV. The salesperson said, "Yes, we have that model but it is in our storeroom, we are not displaying it because it is not moving."

"Why is that so?" I asked. Pointing to the Joy TVs on display, he said. "See for yourself!"

The salesperson then continued, "With Sony, I'm sure that you will not require any service for the first two years, even though there is a two-year service warranty. I'm not so sure about Joy TV." "Do the Joy TV people give a service warranty?" I asked. "They do," said the salesperson; then quickly added, "But when the service engineer of Joy will turn up, if you call him, I'm not sure."

I asked him, whether any special promotional scheme was on, in view of the festive season. He said both Haier and Sony were offering a special discount of ₹5,000 on all models priced above ₹30,000. I kept on asking. "What about Joy, is there a discount going?" He said, "Yes, Joy is offering a discount of ₹6,000 on their model priced at ₹40,000; but sir, do you really want to consider a non-moving model for just an additional discount of ₹1,000?"

I asked, "What common complaints do you get against Joy because of which you really do not feel like recommending it?" The salesperson was surprised at the question. He said, "Sir, I do not know; if you want, I will check up with my service engineer, but he is not here just now. Please leave your phone number with me."

I said, "That is not necessary," and walked out.

I was very angry when I walked out. Then I wondered what our area sales officers and regional sales managers were doing? How could they let this rogue dealer use Joy TV to promote competing brands?"

On my return journey, I did some quiet thinking and came to realize that the buck stops with me. Our dealer development strategy was not able to handle such a rogue dealer.

How many such rogue dealers are there in the market, badmouthing Joy? Do you know Mr. Doshi, Mr. Oberoi? "

Mr. Dinesh Oberoi: "There won't be many. I do occasionally visit dealers in Bengaluru and Mumbai, but I have not come across such a devilish dealer."

Mr. Vivek Doshi: "Sir, we regularly do a dealer satisfaction survey. We do have data on complaints by dealers and dealers' suggestions. But I am sorry that we do not have any reliable information on transactions at the dealers' counters."

Mr. Suresh Chopra: "Thank you Vivek. Dinesh, I bet you visit the dealers with the area sales managers with prior notice. Then they are bound to put up a show for you. Ultimately Joy is the market leader. A dealer can't afford to let us know that he is pushing competitors' products at our cost. So far, we have depended on incentivizing dealers through various kinds of bonuses based on their sales. That does not seem to be effective. The differences in the features of various TV brands are now negligible. The prices are also very comparable. Dealers push a brand on which they have marginally higher commission; or a brand on which the incentive plan is nearing a closing date. We must have a strategy to keep multi-brand TV dealers in line, based on hard data. I do not mind if a few of them do not stock and sell Joy; but I cannot allow them to stock Joy, display it poorly, and then use it to promote competing brands."

Mr. Suresh Chopra continued, "Vivek, quickly put in place a system for market intelligence on transactions at dealers' counters through mystery customers. Cover the five metro cities and 25 other major cities in the next two months. Let us have a clear idea of what is happening at the dealers' counters. Dinesh, you provide the list of the key dealers with the largest sales, to Vivek. Both of you should jointly recommend the best action plan. Give me your recommendations within 10 weeks."

Dealer Audit through Mystery Customers

The action plan decided by Vivek Doshi had the following major components:

- The sample size was 50 dealers in each of the five metropolitan cities, namely Bengaluru, Kolkata, Chennai, Delhi and Mumbai; 10 dealers in each of the 25 other largest cities. The total sample was to be 250 dealers in metropolitan regions and 250 dealers in large cities giving an overall number of 500.

- Vivek Doshi decided to use management students doing their summer projects for mystery customer visits, as these students were abundantly available after their examinations got over in April.
- Each management student will go as a mystery customer to four dealerships per day, spending roughly about one hour at each multi-brand dealership. This means 125 student days are required for fieldwork. Six students working for 25 days would be able to handle this workload. To be safe, Vivek decided to recruit eight students.
- Each student would be trained in the task of acting as a mystery customer. He/She would have a standard story: he/she was looking to buy a good, large, colour TV to be presented at his/her sister's marriage to the newlyweds for their new home. The student will act relatively ignorant, open to be influenced by the salesperson at the dealer's counter.
- The student mystery customer will take a selfie photograph standing outside the dealership with the time and date automatically recorded in the photograph. This will ensure that the student had been at the showroom. Whenever possible, the student will also take a photograph of TV sets on display in the showroom.
- The mystery customer will note the TV sets on display and give comparative marks for display of Joy versus Sony, Haier, Videocon and Phillips.
- The mystery customer will check the salesman's responses to the following questions:
    - What brand does the salesperson recommend for a 48-inch, flat-screen, colour TV?
    - What are the reasons for the salesperson's recommendation?
    - If the salesperson does not recommend Joy as the first preference, then what does he say about Joy when specifically asked?

- What discounts does he offer on various brands?
- Does the salesperson volunteer information on warranty service and quality of service?
- How does he rate the service available for Joy compared with service for the competing brands?
- How pushy is the salesperson for the primary brand that he recommends?

Vivek then recruited eight management students for the assignment to be done for eight weeks and trained them thoroughly for two days. They were all required to do the mystery customer visits for the same four dealers. Their findings were compared and discussed so that the process was stabilized and standardized.

Findings of the Mystery Customers' Audit

The market research team classified the dealers based on two criteria:

- The first criterion was how big the dealer was, as judged by his total sales. This was based on the size of the dealership as indicated by the mystery customer and the total sales of the dealer as guessed by the area sales manager. The dealerships were divided into roughly three equal groups of 175 dealers each. The groups were labelled as large dealers, medium-sized dealers and small dealers.
- The second criterion was the dealer's/salesperson's inclination to recommend Joy. The findings of the mystery customer on various criteria were given numerical weights and an overall index of inclination to recommend Joy was arrived at. The index had a value 10 if Joy was recommended fully and similarly, -10, if the competition for the brand was pushed strongly and Joy was foul-mouthed. Based on this index of inclination to Joy, the dealers were divided into four groups: if the score value of the index for a dealer was above five then the dealers were classified as partner; if the index was between 0 to 5 the dealer was classified as supporter; if the index value was between 0 to -5 the dealer was classified as

detractor; if the score was below -5 the dealer was classified as the devil.

Vivek made the following tables for deciding the overall dealer development strategy:

The system of dealer classification is summarized below in Table 1 and Table 2.

Number of dealers in each class out of 500 dealers surveyed

TABLE 1	**Descriptive Label by Index of Inclination towards Joy**				
	Devils	**Diverters**	**Supporters**	**Partners**	**Total**
Value of index of inclination towards Joy	-5 to -10	-5 to 0	0 to +5	+ 5 to 10	
Large (Top 33%)	30	65	45	40	165
Medium (Middle 34%)	26	65	45	15	170
Small (Bottom 33%)	29	70	50	20	165
Total	85	200	140	75	500

Dealers with extreme scores

	Score= -10	Score = -9	Score= +9	Score= +10
Large (Top 33%)	5	8	6	7
Medium (Middle 34%)	3	5	10	7
Small (Bottom 33%)	4	5	8	4
Total	12	18	24	18

Recommendations by Mr. Doshi and Mr. Oberoi

Mr. Dinesh Oberoi, VP marketing and Mr. Vivek Doshi, general manager, market research sat together to review the findings and prepare recommendations for Mr. Chopra. For additional insights they looked into the regional pattern, but there were no significant differences between the regions. The following is the summary of the observations and recommendations made by the two person team.

We observe:

- The percentage of dealers who are against Joy is almost 50%.
- In a market where the product differentiation and price differentiation are very few and service requirements are low and provided equally by all competitors, the word-of-mouth publicity by the dealer's salesperson is of great importance, particularly because the salesperson is advising the buyer when he/she is making a final decision regarding the choice of brand.
- We must therefore take strong action to curb the negative word-of-mouth publicity and encourage positive recommendations at the dealers' counters.

We recommend the following specific actions:

- Joy should organize dealer conferences in all cities. The conferences should be addressed personally by Mr. Chopra in all the metropolitan cities. The conferences will be addressed by the senior sales manager in other cities. We should make it amply clear that we are using mystery customers to keep a close watch on the word-of-mouth recommendations at the dealers' counter. A written note will be also circulated to all the dealers about the methodology employed.
- Area sales managers should share the findings of mystery customer visits with each dealer by visiting the dealers and showing them dealer-wise reports of mystery customer visits including

photographs of mystery customers in front of their showroom, to ensure total credibility.

- Dealers with a score of -5 to -10 should be told that they are being closely monitored. If their score is found to be below -5 in the next round, which can happen any time during the next 30 days, then their supplies will be discontinued. They will be blacklisted and they will not have any dealing with Joy Consumer Durables for any of the products manufactured by Joy. The action should begin with large dealers having a score of -5 to -10.
- Dealers with a score of 0 to -5 should be told that if their score does not go above 0 in the next two rounds then they will also be discontinued.
- Dealers with a score of +10 should be given a bonus of 10% on the sales made by them during the last three months. This should be prominently announced in the company's newsletter. They should be invited to the head office to receive this bonus at the hands of the chairman.
- Dealers with a score of +9 should be declared a bonus of 5% on the sales made by them during the last three months. This should also be prominently announced in the company's newsletter. These dealers should be given this bonus in a function organized in their city at the hands of Mr. Chopra.
- The mystery customer visits to the dealers should continue once a month for large dealers and once in two months for medium-sized and small dealers.
- All dealers should know that they are being watched by Joy.
- Actions taken should be transparent and consistent.
- This carrot and stick approach should continue at least for one year.

Our recommendations may result in discontinuing of sales through some large and prominent dealers; but that will send a signal to the entire dealer community. The dealers cannot afford to lose their relationship with the largest selling brand in the country. They will fall in line. We will stop foul propaganda at the dealers' counters.

Mr. Chopra liked the recommendations. He also felt that strong action was required to make it known to the dealer community that Joy meant business. He knew that he would be taking on some major dealers who would wait for an opportune time to hit back. He knew that it was a very major decision and therefore he involved the board. He made a presentation at the board meeting and sought their support. Some board members, particularly representatives of the financial institutions, felt that Mr. Chopra should personally speak with the defaulting dealers before taking the extreme action or blacklisting them.

Implementation and Results

Mr. Chopra implemented the recommendations diligently and transparently. He addressed dealers through meetings in all the metropolitan cities. He spoke personally with defaulting dealers requesting them to correct their ways.

Eventually, in the next three months only three large dealers and two medium dealers were blacklisted.

The bonus to dealers with scores of ten and nine was very much appreciated.

The mystery customer survey was repeated amongst all the dealers.

Results after four months showed that dealers with a score lower than -5 had fallen down to 20 in number. There was no large dealer with a score of -9 or -10.

Within a year, dealers with a negative score were less than 40 in number. The dealers with a score of +10 also went up to 67. The sales of Joy televisions, which had grown at an average of 7% during the last three years, showed a growth of 11% during the year in which reports of mystery customers were continuously shared with the dealers.

Chapter 25

Maharani Washing Machines

We were doing dipstick research for the Maharani brand of white goods from New Delhi. Our task was to understand customers' needs, buying behaviour and usage of the washing machines. Of course, the major use was to wash clothes; but we were surprised by the following unexpected findings from our dipstick research.

One

When we surveyed the usage pattern in suburban north Mumbai, we found that in many middle class households the washing machine was mostly idle. The maid servant came and washed the clothes. The home maker did not allow the maid servant to use the washing machine. The home makers said that if they hired a maid servant only for sweeping and wiping the floor and for cleaning the utensils then what the maid charged was not much less than what the maid servant charged if she was asked to wash the clothes as well. This was because the time spent by the maid servant in coming and going was critical and which did not increase or decrease depending on whether she washed the clothes or she did not wash the clothes. Since the maid servant had to be paid almost the same wages, the home maker said, what was the idea of not asking her to wash the clothes? We then asked as to why she bought the washing machine in the first place? No quick answer was forthcoming. Through focused group discussions we discovered that the washing machine was a weapon in the armoury of the home maker in her ongoing cold war with the maid servant. She wanted to convey the message, 'if you think you are indispensable, please remember I have the washing machine and I can also buy a vacuum cleaner and a dishwasher'.

Two

We were at the Good Housekeeping Exhibition organized in Pragati Maidan in New Delhi, standing at the Maharani stall, watching the customers. A wealthy looking Punjabi came to our stall and asked, "Don't you have the top loading machine?" Maharani had only a front loading machine. Our sales person started enthusiastically explaining the advantages of a front loading machine, for example, the table top can be used for storage...The customer was not interested. He walked away. After almost an hour I saw him coming back and going to a competitor's stall of washing machines in front of the Maharani stall. The competitor had a top loading machine. After some discussion, I saw him taking out money and closing the purchase. I could not control my curiosity, and when he walked out of the competitor's stall, I went up to him and asked "Why did you not buy a front loading machine? Why have you bought a top loading machine?" He said, "I am not sure whether I can make good lassi in the front loading machine. I have already installed more than 10 machines, all top loading, in my dhabas on the highway from Delhi to Chandigarh. I prefer a top loading machine for making lassi. Do you have any objections?" I said, "No sir, I stand educated, thank you."

Three

We visited some houses in Delhi to see the working of recently sold Maharani washing machines. To our surprise, the washing machines were still in the receiving room. We were taken aback. The sales manager of Maharani politely asked, "Hasn't our service man come to install the machine and demonstrate it during the last ten days?" The home maker said, "Yes he came. I told him to come after 1 month." I asked, "Why, Why?" The housewife took her time and said, "Once we install the machine in the bathroom, our visitors will not know we have bought a new washing machine."

Four

We went to a large household on the outskirts of Pune. The home maker bought vegetables and fruit for a fortnight from the wholesale mandi so that she saved money. She stayed 20 kms away from the mandi, so she made the trip only once in a fortnight. We asked her how her washing machine was working? Could we see it? She took us to the balcony in which the machine was installed. She opened the door of the machine and took out bags full of vegetables. I said, "Are you using this to store vegetables?" She said, "No. The vegetables are to be kept in the refrigerator. After buying them from the wholesale mandi I wash them carefully to remove the dirt and pesticides. If I keep the wet vegetables in the refrigerator then they tend to get spoiled rather soon. I keep these cotton cloth bags with vegetables in the washing machine and put the machine on the dryer mode. Now these vegetables have been dried very well in the machine. I will now transfer them to the refrigerator and they will keep fresh for almost two weeks. Yes, your Maharani machine is working fine."

Five

If you know of any more uses of washing machines then please contact the author. You will get a good gift!

About the Author

Anand Karandikar

B. tech. (IIT Bombay), P.G.D.M. (IIM Calcutta), Ph.D. (Pune)

Anand is currently working as a Director of VicharVedh, a not-for-profit social organisation, which promotes critical thinking amongst the educated in India. He has been a distinguished professor of Management (Retd.), IndSearch, Pune University, for eight years.

He was the Founder Chairman (Retd.) of Metric Consultancy Limited for 25 years. He established and nurtured this consultancy into to a very large and reputed marketing management consultancy firm in India. He developed a new proprietary methodology of measuring and monitoring customer satisfaction, MOSTER, which is being used by 10 International Market Research agencies operating in 25 countries.

He was a management consultant to more than 50 major Indian companies including Tata Motors, Kinetic group, Force Motors, EID Perry and Ranbaxy.

He has worked on organising landless labour, tribals and cycle rickshaw pullers for their improved livelihood. He was an active volunteer in the People's Science Movement and All India Democratic Women's Association.

He has published three books in Marathi dealing with various social and economic issues. This is his first book in English.